W9-AMT-249

LEO AND THE LESSER LION

LEO AND THE LESSER LION

Sandra Forrester

Alfred A. Knopf
New York

THIS IS A BORZOI BOOK PUBLISHED BY ALFRED A. KNOPF

Visit us on the Web! www.randomhouse.com/kids

Educators and librarians, for a variety of teaching tools, visit us at www.randomhouse.com/teachers

Library of Congress Cataloging-in-Publication Data
    Forrester, Sandra.
    Leo and the Lesser Lion / Sandra Forrester. —1st ed.
       p. cm.
    Summary: In Depression-era Alabama, twelve-year-old Mary Bayliss Pettigrew struggles to understand why her beloved older brother, Leo, died and whether she, miraculously, lived for some special purpose.
    ISBN 978-0-375-85616-7 (trade) — ISBN 978-0-375-95616-4 (lib. bdg.) — ISBN 978-0-375-85366-1 (e-book)
    [1. Brothers and sisters–Fiction. 2. Grief–Fiction. 3. Depressions–Fiction. 4. Family life–Alabama–Fiction. 5. Foster home care–Fiction. 6. Catholics–Fiction. 7. Alabama–History–20th century–Fiction.] I. Title.
    PZ7.F7717Leo 2009
    [Fic]–dc22
    2008040881

Printed in the United States of America
August 2009
10 9 8 7 6 5 4 3 2 1

First Edition

in memory of my grandparents

Evora Thompson Fine
and
Joseph Lloyd Fine

who, in sharing with me their stories of the Great Depression,
always focused on the fun and the fullness of their lives
rather than the hardships

PROLOGUE

I don't remember dying. Not the drowning, not being pulled out of Sweet Springs Lake, not being brought back to life. But just about everybody else in Lenore, Alabama, seems to have the events of that day—March 21, 1932—burned into their skulls. And what they don't know for certain, they're good at making up.

For a long time after, I was more of a curiosity around town than Willard Stokes, who was born with extra fingers and not enough toes and I don't know what all. When people saw me on the street, they'd stop whatever it was they were doing just to gawk. The old men outside the court-house, for instance, spitting tobacco juice into the dust and playing checkers, wouldn't take their eyes off me till I went inside one of the buildings along Main Street—the library, maybe, or Tillett's Grocery to pick up something for my mother—and then they'd crane their necks to watch me come back and turn onto Markham Street, heading home.

Before that day at the lake, one of the old men might

have said without much interest, "There goes Doc Pettigrew's girl."

"Is that Kathleen?" another would ask, squinting in my direction as he mopped at the sweat on his neck with a handkerchief.

"Nah. Kathleen's nearabout grown. That's Mary Bayliss—the little one."

But now the checker players, along with everybody else in town, knew me on sight. I was, after all, the girl who'd come back from the dead.

Once, not too long after that day at the lake, the old men were talking when I passed by, and I heard my name. Then one of them said, "Too bad about the boy. Now, *he* was a pistol."

I hurried on so I wouldn't have to listen to what came next, but I knew they'd be thinking back on every prank my brother had ever pulled. Most folks' favorite seemed to be that Founders' Day when the town leaders came up with the idea of having a parade, complete with haywagon floats and a marching band. And, as expected, the Baptists went all out. Leo said they took every opportunity to strut their stuff because Lenore had nearly as many Catholics and Lutherans as Baptists—owing to the early settlers coming over from Germany—and the Baptist preacher was right touchy about it. And besides that, everybody knew Reverend Scarborough never missed a chance to put on the dog.

So First Baptist raised a great big banner over their wagon that read: *For He is our God; and we are the people of His pasture, and the sheep of His hand. Psalm 95:7.* In keeping with this theme, they'd tethered some real live sheep at the back of the float, while at the front, the reverend and his deacons were all decked out in fake beards and long bathrobes, looking like they'd last been seen around the time of Moses.

I was only three, but I've heard that story so often, it almost seems like I can remember Leo lifting me up on the Baptists' wagon. Like I can see the crowd of onlookers pointing at the float and laughing their heads off, a reaction Reverend Scarborough sure hadn't anticipated. Leo told me how the reverend seemed confused at first and then his face turned red and he looked mad enough to spit cotton. But it wasn't till the parade was nearly over that the preacher finally caught sight of me standing there among the sheep. Leo said I was grinning and waving to my many admirers, wearing our grandmother's floweredy Easter hat. And nothing else.

I can picture the old men outside the courthouse chuckling as they relived that day, and one of them saying, "Yessiree, that Leo was a buster. It's a crying shame what happened, and him so young."

1. SIX OF ONE

It all started with the boat. If Mr. Davies hadn't given Leo that old rowboat, we wouldn't have been anywhere near the lake and none of it would have happened. At first, I'd think about that a lot, even though it didn't change a thing. I couldn't seem to help it.

But that Saturday night in March, two days before my life would change forever, I didn't even know yet that there *was* a boat. I was just sitting in bed scribbling away—with my cat, Rosie, asleep in my lap—feeling pretty near content.

If the neighbors had looked out at our house around eleven-thirty, they would have seen that all the windows were dark except for one of the dormers on the second floor. That was my room. It was way past my bedtime, but I was writing in my tablet like I'd been doing for the past two years, ever since I did that report on the Alaska Territory for Sister Agnes's class and came across something that made me sit up and take notice. I was at the library reading about Alaska in an old *National Geographic* when this one paragraph

4

just leaped out at me. It told how a lady explorer named Dora Keen had risked life and limb to climb a glacier-covered mountain called Mount Blackburn. She faced all kinds of dangers—snowstorms and avalanches and freezing cold—but thirty-three days after starting up that mountain, she became the first woman to ever make it to the top.

Well, I just kept reading that paragraph over and over, soaking up the details. And the wonder of it. Because I'd never heard of a woman doing anything like that before. In school, when the nuns talked about explorers, they were all men, like Christopher Columbus or Lewis and Clark. Nobody had ever mentioned Dora Keen, who, in my opinion, was a sure-dog marvel. And that's when the idea started growing inside my head that I could be an explorer someday, too, just like Dora Keen.

Then I started wondering if there might be other women I'd never heard of who'd done astonishing things and decided to make it my business to find out. Leo and Miss Ida Henderson at the library helped me look through newspapers and magazines, and sure enough, we came across a whole slew of ladies who should have been written up in the history books but weren't. So Leo had one of his brilliant notions—that I write my own book about them—and he bought me a Big Chief tablet at Gilchrist Mercantile to get me started.

We talked over what to call it and finally settled on *Remarkable Women and Their Amazing Adventures*. I printed that on the cover, and then Leo said I should add *By Bayliss Petti-grew*, which I thought was a nice touch. Inside, I wrote about every woman we'd found, and I kept coming up with new ones till all but the last few pages of my tablet were filled with these ladies and their adventures.

Anyhow, that Saturday night in March, I was putting down the facts of Ruth Law flying an airplane from Chicago to New York and setting a new record, but also keeping my ears open. At the first squeak of my mother and daddy's bed-room door, I was ready to scoot under the covers like I'd been asleep all along. But it wasn't anybody in the house who broke the silence; it was the sudden pounding on the front door that startled me so, I nearly jumped out of my skin before recov-ering enough to switch off the lamp.

I sat there holding Rosie, my heart thumping like crazy, while the pounding on the door grew louder and more des-perate. It took a few seconds for me to realize that it was prob-ably just somebody needing Daddy, somebody with sickness in the family or a baby on the way. Not everybody had a tele-phone, especially out in the country, so it wasn't unusual for folks to come by the house at all hours.

Daddy was hurrying down the hall to the stairs, the floor-boards creaking under his feet. Soon the pounding stopped, and I heard a man's voice, gruff with worry, and then my daddy speaking in that calm, steady way of his.

My eyes were beginning to adjust to the dark. I could

6

make out the window at the foot of my bed and a square of night sky that was lighter than the blackness in my room. I was staring out the window, waiting for Daddy to come back upstairs, when all of a sudden something on the other side of the glass *moved*.

Well, I jerked back like I'd just met up with the boogeyman and was fixing to hop out of bed and go running for my daddy, but I held still long enough to take another peek. And what I saw was the shadowy outline of a head and shoulders pressed against the panes. Somebody was out on that roof, hunkered down so he wouldn't be seen. A thief, most likely, intending to break into the house till he heard the commotion downstairs. And now he was just biding his time, waiting for things to get quiet again.

Except . . . I'd never heard of a house being robbed around these parts. Kids might raid a watermelon patch or make off with a few eggs from somebody's chicken coop, but we'd never had what you'd call an honest-to-goodness crime spree in Lenore, at least not that I could recall. And then it came to me. There was only one person in town who made a habit of coming and going at night by way of an upstairs window when there were perfectly good doors he could have used.

Leo, I thought, and let out the breath I'd been holding in.

It was Leo who had shown me how we could go across the roof to the open sunporch outside Mother and Daddy's room and take the porch stairs down to the yard at night to play

7

our tricks. Like the time we dressed up old Mr. Jackson's scarecrow in our grandmother's underwear, and a month later folks were still asking him how his girlfriend was doing. Or that Christmas when Leo and I sneaked over to the manger scene they'd set up in front of Sacred Heart and replaced the baby Jesus with a smoked ham.

The first time we'd slipped out through my window, Leo had used the excuse that the doors to the house creaked too loud. "They'd wake the dead," he said, "and, most surely, Daddy." But I'd been wise to Leo even then. I knew he just liked the thrill of creeping around like a cat burglar.

I was grinning now, wondering what shenanigans my brother had in mind for tonight—till it hit me that since he hadn't let me in on his plans, he must be going somewhere without me, and that grin slid right off my face. We were a team, always had been, and everybody knew it. "When Leo Pettigrew's up to no good," Miss Fanny Douglas used to say, "that sister of his can't be far behind. They're cut from the same cloth—six of one and half a dozen of the other."

So what was Leo doing on the roof without me? Didn't he want me along? The answer to that seemed pretty obvious, and I got this sick, miserable feeling inside. I could have started bawling, but I've never been much for that, so I got riled instead. Leo didn't need me anymore? Didn't want me in on his tricks? Well, that was just fine by me, because I had plenty to keep myself occupied and I didn't need him either.

Just then Daddy came back upstairs. Outside my door, I heard Mother ask, "Who was it?"

"Clyde Mundy. The baby's burning up with fever."

"I'll make some coffee while you get dressed," she said.

After Daddy had gone back to their room and Mother to the kitchen, I lifted Rosie off my lap and went over to the window. Up this close, I could see Leo's blond hair gleaming silver in the moonlight, and the sight of him crouched down out there *really* got my blood to boiling. So I shoved that window all the way up, not even trying to be quiet about it, and blurted out the first thing that came to mind, which was, "*Boo!*"

Leo spun around so fast, he teetered and then lost his balance, falling back on his hands so that his head was pointed downhill toward the edge of the roof. I let out a gasp, just knowing he was about to tumble off and crash to the ground. And in a panic, I realized that if my brother ended up killing himself, it would be all my fault. But in nothing flat, he righted himself and came down hard on his knees so that our faces were only inches apart.

Once I knew he wasn't looking at certain death, I got over the guilt and sorrow and went back to being furious.

"Just what do you think you're doing?" I asked, glaring through the darkness at him. "And you better come up with something good."

2. THE LIONS

"Dadburn it, Bayliss! What are you trying to do, give me a heart attack?"

Even though he was whispering it through the window, I could tell he was put out with me.

"It's your own fault," I said. "You thought you could sneak off without me knowing, didn't you?"

"Hush. They'll hear you."

"What do I care? You could have at least told me."

"Told you what?"

"That you don't want me in on things anymore. You think I give a hoot about a bunch of stupid pranks?"

"Bayliss—"

"I'm getting too old for that stuff anyhow. I'll be twelve tomorrow, in case it slipped your mind."

"Little bit, I'd never forget your—"

"And shouldn't you be giving up all this foolishness, too? Sixteen's kind of old to be climbing out windows."

That's when Leo put his hands on my shoulders and said,

"Take a breath, Miss Mulligrubs, and let me get a word in. I'm not pulling any pranks tonight. You think I'd even want to without you? It wouldn't be any fun at all."

Well, it's a fact that I'd always been putty in Leo's hands, but when I heard those words coming out of his mouth, I believed him. I could feel the last bit of temper and a big load of hurt draining right out of me.

"Then what *are* you doing out there?" I asked him.

"Going to the hobo camp."

My jaw dropped about a foot, and I said, "Leo, have you lost your ever-loving mind? If Mother got wind of this, she'd have a duck fit with a tail on it. And, anyhow, what makes you think you can even find it in the dark?"

"I'll find it."

The way he said it, so casual and sure, I knew. "You've been out there before, haven't you?"

"Just once. I wanted to see it for myself."

"But, Leo, Mother says those hoboes might whop you upside the head for your shoes."

"They aren't dangerous," Leo said, "just down on their luck is all."

Not dangerous? I thought. *My hind foot!*

There was nothing new about drifters jumping off boxcars and showing up at the convent door looking for a hot meal. But since the Depression hit, and so many folks had lost jobs and homes, a lot more had taken to riding the rails.

They'd even built that little shantytown back in the woods near the railroad tracks. Every mother in the county was worried sick about it.

"But if you've already been to the camp," I said, trying to sound reasonable, "why do you want to go back?"

"There's somebody I need to see."

"Who's that?"

"Eugenie Watts."

My jaw dropped again. I knew that name, and so did everybody else in Lenore, what with all the talk about her. She'd come to town a few weeks back, and right away word started spreading that she'd tell your fortune for a dime. Now, ten cents was hard to come by these days, but I'd heard the high school kids were giving her pretty steady business. And our priest was having a conniption about it.

"Leo," I said, "you must've dozed off last Sunday when Father Mueller was warning everybody about that woman. He said Eugenie Watts is an instrument of the devil, and that when we go to her wanting to know what Providence has in store for us, we're committing a sin. And he read that part in the Bible where Saul went to see a fortune-teller, and the next day, Saul *died*."

I thought Leo had something in his throat that he was trying to cough up, but then I realized he was chuckling, real soft so nobody but me would hear him.

"Leo, it's not funny!"

"It's not?" He'd stopped laughing, but I could still hear the smile in his voice. "I was just wondering when you started listening to anything Father Mueller had to say."

Leo had a point. And maybe it *was* a little bit funny, me quoting a priest. But who's to say? Father M. just might know what he was talking about this time.

"Why take a chance?" I asked him. "And what is it you think she's gonna tell you anyhow?"

Leo didn't say anything for a minute. It was too dark for me to see his face, but I had the feeling he was thinking hard about something. Finally, he said quietly, "I *hope* she'll help me figure out what to do with my life."

Then it started making sense. The plan was for Leo to go to medical school and come back and practice with our daddy. Only that was Daddy's dream. Leo had his heart set on going to Auburn and studying agriculture, especially after our grandmother told him she was leaving her farm to him. I'd always known that Leo was meant to be a farmer, and I reckon Daddy should have known it, too. But as long as Leo never came right out and said he didn't want to go to medical school, Daddy could just keep on dreaming.

I used to wonder why Leo wouldn't speak up, and what I decided was, he couldn't bring himself to disappoint our parents. I could have told him from personal experience that this wasn't the worst thing in the world, and that it didn't make a lick of sense for him to go along with Daddy and then be miserable for the rest of his life. But I figured that was something Leo had to work out for himself.

So instead of offering my two cents on the matter, I said, "Then let's get going. Won't take me a minute to get dressed."

I felt around on the floor till I found the overalls I'd worn that day and slipped them on over my pajamas. I was tying my shoes when Leo said, "Maybe you'd better not come—and no, not because I don't *want* you to, but if Mother ever found out I took you to the hobo camp, she'd skin me alive."

"She won't find out," I said.

There was still a pesky little worry at the back of my mind, but I told myself that Saul could have kicked the bucket for any number of reasons besides going to see that fortune-teller. And I couldn't let Leo go to the camp all by himself, could I?

"Who was that banging on the door?" Leo asked as I climbed through the window.

"Clyde Mundy. The baby's sick, and he came for Daddy."

"Then we better wait till Daddy leaves."

Holding on to the window frame to steady myself, I sat down next to Leo. The night was still except for the breeze blowing across my face and a dog barking off in the distance. I lay back against the sloped roof and looked up at the sky. My eyes went past a thousand stars till I found the ones I wanted.

"There you are," I said.

I was real little when Leo first showed me the constellation Leo, and I'd believed him when he told me it was named

14

after him. He'd pointed out the stars that form the outline of the lion. "See, he's lying down," Leo had said. "We're looking at him from the side."

Then he'd shown me three dim stars above the lion's head. "And that's Leo Minor, the Lesser Lion."

"What does *lesser* mean?"

"I reckon it means a little lion, one smaller than Leo."

I remember clapping my hands in delight and saying, "That's like you and me. You're Leo and I'm the Lesser Lion."

From then on, I couldn't go outside at night without looking for the lions, even in fall and winter, when Leo said we wouldn't be able to see them. I loved thinking of my brother and myself that way, always together in a star-bright sky.

"I see Leo Minor's still tagging after me," he said now. "Like a bad penny, that little lion."

"If she wasn't around, you'd miss her."

"Yeah," he agreed, "I reckon I would."

Leo had taught me just about everything I knew that was worth knowing. Besides the constellations, he'd taught me to swim and how to hit a baseball. And it was Leo who'd read to me till I learned how to read myself, and told ghost stories that made me wake up screaming in the middle of the night. The screaming part didn't sit well with our mother, and she'd told Leo that he wasn't to even say the word *ghost* to me again till I was at least eighteen. So, after that, he went to calling the ghosts in his stories phantoms.

I was about to ask him if he remembered all that when I

heard the old Model T start up. And sputter. And stall out. And start up again. Till, finally, Daddy was backing it out of the car shed to the street.

That's when Leo stood up and said, "Come on, little britches."

By the time I got to my feet, he was already going lickety-split across that roof, and I had to pay close attention to keep up without letting my feet slide out from under me.

When we got to Mother and Daddy's room, Leo slowed down and inched past the dormer. I crept along behind him and, in the moonlight, saw him grab hold of the sunporch railing and leap over it. Then he bent down to help me climb up on the porch.

"We're getting good at this," he whispered, and started for the stairs.

Once we were out of the yard and heading down Markham Street, a feeling of pure joy sprang up inside me and spread all the way to my toes and fingertips. It was something about the darkness, and the fact that everybody else was asleep. It was like Leo and I were the only two people on earth.

"Let's run," he said, and reached for my hand.

So we took off down the street through the tunnel of old oaks and maples, laughing and not caring if anybody heard us or not.

3. THE FORTUNE-TELLER

Downtown Lenore was three blocks long, with the churches and businesses lined up on either side of Main Street. Our daddy's office was in the second block, smack-dab in the middle of town. When Grandpa Halsey was still alive, the sign out front had read: *John Halsey Pettigrew, M.D., and Walter Pettigrew, M.D.* Now it just had Daddy's name. I wondered if I'd ever see *Leo Pettigrew, M.D.,* up there, but I figured for a whole dime, Eugenie Watts should be able to tell us that and a lot more besides.

The last block of Main Street was taken up by Burde-shaw's Drugstore—now closed, with the windows boarded up—Tillett's Grocery, the post office, and the Baptist church. Across the street was Sacred Heart: church, con-vent, and school. This was my school, where I'd been lock-ing horns with the nuns for the past six years, and would probably be doing the same for the next six. If I didn't get expelled first. They had rules for everything, those nuns.

It only took a few minutes for Leo and me to get

through town, and then, following the curve of the convent wall, Main Street turned in to Gilly Road. Ahead was nothing but woods, cotton fields, and pastureland, with a farmhouse plunked down here and there to break the monotony.

Walking up Main Street at night was one thing, but now that we'd left the last streetlight behind and were all but swallowed up by darkness, I was thinking that we might ought to reconsider going out to that camp. And when Leo suddenly veered off the road and started down the slope that ran from the back of the convent to the woods, a real bad feeling came over me.

The hill was steep and rocky, and the deeper we went into that hollow, the darker it got. Leo took my arm so I wouldn't step off into a hole and break my neck, but I still couldn't shake my uneasiness. The wind had picked up, and I could hear it stirring the trees, bringing to mind that shivery whisper Leo used when he told his ghost stories. But since I was too old to believe in ghosts, I just breathed in and out a few times to steady my nerves and trudged after Leo into those woods.

The trees were still bare from winter, but the branches overhead were so thick they shut out the last smidgen of moonlight. I couldn't see a thing.

"Are you positive you know where you're going?" I whispered to Leo.

He patted my arm and said, "Don't worry, little bit. The hoboes have beaten down a trail going to the convent for food every day. We'll be there soon."

And sure enough, just a few minutes later, I saw a faint light up ahead. Then the trees started thinning out, and the next thing I knew, Leo and I were stepping into a big clearing with a low-burning fire in the middle. There were maybe a dozen people gathered around the fire talking, their voices too low for me to hear what they were saying. And behind them, at the edge of the woods, were some sagging tents and a few little shacks slapped together from old boards and tarps and bits of tin. Feet were sticking out of most of the tents, and other folks were sleeping under the trees.

Then all of a sudden the talking around the campfire stopped, and faces that were hollow-eyed and none too friendly turned in our direction. All men, I thought at first, but then I spotted the girl. She was staring into the fire without much expression, skinny arms wrapped around her body like she was chilly, even though it was a warm night for March. Dark, tangled hair was hanging in her eyes and down her back, but I could see enough of her face to tell that she was young. Maybe no older than Leo.

Some of the men were young, too—boys, really—and others were as old as the hills, with mouths sunk in where teeth were missing and a week's worth of gray whiskers on their chins. It was one of the old fellas who called out, "Hey there, boy! Leo, right? What you doing down here this late?"

Leo walked over to the fire as if he belonged there, and I stuck to him like a cocklebur. I didn't quite know what to make of these people and kept remembering Mother saying they'd whop us upside the head for our shoes.

"I came to see Miss Eugenie," Leo said, and his eyes shifted to the girl with the scraggly hair.

The old man nodded, and it seemed to me that the others loosened up a little, like they were used to young'uns showing up in the middle of the night to have their fortunes told and were just as glad they didn't have to mess with us. The girl, Eugenie Watts, stood up without a word and started for one of the shacks. The way she moved was slow and weary, making me think she felt a heap sight older than she looked.

My mind was going a mile a minute as Leo and I fell into step behind her. I had a pretty good idea what a fortune-teller was supposed to look like, and this wasn't it. First off, I figured she'd be older. And not so . . . *ordinary*. I thought she'd have on a long, full skirt and be wearing lots of bracelets and a scarf around her head, like the pictures of Gypsy fortune-tellers I'd seen in books. But this Eugenie Watts, in her faded cotton dress with the hem coming loose in the back, was just a girl, not all that different from me. Except for the fact that she was living out here in these woods with no place else to go.

20

She stopped in front of the shack and lowered herself to the ground beside an empty crate that I figured was her table for telling fortunes. There was a candle on top, melted down in the lid of a canning jar till it was just a nub. Eugenie Watts struck a match and lit the candle, then motioned for Leo to sit. I dropped down beside him, but she ignored me. She just held out her hand—which was none too clean—and Leo put a dime in it.

Then she took a pack of cards from her pocket and shuffled them. She was real quick with those cards, but it was her face I was watching. She reminded me a little of my sister, Kathleen, with her dark hair and eyes, only not as pretty. Maybe if she cleaned herself up and had more meat on her bones.

The girl put the pack of cards facedown on the crate. "What is it you want to know?" she asked Leo.

My first thought was, *She's not from around here, not with that Yankee voice.* And my second thought was, *If she was a real fortune-teller, she wouldn't have to ask what he wanted.* That sealed it for me. I no more believed she could look into the future than I could. Leo had just thrown his money away. But then I cut my eyes at him, and his face was about as serious as I'd ever seen it. I knew he still had hope that this girl was what she claimed to be.

"I want to know," Leo said, staring hard at those cards, "what I'm supposed to do with my life."

That was all, and Eugenie Watts seemed satisfied with

it. She took the top card off the deck and slapped it down, faceup, on top of the crate. It's the only one I remember. The king of hearts. Eugenie glanced at the card and said something about Leo being a fair-haired man, which, of course, anybody could see. But Leo just lifted his eyes to her face and nodded, and you could tell he wanted to believe real bad that she knew what she was doing and could untangle all the knots in his life.

She kept turning over cards and muttering something each time. And after she'd gone through a few, it dawned on me that everything she'd been telling him was true. For instance, she said Leo had a sense of fun about him but was also kind and did a lot to help other people. And she said nothing was more important to him than his family. And *then* she said that he was especially close to one member of the family, a girl, and that the two of them were so much alike, it was hard to tell where one ended and the other began. *Six of one and half a dozen of the other,* I thought. And I realized that I was hardly breathing, waiting for her to turn up the next card.

There was some other stuff I don't remember, none of it wrong, but not sounding exactly like Leo either. Then she hesitated, her fingertips resting on the deck of cards, and she said, "The last four cards tell what's in your future."

So Leo and I leaned closer, and Eugenie placed a card down on the crate. And didn't say a thing. I glanced up at her, and she had a puzzled look on her face.

Then she turned over the next card, and the next, still not uttering a word. By this time, my heart was beating fast, and I was getting scared. I can't say why, since I didn't think for a minute she could actually tell the future from those cards, but mostly, I reckon, because of what I saw in her face. At first, her eyebrows were pinched together like she didn't understand what she was seeing, but when she turned over the last card, her eyes got big like maybe *she* was the one who was scared.

And then, before I could figure out what was going on, she just scooped up all the cards and said, "I don't see a thing. Sometimes that happens."

She blew out the candle and stood up, so Leo and I scrambled to our feet, too.

"Here," she said, and handed Leo his dime back.

He was looking about as mystified as I felt. "What do you mean, you don't see anything?" he asked her. "There was a nine of spades. What does that say about me?"

She didn't answer, and her face was blank, like when we'd first seen her sitting by the fire. I wondered if maybe I'd just imagined her looking confused and startled. It all happened so fast, I couldn't be sure.

"Can't you tell me—?" Leo started, but she cut him off.

"I couldn't read the cards." She took a quick step back, as if she couldn't wait to get away from us. "It's nothing to do with you. The gift comes and goes, that's all."

Then she pushed aside a grimy piece of oilcloth tacked over the doorway to the shack and ducked inside.

Leo and I looked at each other.

"I reckon I'm a mystery man," he said, his lips twitching like he was fixing to smile.

I was still feeling uneasy. Even if Eugenie *was* somebody I should have felt sorry for, I didn't like her trying to fool people into thinking she could see the future, and I didn't like her letting Leo down. He was acting as if it didn't matter, but I knew he was disappointed. He'd been counting on her.

I reached for his hand and said, "Come on. Let's go home."

When we passed by the campfire again, the men were talking and not paying us any mind. One was saying, "I hear there's factory work in Illinois. Reckon I'll go see for myself."

"A fellar I met in Birmingham just came from Chicago," another man said. "Told me there's no jobs a'tall up that way."

Leo and I left the clearing. The voices grew softer and softer till I couldn't hear them anymore.

"Well," Leo said when we were deep in the woods, "*that* could've gone better."

"Some fortune-teller," I said. "We should've listened to Father Mueller."

"I guess," Leo said. "But there's one thing I don't understand."

"What's that?"

"Why she didn't just make up something and keep the money."

"Maybe there's set things she tells everybody," I said, "and she forgot her lines."

"Or maybe she saw something too awful to tell," Leo said, but he didn't sound especially worried about it.

"Nah, she's just a big fake, and I'm not gonna waste my time thinking about her."

And I didn't. I put Eugenie Watts right out of my mind. But later, she'd find her way into my head again, and then there was no getting rid of her.

4. TOMMIE DORA AND THE HIRED HELP

In church the next morning, I was half listening to Father Mueller in case he got started on the fortune-teller again, but to tell the truth, my mind was mostly on something else. It was March 20—my birthday—and I was giving myself a good talking-to.

Now don't be disappointed when there aren't any presents, I told myself. *Once this dadblamed Depression's over and done with, we'll have chicken and dumplings for Sunday dinner again, and presents, too. Till then, we just have to be grateful for what we've got.* At least, that's what my mother was always saying. Then she'd tell us how blessed we were, and she was right; I just didn't know to appreciate it then. So that's why, in church with my family that Sunday morning, I couldn't help feeling just a *little* sorry that my twelfth birthday would come and go without a single present to open.

Kathleen was sitting beside me as still as the statue of the Blessed Virgin, hands folded in her lap, gloves so white they'd blind you. Mine had gray stains at the fingertips and were overall dingy, even after Mother let them soak.

All through Mass, Kathleen's eyes never left Father Mueller's face except when we were praying or reading a response. Or when I started shifting around because my heinie had gone to sleep. Then Kathleen would cut her eyes at me and frown, and Leo, who was sitting on the other side of me, would poke me with his elbow and grin. That happened twice before Kathleen hissed at me, "When are you gonna start acting your age?" and I hissed back, "When are you?" even though I already knew the answer. Kathleen was fifteen—exactly one year, one month, and one day younger than Leo—but she'd been *born* old.

Mother was sitting on the other side of Kathleen, then Tommie Dora, then Daddy on the aisle. Tommie Dora was our grandmother, only we weren't allowed to call her that. When Leo was on the way, she'd told Mother and Daddy that becoming a grandma made her feel like she already had one foot in the grave. And what's more, grandmas were expected to sew up costumes for school plays and bake a cake every time the little ones came to visit, and she didn't plan on doing either. So that's how we came to call her Tommie Dora. At her request. This was just one of her many peculiarities.

Once Father Mueller got started talking, he never knew when to quit. Today he was beating the parable of Saint

Luke and the Samaritan to death. But finally, I heard him say the words I'd been waiting for: "*Ite, Missa est.* Go, the Mass is ended." And when I answered back with everybody else, "Thanks be to God," I really meant it.

After we'd made it outside, and the grown-ups had said a few words to Father M., we all gathered on the steps for a good fifteen or twenty minutes of socializing with friends and neighbors. Leo's buddy, Ray Vanzandt, came over, and my best friend, Annie Schumann, squeezed through the crowd to join us.

"Happy birthday," she said, grinning, and handed me a Baby Ruth.

"Annie, it's my favorite," I said. "Thanks."

Most folks were as poor as Job's turkey these days and wouldn't think of spending a nickel on a candy bar. But Annie's daddy owned Schumann's Cotton Gin and Warehouse, and since farmers still needed a place to store and sell their cotton, the Schumanns weren't as hard up as some of the rest of us. Folks still needed doctors, too, but Daddy's patients were as likely to pay him with a bushel of potatoes as hard cash. Lord, but I was getting sick of potatoes!

Annie started talking about the history test we were having on Monday, but my attention had shifted to Tommie Dora, who was heading straight for Yancy Gilchrist. Her lips were pressed thin, and she looked a shade grimmer than usual. I knew what was coming, and it didn't surprise me a bit that my grandmother would pick the most public spot she could find to make a spectacle of herself. In front of the church on Sunday morning. Where else?

Mr. Gilchrist was smiling at Tommie Dora, only it was more of a smirk. And that daughter of his was there in another new dress, and with the same identical smirk on her face, like she had it straight from God that the Gilchrists were better than everybody else, her daddy being the mayor and all. Lila Grace Gilchrist and I had been sworn enemies for six long years, ever since we entered Sacred Heart together. Sometimes, the first time you lay eyes on a person, you just know she's going to be trouble.

"Hey, Tommie Dora," Mr. Gilchrist said, pretending like he was glad to see her.

"Morning, Yancy," Tommie Dora answered, pretending nothing.

Mr. Gilchrist pushed his hat back on his head, and that smile spread to show a lot of teeth. "Looks to me like you've got something on your mind, Tommie Dora. If it's town business, why don't you call the office and make an appointment to come by?"

"No need for that," she said. "I can fill you in right here and save myself a trip."

The two of them together were a sight. Mr. Gilchrist was on the short and scrawny side, while my grandmother would make three of most ladies—in width, I mean—and was close to six feet tall. So there the mayor was, having to throw his head back to look her in the eye, and Tommie Dora peering down at him like she was just itching to take him over her knee and paddle him good. But I was praying it wouldn't come to that.

"I keep the Lord's Day for God and family," Mr. Gilchrist said, that smile of his losing some of its brightness. "Just call Nadine and she'll set up a time."

"Yancy," Tommie Dora said, "I don't reckon God'll hold it against you if you give Him a rest for five minutes and hear me out. Didn't you say in your campaign speeches that having the mayor's ear—anytime, anyplace—was our right?"

"I did say that," Mr. Gilchrist answered, beginning to sound cranky, "and I've noticed, Tommie Dora, that you exercise that right on a regular basis."

This brought some chuckles from the people standing around listening. But Tommie Dora didn't bat an eye.

"The public high school's a disgrace," she said in that blunt way of hers, "and I figured you'd want to see to it before the roof caves in and kills unknown numbers of Lenore's brightest."

"Attendance is way down," Mr. Gilchrist said, trying to edge away, but more folks had gathered to hear what was going on, and he was hemmed in. "So many's dropped out to look for work, the school's half empty."

"What about the half that's full?" Tommie Dora wanted to know. "You willing to tell the folks in this town that their children's lives aren't worth a pinch of snuff?"

Now Mr. Gilchrist was starting to bristle. "I'd send a crew out there first thing in the morning," he said, "but we can't afford it. The town's flat broke."

"You found money to paint your office and buy brand-new furniture for it," she said, pinning him down with those black eyes that could slice through a side of beef. "And I'll wager that fancy carpet took a bite out of the town's budget. I couldn't help noticing the last time I came by to exercise my rights."

The mayor's face was turning red, but I didn't know if that was because Tommie Dora had put him on the spot or because she'd gotten a bigger laugh than him. My daddy was just standing there smiling, and Leo was grinning and looking at our grandmother like she'd just gone ten rounds with Jack Dempsey and left him sprawled in the ring. But I didn't crack a smile. Partly because Lila Grace was glaring at me as if Tommie Dora's carrying on was all my fault, but mostly because I'd seen it too many times, Tommie Dora sticking her nose in and trying to run everything and everybody. Like her going on and on about how I was getting too old to run around town in overalls, and the time she told Mother—right in the middle of Tillett's Grocery for everybody to hear!—that Mavis Quick's grandkids had come down with lice, and since my personal hygiene wasn't the best, it wouldn't hurt to give my head a good dousing with kerosene. Oftentimes I wondered what this town would do for entertainment if my grandmother ever decided to keep her mouth shut. Not that *that* was likely to happen.

About the time Mr. Gilchrist finally made his getaway, Mother and Daddy started easing down the steps. I told Annie I'd meet her at the corner the next morning and took off after Leo for the car.

"You can drive us home," Daddy said to Leo, "and then run that medicine out to Mr. Davies for me."

"No need to drive four blocks," Tommie Dora said. "It'll do us good to walk."

"Are you sure, Mother?" Daddy asked her, but Tommie Dora was already lumbering down the street in the direction of our house.

Then Leo said to Mother, "If you don't need Bayliss to help with dinner, I could use some company driving out there."

I know my face lit up at that because kitchen work was the thing I despised most in life, especially on Sundays, when Tommie Dora was there to boss me around.

"I expect we can manage without you one day," Mother said, and smiled at me, "since it's your birthday. You go on with your brother, sugar, and have a nice ride."

Once we were in the car, I said, "Thanks," and Leo answered, "Anytime." Then we didn't even try to talk because the engine made such a racket you'd have to yell to be heard.

Leo took the curve onto Gilly Road, and we passed the woods where the hoboes lived. Tommie Dora's place was just ahead. She had a big white house that used to be one of the nicest in the county, but it hadn't been painted in recent memory and was starting to look kind of tuckered out, like the rest of Lenore.

As we drove by, I noticed that the porch was knee-deep in cats, as usual. Mavis Quick was always telling folks that Tommie Dora had at least fifty cats wandering through the house on any given day. But that was stretching the blanket some, because I'd personally counted the cats on many occasions, and there were never more than twenty-five or thirty.

About that time, Leo shouted over the engine noise, "Tommie Dora wants us to come out after school this week and help with her spring cleaning. Starting Tuesday."

"Dog bite it, Leo!" I whipped around in my seat to look at him. "We've already been out here every day this month!"

"Not *every* day, half-pint, and that garden wasn't gonna plant itself. You'll be glad when the tomatoes and black-eyed peas come in."

"It'll be us that has to pick 'em! Not to mention the

butter beans and collards and squash. And why do we have to help with the cleaning anyhow? What's Tommie Dora paying Mavis Quick for?"

"She can't afford full-time help anymore," Leo said, "so Mavis only comes in once or twice a week. And Tommie Dora's too frail to do all that heavy work by herself."

Frail? Tommie Dora? I just stared at him like he'd gone round the bend and wasn't coming back. But there was no point arguing because Tommie Dora always got her way, no matter what. And besides that, Leo just *loved* traipsing out to that old farm, even though it meant being in close proximity to our grandmother. It was a known fact that Tommie Dora Bayliss Pettigrew was the most aggravating woman in the county—probably in the whole state of Alabama—and I'd never understand why Leo was so fond of her.

"I reckon she doesn't need full-time help with you and me around," I muttered. "Next thing you know, she'll be hiring us out to milk folks' cows and slop their hogs."

"What was that?" Leo shouted.

I glanced over at him, and he just looked so darned happy. Like there was nothing in this world he'd rather be doing than taking a Sunday drive with his little sister.

"Oh . . . never mind," I said, knowing when I was beat.

5. THE BOAT

The dirt road that led to Sweet Springs Lake was hardly more than a trail through the woods, with weeds growing up between the tire ruts. At first, all you could see was trees, but then George Davies's house came into view.

His place wasn't much, just a three-room cabin with a rusty tin roof and a shed out back where he parked a car even older than Daddy's. Mr. Davies had been the town pharmacist before he retired, and folks said he had money. But you sure wouldn't know it, looking at how he lived.

By the time we got to his driveway, we could see the water. It was a big lake—even Leo couldn't swim all the way across—with one little island in the middle. Trees grew up to the edge of the water, except along a wide sweep of sand just past Mr. Davies's dock where folks came to swim and have picnics.

Leo hopped out of the car and trotted up the steps to the cabin. When nobody answered his knock, he opened the door, stuck the bottle of pills inside, and came back to the car. But instead of getting in, he bent down and peered through the window at me.

"Dinner won't be ready yet," he said. "You want to go down to the water?"

It crossed my mind that Mother wouldn't like me doing that, not in my Sunday dress—which had been Kathleen's first, but Mother had taken it up to fit me—and my good shoes, even if they had seen better days. But I could fix at least part of that. I had my shoes and socks off in a flash, and when Leo saw what I was doing, he took his off, too.

We were crossing the road to the beach, the gravelly sand feeling cool and damp under my bare feet, when Leo said, "Let's go look at Mr. Davies's dock."

That sounded about as exciting as watching our toenails grow. We'd only seen that rickety old dock a million times before. But Leo was already heading off in that direction, so I changed course and went after him.

The dock groaned and swayed a little when we stepped out on it, but it felt sturdy enough to take our weight and we had a good view of the island from there. That island—which, truthfully, was no more than a pile of rocks with a narrow strip of sand and a few stunted cedars—had been of interest to me ever since I'd read about this wildlife photographer named Osa Johnson. She'd been captured by headhunters on an island in the South Seas, and they were about to chop her head off when she brought out some pictures she'd taken of them. And since those headhunters had never seen a camera, they thought Osa Johnson had worked some kind of magic and spared her life.

Now, I knew I wouldn't find any headhunters at Sweet Springs Lake, but that island seemed magical to me anyhow, and I envied Leo being able to swim out there. Every summer I'd ask Daddy to let me try, and every summer he'd say, "You're not strong enough yet. Maybe next year."

We were about halfway down the dock when I noticed the rowboat. It wasn't new, but somebody had done a nice job fixing it up. That boat just shimmered in the sun, as white and clean as Kathleen's Sunday gloves against the dark green water.

"You reckon this is Mr. Davies's boat?" I asked Leo.

"It used to be," he said. "Belongs to somebody else now."

"Who?"

"What's the name on the bow?"

I bent down to read the words painted on the boat. Then I straightened up real quick and looked at Leo, not understanding.

"It says *Mary Bayliss*. But that's me, Leo. What does it mean?"

"It means," Leo said, a smile tugging at the corners of his mouth, "that it's your boat. Happy birthday, little bit."

I must have stood there with my mouth hanging open for a full minute. Then I threw my arms around Leo's neck, and he made a show of gagging and gasping like I was choking him to death. But he was smiling big now, and so was I.

"As I live and breathe," I said when I'd finally let go of him and squatted down for a closer look at the boat. "But how did you—? Is this really—? Well, I declare."

"So you like it?"

"It's the best present anybody ever gave me," I said. "But where did you get the money for a boat?"

"Didn't need any. Remember back in the winter when we had that ice storm and I cleared away those pines that fell on Mr. Davies's house? He gave me the boat in payment. Course it needed some work. Daddy bought the paint. And it was his idea for you to come see it when I brought Mr. Davies his pills."

About that time, something wonderful occurred to me. "Leo!" I said, grabbing hold of his arm. "I'll be able to take the boat out to the island! You want to right now?"

He was slow in answering, so I said, "I know, it's nearly dinnertime."

"But we don't have to be at Tommie Dora's till Tuesday," he said. "We can come back tomorrow after school, and I'll teach you how to row."

I perked up at that, but then I remembered. "Dadburn it! I'll have to help Kathleen fix supper."

Since Daddy had to let Pearl Allbright go when he couldn't afford to pay her anymore, Mother was working all day at Daddy's office, and Kathleen had taken over most of the cooking. I was supposed to give her a hand, except when Tommie Dora needed Leo and me out at her place, and that suited my sister just fine. She dearly loved telling me what to do.

But Leo just grinned and said, "We'll get around that somehow."

He sounded so sure, I figured he must have a plan in mind. So I was practically floating up out of my seat all the way home, thinking, *I have a boat. I-HAVE-A-BOAT!*

But that wasn't the end of my birthday. When we walked into the kitchen, there was no mistaking the smell coming from a skillet on top of the stove. "Chicken!" I shouted. "We're having fried chicken!"

Then Mother was herding us into the dining room, with Kathleen and Tommie Dora bringing in the vegetables and biscuits and a big bowl of milk gravy, and Mother carrying the platter heaped with chicken. It was the first time we'd had meat since I don't know when, and as soon as Daddy said grace, Leo and I were reaching for the drumsticks.

I didn't see how my birthday could get any better, but after we finished eating, Mother brought four presents to the table and put them down in front of me.

"Open this one first," she said, handing me a package

wrapped in tissue paper and tied with a blue ribbon. "It's from Daddy."

So I tore into that paper, pretty sure I'd find a book inside. And I did. Daddy told me it was about this proper English lady named Mary Kingsley who took off to explore the jungles of Africa and got more than she'd bargained for, what with all the snakes and crocodiles and tribes of cannibals. I could tell right off this was my kind of book.

Mother was frowning at Daddy because my interest in traveling to far-off places, and maybe living a short but eventful life, worried her some. But it was Tommie Dora who said, "Walter, why do you encourage her? All these stories about folks getting gobbled up by cannibals and burning to a crisp in airplane crashes are just plain morbid. It's a mystery to *me* why Mary Bayliss can't read *Rebecca of Sunnybrook Farm* like every other girl in town."

But I didn't pay her any mind because I was already opening Mother's gift. It was a bookmark, with a cat curled up next to a stack of books and my name along the edge, all done in needlepoint. The cat was black and orange and white, like Rosie. Everybody said how pretty it was, and Tommie Dora remarked that she'd never had the patience for needlework, which came as no surprise to anybody, and then Kathleen handed me her present.

Gloves. My sister had given me brand-new, spanking white gloves, and she'd even taken the trouble to write out instructions on how to wash them and pat them dry with a towel and keep them looking nice. What more can I say about Kathleen's gift?

There was one present left to open. From Tommie Dora. I was a little anxious as I ripped off the paper because, really, you never knew what my grandmother might do. But when I saw the corner of another book, I started to get excited. Till I read the title: *Rebecca of Sunnybrook Farm*.

Leo cracked up, and everybody else was snickering, even me. But Tommie Dora was dead serious, looking first at one face and then another, saying, "What's so amusing about *Rebecca of Sunnybrook Farm*? It's a classic."

I don't reckon I'll ever forget a minute of that day, but Tommie Dora kept snapping pictures just to make sure we had it all down in black and white. In the one she framed for me that's been on my bookcase ever since, we're all standing around the table with big smiles for the camera, and the first thing you notice is how much Kathleen favors Mother and how Leo's the spitting image of Daddy. And how I'm the oddball. My hair isn't blond like Leo's or dark like Kathleen's, but just plain brown and bobbed short, so in the picture it looks like a gray cap pulled down over my ears. And while everybody else is tall and thin, I'm short and kind of sturdy. The only way you'd know I belong to this family, and wasn't left on the doorstep by Gypsies, is the fact that I have the Pettigrew eyes. They're as blue as Daddy's and Leo's, only you can't tell that from the photograph.

So, anyhow, that was my twelfth—and best—birthday. But when I crawled into bed that night, about as content as I ever remember being, I had no way of knowing that the day would come to mean even more to me as time passed. That later, I'd look at the picture of all of us together and think, *This is what we lost.*

6. THIS MORNING IS A GIFT

"Bayyy-liss! Breakfast!"

At the sound of my mother bellowing up the stairs, I opened my eyes just enough to see that the sun was up and, judging from its brightness, had been for some time. It was the morning after my birthday. Daddy would have already left for the office, and if I didn't shake a leg, I'd be late for school. Since I still had Bible verses to copy after my last run-in with Lila Grace Gilchrist—which *she* started, but Sister Annunciata wouldn't listen—I knew I'd better not press my luck. But I'd stayed awake reading the book Daddy gave me till all hours, and the last thing I wanted to do was leave that bed.

It couldn't have been more than two seconds later when somebody jerked the quilt off me, and then Mother was yelling in my ear, "Rise and shine, sugar! This morning is a gift."

This morning is a gift. I'd heard those words hundreds—probably *thousands*—of times in my life. Mother would say them on steamy summer mornings and frosty winter ones. On any day she judged to be especially fine. And my mother seemed to think *most* mornings were especially fine.

"Come on, get up," she said, swatting my bottom with her hand.

I opened my eyes, but just barely.

"Don't you want breakfast? Eggs, bacon, and biscuits with honey?"

My eyes popped all the way open. "Did you say *bacon?*"

Mother smiled. "Mr. Taylor paid for his appendectomy this morning."

She knew she'd gotten my attention, so she didn't linger, and I was up and jerking a dress over my head by the time she left the room. I was wide awake as I followed the smell of frying bacon down the stairs to the kitchen.

I'd expected to find my brother and sister sitting quietly at the table, too busy chewing and swallowing to say more than *Pass the biscuits, please.* So when I opened the kitchen door to the sounds of a wail and an earsplitting clatter, I was taken aback.

I saw right off that Daddy and Leo weren't there. Mother was standing at the stove over a skillet of popping bacon, and Kathleen was at the table with two little boys, a squalling baby in her lap. One of the boys was stuffing a whole biscuit into his mouth, the honey dripping down the front of his grimy shirt, and the other one was banging a spoon on the table like he was hammering nails.

The Clark boys. They lived four doors down, in the worst-looking house on the street. Nobody could remember its original color because all the paint had peeled off years ago, and their daddy didn't bother keeping the grass cut, so by the end of summer, that yard was a nesting place for everything from rats to copperheads. Everybody on Markham Street hated to see the Clark boys coming because they were always up to meanness, throwing rocks at windows or tying firecrackers to the tail of some poor cat. Mother and Kathleen felt sorry for them when they came to the door begging for food, but I wasn't that charitable. Fred was eight and Henry was six, and I figured that was plenty old enough to know better than to torture innocent animals.

Kathleen was sticking a spoonful of mush into the baby's mouth and cooing, "Isn't that good, Martha Jo? Yum, yum. Let's have some more."

Mother glanced up from the stove and said to me, "Go on and sit down," like time and patience were running short. "You leave for school in ten minutes, fed or not."

So I slumped into a chair as far away from the Clarks as I could get. Mother plopped a pile of scrambled eggs, two pieces of bacon, and a biscuit on my plate, and out of the corner of my eye, I saw her give Fred and Henry two pieces of bacon each—not their first helping, I was sure.

I started to ask what they were doing at our house, but all I got out was, "Why are—?" before my mother broke in with, "Mr. Clark's gone to Birmingham to look for work, and Mrs. Clark has an appointment with Daddy."

"She's expecting again," Kathleen said, smiling like this was *good* news. "I said I'd see Fred and Henry off to school and watch Martha Jo."

I took a bite of bacon and cut my eyes at Kathleen. "Aren't you going to school?"

"I'll be a little late," Kathleen said. "Mother wrote me a note."

Well, Mother never wrote *me* notes when I was late, but given a choice between going to school and looking after the Clarks, I'd take school anytime. Kathleen was crazy about kids, but I didn't have much use for them myself. I was always scared they'd fall out of a tree and break a leg or hang themselves on the clothesline, and then I'd be the one to have to answer for it. And *these* kids smelled like sour milk and other things I didn't care to think about.

Eating my bacon in tiny bites to make it last longer, I stared out the window and tried to forget the Clarks were there. Then something brushed against my leg, and I looked down to see Rosie at my feet, her green eyes fixed on the bacon in my hand.

"But it's my last bite," I said.

I stared at the cat and the cat stared back. Finally, with a sigh, I dropped the piece of bacon to the floor.

I was putting my dishes in the sink when Leo came into the kitchen carrying his schoolbooks.

"You just getting up?" I asked him. "Well, you're too late. The bacon's gone."

"Leo's already eaten," Mother said. "*He* was up on time."

Then the baby started crying again, Henry went back to banging his spoon, and Mother was shouting over the noise, "Get your books, Bayliss. Leo, y'all go on without me; I have to finish these dishes. Have you both got your homework? Don't dawdle now."

Leo and I made a beeline for the kitchen door, and it was a pure relief to get out of there. We were coming around the side of the house when I saw Harry Burdeshaw across the street, polishing the hood ornament on his daddy's Packard. That car was real fancy, painted a dark red that Harry said was called cranberry, with shiny black fenders and chrome trim. Mr. Burdeshaw had special-ordered it before he knew he was going broke. Then he'd tried to sell it, but nobody in these parts had that kind of money, except for Yancy Gilchrist, and he already had a big, fine car.

When Harry looked up and saw us, he waved, and his dog, Jack, came loping over to greet us. Leo always said, to look at that dog, you'd figure he was part grizzly bear and part werewolf, but inside, he was pure sugar. And as if to prove it, Jack leaned all of his ninety pounds against my hip and stuck his big head into my hand for some petting.

I was picking beggar's-lice out of his fur when Harry ambled over to join us, carrying *one* book. Those public school kids didn't know how good they had it.

Harry was fourteen but looked younger. He had a mess of dark hair that I'd swear he cut himself, most likely with the hedge clippers, and was so skinny, Tommie Dora always said, "That boy's all elbows and freckles."

"I got me a new job," Harry said, "working for Elroy Johnson."

"Don't you have enough jobs already?" I asked him.

Harry worked for anybody in town who could afford to pay him, mostly raking leaves and mowing lawns. But he wasn't above chopping wood and painting fences either.

"Mama's had another pay cut," he said. "She's only bringing home forty dollars a month now."

Miz Burdeshaw used to make three times that much teaching second grade at the grammar school, but the state just kept chipping away at teachers' salaries. They said Alabama was running out of money. And Harry's daddy, who took over as the town pharmacist after Mr. Davies retired, owned Burdeshaw's Drugstore but had to close it down back in the fall. Leo said Mr. Burdeshaw went broke because he let folks have their medicines even when they didn't have the money to pay for them, which was most of the time. Then he couldn't find a job close to home and had to go off to St. Louis to work in his brother-in-law's dry goods store. The Burdeshaws needed every penny Harry could bring in.

"What are you doing for Elroy Johnson?" Leo asked him.

"Loading the rolling store," Harry said. "Two hours on weeknights and Saturday mornings. He's gonna pay me six dollars a week."

"Six dollars," I said. "That's good money."

Elroy Johnson's rolling store was a big enclosed truck that he drove all over the rural parts of the county. He came by Tommie Dora's on Tuesday mornings, and she'd trade eggs for whatever she needed, everything from cornmeal to headache powders to that smelly stuff she used to bleach her mustache. Only we weren't supposed to know about that.

Leo and Harry were talking about what would happen if cotton prices fell again, and I was wondering why they cared, since none of us grew cotton, when I noticed Mother on the back porch shaking the kitchen rug over the railing. She saw us standing there and came out to the street.

"Didn't I tell you not to dawdle?" she asked, frowning at Leo and me. But then her eyes settled on Harry, and her face softened considerably. "Morning, Harry. Your mother told me you have a new job. Just don't take on too much now, you hear?"

"Yes, ma'am," he said.

"What you need is a little fun."

"Yes, ma'am," he said again.

Mother and Daddy thought a lot of Harry. Daddy said he was an enterprising young man with a bright future ahead of him, and Mother agreed. But she worried about him working too hard and not having enough time to be young and carefree.

She was studying his face and seemed to be pondering something. I figured she was trying to think up some kind of fun for him, but I sure didn't expect what came out of her mouth next.

"Bayliss," she said, "why don't you and Harry and Leo launch that boat of yours this afternoon? Kathleen can get supper by herself."

And I have to say, those words were like a gift from heaven. It was as clear as day that God *must* have had a hand in it. And not being one to question the Lord's plan—and not wanting to give my mother a chance to change her mind—I looked at Leo and Harry and asked quickly, "Y'all want to?"

"Sounds good to me," Leo said, and then winked at me like he'd arranged the whole thing.

Harry's face had lit up, but now he caught himself. "I don't know," he said. "I start work tonight."

"But that's after supper, right? Come on, Harry," I said. "We'll be home before dark."

"Well . . . I reckon I could."

Mother was smiling at him, but then she snapped back to the present and said, "Get a move on, Bayliss. You can't be late *again*."

"We'll come get you after school," I said to Harry as Mother gave me a little push toward the street.

From that last glimpse of his face, I could tell Harry was still questioning whether he should go with us, but he deserved some time off, and I knew he'd be glad once we got to the lake. I remember thinking, *This is going to be the best afternoon! One I'll never forget.*

7. SWEET SPRINGS LAKE

After school, Leo and I changed clothes as fast as we could and then trotted over to Harry's house. He was already waiting for us on the front steps. As we started down the street, Miz Burdeshaw stuck her head out the door and yelled, "Y'all be careful now!"

"Yes, ma'am!" I called back, but I wasn't thinking about being careful just then. In my mind, I was already out on that lake with the oars in my hands and a cool breeze blowing off the water into my face.

When we got to Daddy's office, I noticed that the lot out front was filled up with mules and wagons. "Daddy's gonna be here awhile," I said.

But Leo and Harry had already gone on to Gilchrist Mercantile next door and were looking in the window. I figured Leo was hankering after one of the new fishing rods Mr. Gilchrist had on display, and Harry, most likely, was eyeing the lawn mowers. I knew I'd guessed right about Harry when he let out a low whistle and muttered, "Eighty dollars for a power mower. Who's got that kind of money?"

"Not me," Leo said cheerfully. "I reckon I'll have to keep on using the old Leo-powered model." Then he started singing, "I'm sad and weary, I've got those hungry, ragged blues."

They played that a lot on the radio. Songs about empty pockets and lost dreams seemed to touch a chord in folks these days.

Harry and I joined in, and we were all still singing when Tommie Dora's house came into view. That's when I clamped my mouth shut and started walking faster.

"You're stepping out all of a sudden," Leo remarked.

"I don't want her seeing us," I said. "I'll scrub every last floor in her house tomorrow, but *today I'm going out in that boat*."

Leo winked at Harry. "I reckon she's going out in that boat," he said.

We made it past the house without Tommie Dora calling us back and took the turnoff to the lake. When we got to Mr. Davies's place, Leo stopped and wiped his sweaty face on his shirtsleeve.

"Good gosh a'mighty, it's hot for March," he said. "Y'all wanna take a dip?"

"No," I said, "you're gonna teach me how to row, remember? Besides, it's too early for swimming. You don't see anybody else out there, do you?"

The beach and the sandstone cliffs just beyond were deserted. But come May, families would be spreading out picnic dinners on the sand, and us kids would be scrambling up the sides of those cliffs and leaping off into the lake. There were rocks just beneath the surface of the water on the far side of the cliffs, but we'd been coming here long enough to know where it was safe to dive. Even so, some mother was always yelling to her children, "Mind you steer clear of the rocks! You'll crack your heads open or worse!"

"See," I said to Leo, "nobody's here. Not even any boats."

"Except yours," Harry said, and started down Mr. Davies's dock.

When I saw the *Mary Bayliss*, shining white and more beautiful than I'd remembered, goose bumps popped up on my arms.

Harry studied the rowboat from one end to the other, and then he said, "You did a real good job, Leo. She's a beauty."

Then Leo lowered himself into the boat, and Harry and I climbed in after him.

"I'll row first," Leo said. "Keep your eyes on me, Bayliss, so you'll know how to do it. Harry, can you untie that rope?"

Leo pushed off from the dock, using an oar to turn the boat around, and started to row. I watched how his arms moved and how the oars sliced through the water. *Looks simple enough*, I thought.

Sunlight reflecting off the water nearly blinded me, and the sun was hot on my face and arms. But there was a breeze, just as I'd imagined it, sending little waves across the surface of the lake. And now that we were moving away from shore, everything looked different. The trees pressing in seemed bigger, and when I peered into the water, it didn't look dark at all, but clear enough for me to spot little fish swimming around the boat. And the island! I could make out details I'd never seen before. There were hollies and small water oaks growing in among the cedars, and bits of twisted driftwood on the sand that sloped down from the trees. The island would be the perfect place to camp this summer, but what I wanted to do right now was go out there and take a look around.

"You wanna try it?" Leo asked, and I nodded.

The boat rocked gently as we switched places. I sat down and picked up the oars, intending to head straight for the island. But I soon found out that rowing wasn't as easy as it looked. For one thing, the oars were heavy, and pulling them against the water put me in mind of dragging fence posts through molasses. Then there was the problem with my arms, which didn't seem to want to work the way Leo's had and before long were starting to ache. Leo must have seen I was having trouble because he commenced to telling me to do this and do that, and I got so bumfuzzled, none of it made any sense.

But I wasn't about to let him think it was too much for me. So I kept inching toward the island, gritting my teeth and grunting with every wobbly stroke, till my shoulders were throbbing and the palms of my hands were rubbed raw, and I just had to let go of those oars and rest a spell.

I reckon Leo could see that I was tuckered out, but all he said was, "It's hot as blazes out here. Why don't I row us back and we'll sit in the shade awhile?"

That was Leo's way, wanting to spare my feelings. So I nodded and squeezed past him to sit down next to Harry, trying not to show how sorely disappointed I was.

Leo brought the boat into a shady spot at the far end of the beach. While he was tying it to a scrawny pine, I got out and headed up the moss-covered side of the cliffs, following a zigzagging path that my feet knew by heart. I'd just reached the top, about thirty feet above the sand, when the boys started up after me.

My spirits were dragging and I wasn't in the mood to have them lifted, so I sat down with my back to Leo and Harry and looked out over the lake. The wind had picked up, making the water choppy. My eyes drifted over to the island, and I thought, *I'll never be able to row out there on my own. A new boat and what good is it to me?*

Then Leo and Harry came to sit on either side of me.

"You know, little bit," Leo said, "I was about your age when Mr. Vanzandt took Ray and me fishing and let us try rowing. And I didn't make it nearly as far as you that first time."

I just kept staring straight ahead and didn't say anything.

"You need to build up your muscles is all," Leo said.

Harry reached into his shirt pocket and brought out three lemon drops. "Elroy Johnson gave 'em to me," he said, popping one into his mouth and holding out the others to Leo and me.

As I sat there in the sun with the sweet-and-sour taste of the candy in my mouth, the aching in my shoulders began to ease up. Then my eyelids started to droop, and I yawned.

About that time, Harry yawned, too. "Wake me when it's time to go," he mumbled, and stretched out on the smooth surface of the rocks.

Leo unfolded his long legs and stood up. "I think I'll go for a swim," he said.

"Are you plumb crazy?" I asked, squinting up at him.

"Nope. Just hot."

He dropped his shirt at my feet and took off his shoes and socks. Then he walked to the edge of the cliff, gave a little bounce on the balls of his feet, and jumped. I leaned over the side just in time to see him disappear beneath the water. Seconds later, he came bobbing up again.

"It's great!" Leo yelled, pushing the wet hair back from his face. "*Freezing*, but great."

"Don't blame me if you get the grippe!" I called back.

I glanced at Harry, who was lying there with his eyes closed and hadn't moved, and then looked back at my brother. He was swimming toward the island.

I yawned again, thinking that I had to stay awake till Leo got back. But my eyelids were so heavy. Maybe I'd just close my eyes for a minute but not go to sleep. Because Daddy was always telling us, "Watch out for each other in the water."

But I could rest my eyes. No harm in that.

I lay down next to Harry, barely aware of the clouds moving across the sun, filtering out some of the light. The heat from the rock seeped through my shirt, toasting my skin. I turned on my side and slipped an arm under my head to cushion it.

This was what I needed. Just a few minutes to lie here and think about things. I felt better about the boat after what Leo said. And I *would* learn to row it.

I woke up with a start. It was so dark, I thought I'd been asleep for hours. Still groggy, I looked at the sky and realized that the sun was hidden behind a big black cloud. Then I heard the rumble of thunder.

"Wake up," I said to Harry, nudging his arm. "A storm's coming."

I got to my feet and looked out over the water for Leo,

expecting to see his head bobbing on top of the waves. But there was no sign of him. My eyes dropped to the beach below. It was deserted. So where *was* he? He couldn't have just vanished. Then a terrible thought shot through my mind, jolting me. All of a sudden I felt weak. And scared. *Please, God*, I prayed, my eyes darting back across the water to the island. And that's when I saw him, ambling down the sandy slope from the trees, then stooping to pick up a pebble or something at his feet.

Well, if that didn't beat all! I was shaking now, but I wasn't scared anymore—I was mad! Here I'd been thinking Leo had drowned, and all the while he'd been lollygagging on that island.

Harry had come to stand beside me. We watched Leo walk slowly along the narrow beach, head down, eyes searching the sand.

"What's he doing?" Harry muttered. "You think he doesn't see those clouds?"

I shrugged, frowning, then started shouting Leo's name. Harry joined in, but Leo couldn't hear us, so I tried waving my arms to get his attention.

Leo finally looked up and saw us. He nodded and pointed to the sky to show that he knew about the storm. Then he started doing a silly little dance on the sand.

"Dadburn it!" I yelled at him. "Quit fooling around and get back here!"

As if he'd heard me—which didn't seem likely over the rising wind—Leo stopped dancing and began to wade out into the water. When it was up to his waist, he dove in.

Another clap of thunder sounded, closer this time, and I felt the first drops of rain on my face. The wind was whipping across the lake, causing whitecaps to form on the waves.

"The water's pretty rough," Harry said, sounding worried.

But I was barely listening. The rain was coming down harder, and I was having trouble seeing Leo. I moved toward the edge of the cliff.

"Don't go any closer," Harry said. "You're making me nervous."

A flash of lightning lit up the sky. Startled, I blinked and, in that instant, lost sight of Leo. All I could see was water. Just endless gray waves rising in foamy peaks, then falling, then rising again.

I clutched Harry's arm, my nails digging into the cloth of his shirt. "I don't see him!"

"There," Harry said, pointing.

At the tip of Harry's finger, I spotted him. "Come on, Leo," I whispered. *Please, God . . .*

The rain was beating down now, and Leo was still a long way from shore. Thunder shook the air and made Harry and me jump.

"I think I better get somebody," he said.

I gave a jerky nod. "Mr. Davies. Yeah, Harry, go get him."

Harry took off down the side of the cliff. I pushed the wet hair out of my face, straining to see through the rain. My eyes were on Leo when he went under. A few seconds later, he surfaced again, but I could tell something was wrong. He was holding his arms over his head, his hands clenched into fists.

Fear grabbed me, taking my breath away. I cried out for Harry, but Harry was gone. Then Leo sank under the waves, and I knew I couldn't wait for help.

Not stopping to think, I took a step toward the edge of the cliff. I didn't expect the mossy rocks to be so slippery. It happened so fast, I didn't even realize that my foot had slid out from under me.

I wouldn't remember much of what came next. Falling into space. Hitting the water. Smashing against the rocks. Then . . . nothing.

8. DROWNING

I don't remember being taken to the hospital in Birmingham. I don't remember being poked and jabbed and x-rayed, any more than I recollect Mother sitting beside my bed for two days and three nights without ever closing her eyes.

The nurses said I was off in my own shadowy world, in a deep sleep most of the time. Then suddenly I'd be choking and gasping, clawing at the bedsheets and kicking them into a tangle. I don't remember any of that either, but later on one of the doctors told me that at some level I must have known I was in trouble, and all that thrashing around was me trying to save myself from drowning.

I don't remember the nurses trying to comfort Mother and Daddy by saying what a fighter I was. The only words I *do* remember were spoken by a young nurse who looked down at me and said, "It's a miracle she survived, poor little thing."

A *miracle*. That was the first time I'd hear those words, but it wouldn't be the last.

9. SURFACING

This is the second thing I remember: feeling scared. *Really* scared. And looking up at my mother and saying, "Leo." She was holding my hand, and I felt her jerk when she heard his name. And in that sickening instant, I knew. That's when somebody started screaming. It was a raw, heartbreaking sound like nothing I'd ever heard before. Then Mother was bending over me, whispering, "Hush now, hush, sugar," and I realized the screams were coming from me.

The next thing I remember is Daddy sitting beside my bed, looking exhausted and a lot older than he should. He put his hand on my arm and said, "You fractured a bone in your spine. They'll give you shots of morphine for the pain." He said, "You hit your head and back on the rocks." And that's all I remember.

It took at least two more days, maybe three, for me to come all the way back. For me to really understand what was going on. I wanted to ask what happened to Leo, but I was too scared. Because I knew just saying his name would upset Daddy and bring back that look to my mother's eyes. I tried to find a word to describe the look—*If Leo were here,* I thought, *he'd be able to tell me*—but I couldn't come up with one on my own that came close. And I thought, *Maybe there aren't any words for something this terrible.*

Then a memory flashed into my mind, so unexpected it startled me. Grandpa Halsey and I were walking in the woods. I must have been five or six. The leaves over our heads were red and yellow. Leaves as bright as sunflowers were falling from the trees all around us. I'd been happy that day. Happy to be in the woods with the leaves dancing in the air. Happy to be with my grandpa.

But then it all turned horrible. We found the dog, a big tan and white collie. Somebody had shot him, and he was lying there on his side, the yellow leaves under his body turning red from the blood oozing out of his chest. At first, I thought he was dead, but then I saw one of his back legs twitch and heard the wheezing when he tried to breathe.

Grandpa Halsey said a hunter must have mistaken the dog for a deer. He took my hand and tried to pull me away, saying he had to go get his gun, but I wouldn't leave the dog. Grandpa finally had to pick me up and carry me back to the house, but not before the collie lifted his head, so weak his whole body trembled with the effort, and looked straight into my face. There was pure misery in that dog's eyes, and they seemed to be saying, *I don't understand. Why is this happening to me?* But there was nothing I could do. It was Grandpa Halsey who took his rifle back to the woods, while I crawled up under the porch off the kitchen, crying so hard I threw up. That's where I was when I heard the crack of a rifle shot and knew it was over.

Crouched under the porch, sobbing, I hadn't been able to imagine anything worse than that happening. But now it had, and I understood, *truly* understood for the first time, how bewildered that poor old dog must have been. Maybe that's what I'd seen in my mother's eyes when she heard Leo's name, her asking herself, *Why is this happening?* So I wouldn't say it again, the name I loved best in the world.

I lay there wondering why nobody had ever told me how hard life is. How everything can change in a second, and once it has, there's nothing you can do to make it right again. Even a dying dog had known that before I did.

Now I woke up at every sound. I'd open my eyes and lie real still because the pain in my back was bad. Moving even the tiniest bit would send it shooting down my backbone from that broken place between my shoulder blades. But the break would heal. My daddy had said so. It was the other broken place he didn't mention. The one so deep inside, the doctors would never be able to find it, even if they cut me wide open. There weren't any shots for that kind of pain. I was sure there was no help for it at all, and that there would be no end to it. And because I was alive when my brother was dead, this seemed only right.

The doctors said I was out of danger. That first night, they'd told Mother and Daddy that I might not live and, if I did, there was a chance I'd have permanent brain damage. So everybody seemed happy that I could count to ten and knew what month it was. Now Mother was going home with Daddy at night and coming back in the morning, looking awful, her face the color of oatmeal except for the purple smudges under her eyes. She'd kiss me on the cheek and ask if I'd slept well, and I'd say, "Yes, ma'am." Then Daddy would come in, looking tired to death and all hunched over like he didn't have the strength to hold his head up. He'd ask me if I'd had a good breakfast, and I'd answer, "Yes, sir," although I couldn't have said what it was I'd eaten.

There was one doctor with a long, sad face who came in every morning to examine my back and ask me to describe the pain. Since the pain never changed, I didn't know why he bothered. But he was kind, and I always felt a little better after he'd been there.

"Healing will take time," he told me, "but in three or four months, you'll be as good as new."

I felt sorry for the doctor when he said that. I knew he wanted to think of me getting well and strong again, so I didn't tell him the truth: that I'd never be the same. That *nothing* would ever be the same.

One morning, when I was propped up in bed eating my breakfast—real slow because it hurt to lift the fork to my mouth—a young nurse came in.

"Morning," she said, and smiled at me. "How are you feeling?"

I didn't recall having ever seen the nurse before, but her voice seemed familiar.

"You probably don't remember me," she said, setting a tray on the bed beside me, "but I was here the day after they brought you in."

And then I did remember. "You said it was a miracle I was alive."

"Why, bless your heart," the nurse said in surprise. "Imagine, you hearing that."

"Do you really think it's a miracle?" I asked her.

The nurse was wiping my arm with something cold, but now she looked up. "You were in the water a long time, and you weren't breathing when they pulled you out. Your heart had stopped." She smiled again and said, "Yes, I believe it's a miracle. I reckon there's a reason why you were saved. God must have a special purpose for you."

I thought, *A special purpose? But Leo was the special one. Why wasn't he saved?*

"You've been given a second chance," the nurse went

on as she stuck the needle into my arm. "You just have to figure out what you're supposed to do with it."

I'd never thought about needing a reason for being alive. It was too much to take in all at once. So I closed my eyes and waited for the shot to do its work.

10. HOME

Three days after Leo's funeral, they let me go home. It hurt to sit up, so I was lying in the backseat, and even though Daddy drove slow, when he hit a bump, it felt like somebody was stabbing me in the back with a butcher knife. By the time he turned in to our driveway, it was all I could do to keep from crying.

Those days and nights in the hospital, when I'd felt tears pressing on my eyeballs till they ached, I'd wished I could just give in to it and start bawling. Only I was never alone for five minutes, what with all the nurses trotting in and out, and I hadn't wanted to go to pieces in front of folks I barely knew.

But more than that, I didn't want to break down because my mother and daddy hadn't shed a tear—not once since Leo died. At least, not that I'd seen. They'd seemed like strangers, all stiff and careful and talking about things that didn't matter. I'd wanted to tell them to stop pretending—I'd wanted to *scream* it—because I couldn't stand them acting like nothing had happened. Leo was gone, and all the pretending in the world wouldn't change that.

But then I'd found myself doing the same thing, babbling nonsense about the pot of violets Kathleen had sent me or the rice pudding I'd had for dessert the night before, because it hadn't seemed right to make Mother and Daddy hurt any more than they already did. And because it had scared me to think of what could happen if they suddenly started talking about what was really on their minds, what was weighing them down every minute of the day. They might fall apart, and then so would I. And once it all came spewing out, what if I ended up saying something ugly that I couldn't take back? So I tucked away a lot of feelings at the back of my mind where I wouldn't be tripping over them all the time.

Now that I was home, all I wanted to do was go to my room and be by myself. But even getting out of the car was a struggle, and crossing the grass to the porch with my mother and daddy helping seemed to take forever. And then there were the porch steps to climb.

Rosie was asleep in the swing. Before all this happened, I would have scooped her up and planted a kiss between her ears, but today I barely noticed she was there.

When Daddy opened the front door, Kathleen came rushing down the hall toward us, smiling and anxious.

Then her eyes settled on my face, and all of a sudden she wasn't smiling anymore.

"Do I look that bad?" I asked her, not really caring.

"No, not at all," Kathleen said real quick. "You look . . . good."

"You two can talk later," Mother said. "We need to get Bayliss to bed."

Daddy helped me up the stairs and down the hall to my room. Mother had gone ahead. When I finally got there, I saw that she'd turned back the quilt and top sheet and had the bed ready for me.

I was hurting something awful, but after Daddy left, I had to stand there while Mother took off my clothes and got me into a pair of pajamas. My back was on fire and my legs were shaking like they were about to give way, but the worst was still to come. Sitting down on the edge of the bed and easing my body under the sheet was pure torture. Mother went over to the window to pull the shade, and I just lay there with my eyes closed, hardly breathing, while I waited for the pain to let up.

After she was gone, I stretched out my arms and legs, trying to get more comfortable. It didn't help. I had thought I'd feel better once I was home and in my own bed, away from the noise and all the people coming and going. I'd pictured myself snuggled up under my blue and white quilt, cozy and safe, like when I was little and had the measles and my mother brought me cinnamon toast and cocoa on a tray. But this was nothing like having the measles. And lying there in the quiet, I realized that I missed all the commotion in the hospital. It had kept me thinking about what was going on around me, but now I had nothing to fill my mind and troublesome thoughts were starting to creep in. Like Leo's door.

When Daddy and I had gotten to the top of the stairs, I'd noticed right off that every door was open except for Leo's. That bothered me, but Mother was hurrying past to get the bed ready, and I'd had to shift my attention to making it a few more feet.

Now, staring at the ceiling, I remembered that closed door. It seemed like somebody was trying to shut out any reminder of Leo. Had they already packed up his books and ship models? Given his clothes away? I found myself getting agitated, because nobody had the right to get rid of Leo's things.

I drifted in and out of sleep. Once, when I opened my eyes, I found Rosie lying in the crook of my arm with her head on my shoulder. Even that light pressure hurt my back, but I wouldn't have dreamed of making her move. When I woke up again, Rosie was gone, and Kathleen and Tommie Dora were standing just inside the doorway.

I was surprised to see my grandmother, who went out of

her way *not* to visit sick people. Tommie Dora was the first to admit that sickrooms made her fidgety, and that by the time she left, most folks wished she'd never come at all. But here she was, wearing her good navy-and-white-dotted dress, and she'd pinned down that wiry hair of hers so that it was hardly sticking out at all. I could tell she'd gone to a lot of trouble to make herself presentable.

She dragged the desk chair over to the bed and sat down.

"So how are you feeling, Mary Bayliss?"

"All right."

"Are you in much pain?"

I was struggling to sit up, and it felt like a hand was squeezing my spine, about to snap it in two. But I still noticed something different about my grandmother's voice. It sounded almost . . . *kind*.

"No, ma'am," I said.

"Don't you fib to me, Mary Bayliss Pettigrew." Now she sounded aggravated—meaning, she was back to normal. "I'm not so old and addled that I can't tell when somebody's suffering. And *you've* seen better days!"

Kathleen, who was usually so eager to please any grownup it was sickening, frowned at Tommie Dora like she was warning her, which made me realize that I *must* look awful.

"Kathleen," I said, "will you hand me that mirror off the dresser?"

My sister seemed to get nervous all of a sudden. "Mother wants you to rest," she said, fluttering around and letting her eyes light on everything but me. "We should leave so you can—"

"Oh, for crying out loud," Tommie Dora said, "let her have the mirror." Then she looked at me. "Don't get upset by what you see, Mary Bayliss. It's only temporary."

Kathleen brought me the mirror and gave our grand-mother another look, as if to say, *All right. Just don't blame me when she gets hysterical.* But when I held the mirror up and saw my reflection, I was too shocked to make a sound. My face looked like a big mound of rising bread dough, all puffed up and faintly yellow, with dark purple bruises down one side that were the exact same color as blackberry jam. Blood had pooled in my eyes so the whites were red and liquidy, and to top it off, my hair was stiff and plastered down like a skillet full of grease had been dumped over my head. I understood now why Kathleen hadn't wanted me to see myself. I looked like death eating a cracker.

I let the mirror drop to the bed. There was a new sad-ness in my heart, one more thing to grieve over. I didn't think I could take much more. But then I pictured myself dissolving into a puddle of tears in front of my grandmother, and that's what saved me. I wasn't about to start blubbering like a baby with Tommie Dora there! Why had she come anyhow? She sure wasn't helping. It was all well and good for her to tell me not to get upset, but *she* didn't look like a monster. *Her* back wasn't broken. The only thing wrong with *her* was being old. But I was young. I was supposed to be strong and healthy, not all beat up like I'd been trampled and left for dead. What if my face stayed like this? What if my back never got better? How could I bear it?

Tommie Dora was just sitting there watching me.

Finally, she said, "Mary Bayliss, as hard as this is for the rest of us, I know it's hardest of all for you." And there it was again, the kindness in her voice. "But you'll get through it, and I'm gonna be here to see that you do. So what do you have to say about that?"

I didn't have any idea how to answer her, so I said the first thing that popped into my head, which was, "I need to wash my hair."

One of Tommie Dora's eyebrows arched like a bird's wing. Then her lips started twitching, and I thought for a second she was fixing to smile. But she nipped that in the bud and frowned instead. "We'll take care of it tomorrow," she said.

It wasn't till my grandmother had left that I realized something that made me feel ashamed. All I'd been thinking about was myself. How I looked and how I felt. And how much I missed Leo. But Tommie Dora had lost him, too, and even if she wasn't one to make a fuss over her grandkids, there was no doubt in my mind that she'd loved him. She had to be all torn up, and yet she seemed like the same old Tommie Dora. Except for those few moments of being almost nice.

But Tommie Dora could handle anything. I'd never seen her fall apart and was pretty sure I never would. I wondered if she'd cried at the funeral, but that just made me feel worse. Because *I* should have been there. It was *my brother* they'd buried.

I still couldn't believe it. That he was gone. That I'd never hear him call me Miss Mulligrubs or little britches again.

And right before I fell asleep, I had one last thought: *Now there's nobody for Tommie Dora to leave the farm to.*

11. THE HARDEST THING

I'd just finished breakfast the next morning when Tommie Dora came barging in and started giving orders. Mother was to help her get me out of bed so they could wash my hair. Kathleen was to go find a big pan to fill with water.

"I can't bend over," I said to Tommie Dora as she steered me into the bathroom.

"All you have to do is get into the tub and stand there."

"I can't stand for long either."

"Mary Bayliss, you can do this," Tommie Dora said. "You're tough as an old boot."

I wasn't sure if she meant that as a compliment or not, but before I could puzzle it out, she had me in the tub.

Tommie Dora directed Kathleen to fill the pan with warm water. While Mother held on to me, my grandmother poured the water over my head, shampooed my hair, then rinsed it. By the time they got me dried, dressed, and back in bed, I was feeling weak and sick to my stomach from the pain.

But a while later, when visitors started coming, I was glad that my hair was clean at least. I didn't want to see anybody—or have them see me looking this sorry—but folks in Lenore believe in paying their respects when somebody's laid up, and nothing short of smallpox would have kept them away.

Mavis Quick was the first to arrive, and right behind her came Jewel Clark, which worked out well since Mavis liked nothing better than remarking on how poorly the patient looked and having somebody there to agree with her.

"See how her face is all swoll up?" Mavis asked, peering down at me.

"My uncle Stub looked just like that before he died," Jewel said. "Kicked in the head by a mule."

"You see all that blood in her eyes? That can't be good."

"No, ma'am," Jewel said, shaking her head. "Not good a'tall."

Then Mavis said to me, "Baby girl, you're lucky to be alive. George Davies told us it was a miracle, and I reckon he was right. I didn't know how bad off you'd be."

That was when Kathleen, who'd been standing by the door listening, hurried in to show them out. Only, before I could fully appreciate the ladies' departure, I heard somebody else coming down the hall. But it was just Miz Burdeshaw, who'd never think of comparing me to kin that was now deceased, toting a stack of old *Ladies' Home Journals* for me to read. And then Miss Ida Henderson stopped by on her way to the library. She'd cut out a newspaper article about an aviator named Ruth Nichols who broke her back in five places when her plane crashed and still went on to set a new world's distance record.

"Be sure to write about her in your book," Miss Ida said. "Ruth Nichols should be a particular inspiration to you."

Other ladies from the neighborhood and from church came parading through all morning, some bringing spring flowers from their yards, and almost every one of them remarking that it was a miracle I was still alive and kicking. Miz Mayhew, an old woman who was every bit as sharp-tongued as Tommie Dora, twice as nosy, and spiteful to boot, asked me if the doctors expected me to ever walk again. And judging from the sly look on her face, I was pretty sure she was hoping not. But Kathleen must have been afraid I'd haul off and slap her because she was rushing the old biddy out of the room before I had time to answer.

It was getting close to noon, and Kathleen had gone downstairs to warm up some of the food folks had brought, when I heard my mother talking to somebody in the hall. Then I recognized Annie's voice.

Annie Schumann had been my best friend since first grade, and there'd never been a time in the past six years when I hadn't welcomed a visit from her. Till now. The truth was, I didn't care to have her see me like this, all crippled and looking the way I did. I could just picture the shock—and the pity—on her face when she saw me, and I wasn't up to that just yet. So I pulled the quilt over my head and pretended to be asleep.

The door creaked open. Then I heard Mother whisper, "All the visitors must have worn her out. But you're just what she needs, Annie. Why don't you come back in the morning?"

I lay there with my head covered for a long time after they left. I knew Mother wouldn't understand why I didn't want to see my best friend. She'd say, *So what if Annie feels sorry for you? Wouldn't you feel sorry if she'd been the one to get hurt?* But I could just see Annie running down Main Street to meet me before school, with that blond hair bouncing on her shoulders and those long legs pumping. Annie was always in a hurry. And Annie hadn't changed. She could still run, and she could still climb the ladder to her tree house and swing back to the ground on the rope Leo had put up for us, while I was shuffling down the hall to the bathroom like an old lady.

After dinner, I slept for a while and woke up hurting. Rosie was stretched out in the chair beside my bed. I was talking to her, trying to shut out the pain, when the door suddenly swung open and there were two nuns in black habits standing on the threshold. The young, pretty one was my teacher, Sister Boniface, and the old, grumpy one was Sister Annunciata, who had probably punished me more times over the years than all the other kids at Sacred Heart put together.

They came over to the bed, and I tried to sit up, but Sister Annunciata said, "Lie still, Mary Bayliss. We aren't staying long. We just came by to see how you're feeling."

"I'm fine, Sister."

"I doubt *that*," Sister Annunciata said in that stern voice that made you think you were in trouble even when you weren't. "But you will be."

"Before you know it," Sister Boniface added, and smiled at me.

Of all the nuns, Sister Boniface was my favorite. Besides being beautiful, she was kind and caring, exactly what a nun ought to be—and, I thought, cutting my eyes at Sister Annunciata, too often was not.

I asked them to sit down. Sister Boniface shook her head, but Sister Annunciata said, "For a minute," and plopped herself down in the chair. Luckily, Rosie made it to the floor in time to avoid suffocation, but just by a whisker.

Now, I thought, *they'll start in on how God saved me for a purpose.*

But Sister Boniface talked mostly about schoolwork,

telling me not to worry about my assignments, that my grades were high enough for me to pass even if I didn't make it back before the end of school. And Sister Annunciata said I wasn't to worry about *anything*, that it was my job to heal and get my strength back. Then Sister Boniface said she'd bring me some books from the school library. The whole time they were there, they didn't utter the words God or *miracle* even once, which was peculiar, them being nuns and all. And after they left, it occurred to me that Sister Boniface, and even Sister Annunciata, hadn't seemed to care much *why* I was alive, just that I was.

I lay in bed that night thinking, *Why did God take Leo and not me?* Back at the hospital, I'd asked myself that over and over, and never could come up with an answer. But now I was wondering if maybe that nurse had been right. *Had* I been saved for something special? But who was going to tell me what that something special was?

Then, out of the blue, I remembered the fortune-teller: Eugenie Watts saying she couldn't see Leo's future in the cards, and Leo saying that maybe she'd seen something too awful to tell him. It could drive you crazy—wondering if she'd known and, if so, why she hadn't warned him. I squeezed my eyes shut, not wanting to think about it. Not wanting to think at all. About the hardest thing, especially. That it was my fault. That if I hadn't been so set on taking that boat out, Leo wouldn't have even been at the lake and he'd still be alive.

When the worst thing in the world happens, you look back and see all kinds of ways you might have been able to stop it. If only you'd known to do this instead of that. But it's too late then, so it just eats at you.

12. FIRST STEPS

Annie came back the next morning before school. I heard her in the hall telling Kathleen that her mother had sent me some oatmeal cookies. I felt a little guilty, especially considering the cookies, but not guilty enough to face her, so I pretended to be asleep again.

"I'll wake her," Kathleen said from the doorway. "She'll want to see you."

"You think so?" Annie asked, and I heard something unfamiliar in her voice. She sounded hurt. "That's all right," she said. "Just let her sleep."

Daddy checked on me when he came home at noon, and since the pain was no better, I thought about telling him I could use one of those shots they gave me in the hospital. But he seemed so hopeful when he asked how I was feeling, I ended up saying what he wanted to hear.

Mother had fixed chicken and dumplings, and she looked almost excited when she brought in the tray. Not so long ago, a meal like this would have been something for

Leo and me to celebrate, like when we'd had fried chicken on my birthday. But without him here to enjoy it with me, the sight of those dumplings just made my heart ache.

After Mother left, I ate a little bit, but I didn't have much of an appetite and ended up giving most of it to Rosie. She was taking a bite off my fork when I looked up and saw Harry standing in the doorway.

He held up a hand and said, "Hey."

"Hey, yourself. Come on in."

Harry was never in a rush, but I thought he took longer than usual to sidle over to the bed.

"Why aren't you in school?" I asked him.

"I just came home for dinner. Thought I'd stop by and see how you're doing."

His eyes didn't quite meet mine, and I could tell he was feeling awkward, which was strange since Harry had been running in and out of our house for as long as I could re-member. He was almost like a second . . . a second brother. Was he uneasy because of Leo? Because he hadn't been able to save him? But Harry must know I didn't blame *him*. He'd gone for help. I remembered that much. None of this was Harry's fault.

He reached out to scratch Rosie behind her ears, still not looking at me.

"You went for Mr. Davies," I said, and Harry's head jerked up. "Then I slipped and fell. That's the last thing that's clear in my mind. Nobody's told me the rest—you know, who got me out of the water and all."

Harry's face was chalky, every freckle seeming to pop out at me. "James and Albert, Mr. Davies's sons, were at their dad's place when it happened, and they all came to help. James and I climbed to the top of the cliff, but you weren't there. Then we saw you in the water, on the side where the rocks are. Your eyes were closed, and you were so still, I thought you were dead." His shoulders sagged like the memory was a heavy weight. "It was James who pulled you out and then went to get your daddy. And Mr. Davies got you breathing again."

This was the first time I'd talked about that day, and it was scary. But there was something else I needed to know.

"Who found Leo?"

Harry's eyes dropped to the floor. "Albert and I took the boat out to look for him, but . . . it was too late."

I was feeling sick. The few bites of dumpling I'd eaten were rolling around in my stomach and threatening to come back up. "Anyhow," I said, "you tried."

He was staring out the window, looking hard at nothing. "But trying wasn't good enough, was it?"

I didn't leave my room for two weeks except to go to the bathroom. Mother was in and out, and Daddy and Kathleen spent time with me before they left for the day and in the evenings, but my constant companion was Rosie. She stayed at my side while I looked at the magazines Miz Burdeshaw had brought and while I napped. I napped a lot.

Annie didn't come back, but Harry stopped by every morning before school. And late in the afternoon, either Tommie Dora or Sister Boniface would come read to me. They were taking turns.

When Sister Boniface had mentioned bringing books from the school library, I'd expected them to be Bible stories. So I was surprised when she came in with *Treasure Island*, which I'd never read but remembered Leo liking a lot. That first day, my back was giving me a fit, and I was gritting my teeth when Sister Boniface sat down and started reading. But it wasn't long before the book grabbed my attention and held it. By the fourth or fifth page, I was so caught up in the story, I hardly thought about the pain.

Sister Boniface would mark where we left off, and the following day Tommie Dora would begin with the next chapter. Tommie Dora had never read *Treasure Island* either and liked it as much as I did, so I'd fill her in on what she'd missed the day before.

But one afternoon, instead of opening the book, Tommie Dora just sat there studying my face. Finally, she said, "The swelling's gone down. Have you looked at yourself?"

I shook my head. Mother remarked every day that my

face was getting better, but mothers are supposed to say things like that.

"Then it's time you did," Tommie Dora said, and handed me the mirror.

My eyes were still on her instead of my reflection.

"Go on," she said.

So I looked and saw that the swelling was gone and the bruises had faded till you could just barely see them. Even the whites of my eyes were truly white again and not blood-red.

I was smiling into the mirror when Tommie Dora said, "All right. That's enough vanity for one day." Then she opened the book and started to read.

We'd gotten to the part where Jim and the others go inside the cave and see piles of coins and gold bars—and Tommie Dora was just as anxious to find out what was going to happen next as I was—when Daddy stuck his head in and said, "Supper's nearly ready. Stay and eat with us, Mother, and I'll take you home after."

Then Daddy looked at me and said, "I think it's time you started coming to the table, baby. You need to be moving around more. Try walking to the corner tomorrow."

Tommie Dora agreed. "It's the only way you'll get your strength back."

"But I still hurt," I told them, "especially when I'm not lying down."

"You'll heal faster if you walk," Daddy said. "I want you to go a little bit farther every day. Just don't twist or bend down, and don't lift anything."

"Mary Bayliss, I'll come early tomorrow and walk with you," Tommie Dora said. "We can be back before Sister Boniface gets here."

It sounded like a bad idea to me. All that walking was going to be painful, and there was no telling *who* we'd run into. But with the two of them ganging up on me, I didn't have much choice.

The next morning, I managed to put on a shirt and a pair of overalls by myself. But I was so worn out from the effort, I slept till dinner. After we ate, Mother helped me with my socks and shoes, and then I shuffled out to the porch to wait for Tommie Dora. By the time Daddy dropped her off, I was hurting and aggravated.

Before she'd even reached the porch, I said, "I need to rest."

"You've been resting for weeks. Come on, it won't kill you to walk a block."

Grumbling a little, I started down the porch steps, holding on tight to the railing. I used to fly down those steps, but now I was scared of falling.

Tommie Dora took my arm and led me down the driveway to the street. My legs were already feeling rubbery. But when I told her as much, hoping we'd turn around and go back inside, all Tommie Dora said was, "See how weak you are from lying up in bed?"

From then on, we walked every afternoon. I truly hated those walks. I'd catch folks like old Miz Mayhew or Jewel Clark peeking around their snowball bushes or out the front window at me, just dying to see what kind of progress Lenore's walking miracle was making. I reckon the only difference between me and the bearded lady in the circus was, folks had to pay to see the bearded lady. But since nothing exciting ever happened in this town, I figured I'd better get used to being the main attraction for a while.

After we'd been walking for a few days, I had to admit it was getting easier. But I still couldn't pick up Rosie or wash my own hair. I couldn't even get out of bed without the pain grabbing me. And some mornings I was so stove up, I felt as old as Tommie Dora.

But I was trying not to complain too much. Because I'd been thinking, what if God heard me and decided I didn't *deserve* a second chance?

Mother had just left my room after saying good night, and I was fixing my arms and legs in the most comfortable positions possible, when I heard her say, "What were you doing in there?" like she was accusing somebody of something.

And Kathleen started stammering, "I was . . . I was just . . . looking at his clothes, wondering if . . . if maybe we shouldn't give 'em to somebody who can use 'em."

I lay real still, waiting for my mother's answer.

"We will," Mother said, her voice so low now I could barely hear it. "One day."

The next morning, Kathleen was wearing a shirt of Leo's over her pajamas. And a few days later, on my way downstairs for my walk with Tommie Dora, I saw that Leo's door was open and Mother was inside filling a box with his clothes.

I should've said something, maybe kept her company while she packed it all up, but I reckon I wasn't ready to admit that Leo wouldn't be needing those clothes anymore. Sometimes I'd even forget for a minute that he was gone. I'd walk into the kitchen and expect him to be sitting at the table, grinning. Or I'd see something move out of the corner of my eye and think it was Leo walking down the hall. But the feeling that he was still with us was strongest at night when I was in bed and everything was quiet. Lots of times I'd sense his presence, even though I couldn't see him. But when I'd say his name, he didn't answer. Maybe it only seemed real because I wanted so much for it to be true.

I was still thinking about Leo when I went outside to the porch. I wondered if Mother and Daddy and Kathleen ever had the feeling that he was close by. And Tommie

Dora. Did she sometimes think she caught a glimpse of him out there hoeing in her garden?

The Model T was turning in to the driveway. Daddy waved to me, and Tommie Dora got out and headed for the porch. Watching her climb the steps, huffing and puffing a little and glaring at a wasp buzzing around her head, I couldn't help smiling.

"What are you grinning at?" she asked, sounding cranky. "I'm old and I'm fat and I don't move like when I was young and skinny."

"I'm just glad to see you," I said.

13. A REVELATION

When school let out in May, and Kathleen was home to stay with me, Mother went back to work at Daddy's office. Much to my relief. I didn't need anybody taking care of me now that I could do most things for myself, as long as I didn't have to lift anything or bend down—so somebody still had to tie my shoes. And the truth was, Mother had been getting on my nerves.

It seemed like every five minutes she'd be asking if I needed something, or I'd glance up and find her studying my face, looking for *what* I didn't know, but it was bothersome. And besides that, she'd been growing more restless by the day. She'd scrub and rescrub every floor, every cabinet, every *doorknob,* till I started thinking twice before walking through a room for fear of tracking in a speck of dirt. Now don't get me wrong. Mother had always kept a nice house, but I'd never known her to iron my underwear or take a toothbrush to the bathroom tile before. She just couldn't sit still.

Everything else was out of kilter, too, and it wasn't just Leo not being there. Like one Sunday morning we were all at the breakfast table and I noticed that Mother and Kathleen had on their good clothes, but Daddy was wearing an old shirt with paint stains on it. That's when it came to me that Daddy hadn't been to Mass once since I got home from the hospital, and that wasn't like him. The only time he ever missed being in church on a Sunday morning was when a patient needed him. Course, I wouldn't have been able to sit in one of those hard pews without my back seizing up, but there was no reason for him not to go.

So I said, "Daddy, why don't you go to Mass with Mother and Kathleen? You don't have to stay with me. I'll be fine."

And from the sudden tightening of his mouth, and the way Mother's and Kathleen's eyes darted to his face, I knew right away that I'd said something wrong. But for the life of me, I couldn't figure out what it was.

Then Daddy said quietly, "Maybe next Sunday." And Mother commenced to talking about what she was planning for dinner, ticking off every vegetable, as well as the spoon bread and iced tea, and it was pretty clear that she just wanted to change the subject.

The way they were acting was perplexing and made me wonder what they all knew that I didn't. So when Kathleen left to get her pocketbook and gloves off the hall table, I went after her.

"Kathleen," I said, "why isn't Daddy going to Mass? If it's because of me—"

"No, no," she cut in, "it's not you. Daddy's just hurting. And confused. He can't understand all this. . . . Why Leo . . . Why God let it happen."

"You mean he's blaming God for Leo drowning?"

"Not *blaming* Him," Kathleen said quickly. Then she sighed. "Well, I guess he is. And going to church doesn't bring him comfort right now, not the way it does Mother. She tried to get him to talk to Father Mueller or to pray about it, but Daddy said he didn't see the point. He's just grieving and torn up, Bayliss. Father Mueller told Mother that sometimes folks get so angry when something like this happens, they just have to get mad at *somebody*, but that he'll get over it and we're not to worry."

I didn't tell Kathleen this, but I wasn't worried about Daddy being mad at God. I could even understand why he might be, since I was having some trouble myself figuring out why God hadn't saved Leo, when it would have been so easy for Him to do.

"Just don't mention Mass to Daddy again, all right, Bayliss?"

So I didn't. And every Sunday morning, Daddy and I stayed home while Mother and Kathleen went to church.

Just as spring had come early that year, the full heat of summer was already settling over the town. I'd wake up in the mornings with my hair damp and my pajamas sticking to my back. And I'd wake up hurting, but the pain was beginning to change. It wasn't so much a fierce stabbing that grabbed my attention as a nagging ache that I could sometimes ignore.

Tommie Dora and I were still walking, and now she was the one who came home dragging. One afternoon she took longer than usual to climb the porch steps and then sank into the nearest rocker. I sat down in the chair next to hers.

"Well, Mary Bayliss," she said when she'd caught her breath, "I don't reckon these old legs can keep up with yours anymore. Tomorrow you can strike out on your own."

I was startled by this announcement, but even more so by my reaction to it. The thing was, I hadn't minded Tommie Dora's company nearly as much as I'd expected to. I'd seen early on that folks weren't as likely to ask nosy questions when she was there, and besides that, the time I spent with my grandmother had turned out to be kind of comfortable. She didn't hover and make me feel like an invalid, and she never once said anything just to cheer me up. Whatever words came spilling out of Tommie Dora's mouth were as honest and plainspoken as she could make them. And even though we never talked about Leo, I knew she'd be willing to, whenever I was ready. Tommie Dora wasn't one to shy away from something just because it was hard.

"We won't walk so far," I told her.

"Don't even think about slacking off," she said. "Just look how it's helped."

I was staring down at my hands, not wanting to let on how disappointed I was.

"Course, I'll still come see you," Tommie Dora went on, "and your daddy can bring you out to the farm to visit."

I looked up at her. "Or I could walk."

Tommie Dora raised her eyebrows. "All the way to my house? You're not strong enough for that yet."

"I'm plenty strong," I said.

"Well, all I can say is, I admire your gumption, Mary Bayliss."

And that was a lot coming from Tommie Dora. I couldn't remember her ever saying she admired *anything* about me before.

So the next afternoon, while Kathleen was listening to one of her soap operas on the radio, I called out from the hall, "I'm going for my walk."

"Say hey to Tommie Dora for me," Kathleen called back.

I hadn't told anybody I'd be walking alone, or where I'd be going, but I figured Kathleen would be wrapped up in her programs and wouldn't notice how long I was gone.

It wasn't till I turned onto Main Street that I realized I was still attracting attention. Some folks spoke and asked how I was doing, but others, like the old men in front of the courthouse, just stared a hole through me. And without Tommie Dora there, I felt conspicuous. But then I thought, *So what? Let 'em get an eyeful.*

It took longer to reach Tommie Dora's than I'd planned on, and by the time I turned in to her driveway, my legs were about to buckle and my back was burning like somebody had set a match to it. But the look of astonishment on my grandmother's face when she opened the screen door made every step worth it.

"Well, if you don't beat all," Tommie Dora said. Then she told me to sit down before I fell over and went inside for a pitcher of lemonade and a plate of tea cakes Mavis Quick had baked that morning.

We were sitting there on the porch sipping and nibbling and rocking, surrounded by at least a dozen of Tommie Dora's cats and the sweet smell of jasmine, when I noticed Harry coming down the road with a hoe over his shoulder.

"What's he doing?" I asked Tommie Dora.

"He's been coming just about every day to work in the garden," she said.

Because Leo can't, I thought, and that ache I carried around in my chest all the time swelled with longing. I'd give anything to see Leo walking up and down those rows, hoeing with care so as not to break the tender plants, and even whispering encouragement to them. This was *his* garden, and, unreasonably, I felt a twinge of irritation that Harry was taking it over.

"I offered to pay him," Tommie Dora said, "but he seemed offended. Said he didn't take money from friends. Come on up here!" she yelled to Harry, and went inside for another glass.

After that, I'd go out to Tommie Dora's nearly every afternoon. I wasn't up to working in the garden yet, but she still found plenty to keep me occupied. One day it was polishing the silver; the next, pasting a boxful of old photographs into an album. She'd sorted the pictures by year, so all I had to do was place them on the pages in the same order. But I had questions about a lot of them, and that slowed me down some.

There was this one picture of a pretty girl sitting on a bench under a magnolia tree. "Who's this?" I asked Tommie Dora, and just about fell out when she said it was her.

"I was visiting my cousin Edith in Montgomery," she said.

I had serious doubts that this sweet-faced and *slender* girl was really my grandmother, but then I noticed the eyes. Even in the blurry photograph, they looked sharp enough to cut through hard cheese.

Then there was the picture of the nun. She was standing in front of a stone building that was probably Sacred Heart Convent, wearing the white wimple and dark veil of a Benedictine. I studied her face, but she didn't look like any of the sisters I knew, so I showed the picture to Tommie Dora.

"That's my sister Edna Earl."

My head shot up, and I said, "You've got a sister who's a nun? How come I never heard about her?"

"Edna Earl died young," Tommie Dora said. She took the photograph from me and looked at it. "Before your daddy was born. After she took her vows, she was called Sister Mary Julian."

I had an intense and immediate curiosity about this great-aunt who I hadn't even known existed before now, and I started firing questions at my grandmother. What did Edna Earl die from? How old was she when she died? Why had she become a nun? And why in Sam Hill hadn't somebody talked her out of it?

Tommie Dora appeared a little dazed, as if maybe she herself had forgotten about this long-dead sister, but she didn't seem to mind answering my questions. Edna Earl had died at the age of twenty-seven from a weak heart, something she'd been born with. She'd always been a quiet, studious girl and loved going to Mass, so nobody was surprised that she had a vocation. And their parents hadn't tried to change Edna Earl's mind because they were proud of having a child enter the religious life.

"Well," I said, "I never expected this. Imagine, me being kin to a *nun*."

Tommie Dora looked irritated. "No need to make such a fuss over it," she said. "Most Catholics in this town have had a nun or a priest in the family at one time or another."

"Still and all," I said, "who'd have ever thought *you'd* be kin to a nun?"

That night, I dreamed I was lying in bed when the door slowly opened and a nun walked in—only it was more like she floated, she was so graceful and light on her feet. I couldn't see her face in the dim light, but I knew it was Edna Earl. And sure enough, she came over to the bed and said, *I'm Sister Mary Julian, your long-dead great-aunt.* So I said, *But if you're dead, how can you be here talking to me?* And Edna Earl said the best thing I'd ever heard. She said that the dead can come back anytime they want to!

I lay there staring at my great-aunt and feeling so relieved, I couldn't help crying a little. *Then Leo can come back?* I asked her. *I'll be able to see him and talk to him?* And Edna Earl said, *He'll come back once you've done something to earn it, Mary Bayliss.* I sat straight up in bed and said, *Just tell me what to do.* But Edna Earl had turned away and was floating toward the door. *Please!* I called out to her. *Tell me how I can see Leo!* The nun looked back over her shoulder, and then she said, *You know what to do, Mary Bayliss. You must find your special purpose.*

My heart sank. *I've tried,* I said, *but I haven't been able to figure it out. Can't you help me? You're a nun, and even though you're dead, aren't you still supposed to help people?* And after a long silence, Edna Earl said, *You must change your selfish ways, as I did when I gave my life to God. You must show by your thoughts and deeds that you deserve being brought back from the dead.*

Then I woke up. My eyes darted to the door looking for Edna Earl, even though I'd already realized that I'd been dreaming. But maybe this was how dead people came back to visit the living. Maybe that's how I'd see Leo again, in a dream—or something that seemed like a dream but wasn't.

I sat up slowly, shrugging my shoulders to ease the ache in my back and thinking hard. Edna Earl had said that Leo would only come back once I'd found my special purpose. *You must change your selfish ways . . . show by your thoughts and deeds that you deserve being brought back from the dead.*

And that's when I knew. My mind was still a little foggy with sleep—and with uncertainty, because I wasn't at all sure that a dead nun had really spoken to me. It was like something from one of Leo's ghost stories, our great-aunt the nun coming back to haunt us. But it was *possible* that Edna Earl had come here to help me. Because finally, after all these weeks, I knew what my special purpose was. It was so obvious, I wondered why I hadn't been able to see it before. Why I'd needed a ghost to make me understand.

14. MOVING ON

"Morning, Mary Bayliss," Sister Boniface said as she came up the porch steps. "I've got another book for you by Robert Louis Stevenson. I think you'll like it as much as *Treasure Island*."

"Thanks, Sister!" I was shelling peas for Kathleen to cook for supper and was glad to have a reason to take a break. "Would you like some iced tea? Kathleen just made it."

"No thank you." She sat down in a rocker and dabbed at her face with a handkerchief. "But I'll enjoy this cool shade with you for a few minutes."

Now that I was up and around, there was no need for Sister Boniface to read to me, but she still came by with books. This new one was called *Kidnapped*.

I set the pan of peas down at my feet and took the book from her. It looked pretty good, judging from the bits I read as I flipped through, but I had something else in mind right now.

"I reckon there must be lots of books on saints in the school library," I said.

Rosie had come up on the porch and was dipping her paw into the peas. Sister Boniface was watching her. "There are," she agreed, and then smiled when Rosie snagged a pod and flipped it out of the pan.

"Could you bring me some of those, Sister?"

"You want to read about saints?" She gave me a questioning look.

"Yes, Sister. Especially the ones who started out bad. The kind who ran wild when they were young and then, later in life, saw the light and turned holy."

I reckon she couldn't have been more surprised if I'd asked for a book on hootchy-kootchy dancers. "I don't recall you ever being interested in saints before," she said.

"That's because I wasn't. But now I am."

"I see," Sister Boniface said, but I could tell that she didn't see at all.

The next day, I was about to head out to Tommie Dora's when there was a knock on the door. It was Sister Annunciata.

I invited her in, but she said, "No, I have other stops to make. I'm just dropping these off for Sister Boniface."

She handed me four books, the top one titled *The Life of Saint Augustine of Hippo*. After I thanked her, I figured she'd be on her way, but she didn't seem to be in much of a hurry.

"So, Mary Bayliss," she said, "are you really planning on reading all these books?"

Well, let me say right here that Lila Grace Gilchrist was always lugging home books on Jesus and Mary and whatnot, just to impress the nuns, and I'd never once heard Sister Annunciata ask *her* if she was actually going to read them. Which she wasn't. But I intended to read every page, so I said, "Yes, Sister."

She looked at me like she didn't believe it for a second.

"And you asked specifically for ones who'd sown their wild oats?"

"I figured I'd have more in common with them," I told her. "The ones who didn't take naturally to being holy, I mean, and had to work at it. I want to figure out how they did it."

The corners of Sister Annunciata's mouth lifted just a hair, like she'd thought of a joke but wasn't sure if it was funny or not. "Don't tell me you have it in mind to become a saint, Mary Bayliss." If it had been anybody else, I'd have said she was teasing me.

"Oh no, Sister. I'm gonna become a nun."

"A nun. Well, now." She just stared at me for a minute, and then she said, "You know, I believe I will come in. I want to hear all about this."

We went to the living room, and a startled Kathleen turned off the radio before hurrying to the kitchen to fix us something to drink. Sister Annunciata sat down in Daddy's chair and said, "All right, Mary Bayliss. Why don't you start at the beginning?"

So I told her about folks saying that God must have a special purpose for me, what with Him letting me come back from the dead and all, only I hadn't been able to figure out what that purpose was. Not till Edna Earl came to me in a dream and made me see that I was supposed to give up my selfish ways and devote my life to God.

"This probably comes as a surprise," I said.

"You could say that," Sister Annunciata answered.

"I know I've caused you and the other sisters some trouble over the years," I said, "but that's all in the past. When I come back to school, you're gonna see a whole new person."

"To tell the truth," Sister Annunciata said, her forehead wrinkling like she was giving this some thought, "I never saw much wrong with the old person. Nothing that time and growing up a little wouldn't take care of."

Well, this was news to me. I'd always figured the nuns thought I was about two sinful deeds away from a jail cell. Not to mention a long stretch in purgatory.

"We all have a purpose in life," Sister Annunciata said as she settled back in Daddy's chair, "but I'm not sure we find it by *looking* for it. I think maybe it has to find us. It could be that *your* life is supposed to be about—oh, I don't know, maybe helping your neighbors or being a loving wife and mother. But if you're patient, I reckon it'll make itself known to you one of these days."

"It already has," I said. Hadn't she been listening at all? "I know I'm meant to be a nun, and I want to start practicing right away."

"Practicing?"

"You know, doing good deeds. Will you help me come up with some, Sister?"

She was gazing at the ceiling like she was thinking again. Or maybe praying. Then she looked back at me and said, "Right now you need to concentrate on getting well. But later on, if you still feel this way, come see me and we'll talk about finding some charity work for you."

"Thank you, Sister. But I just want you to know, my mind's made up. I'm serious as all git-out about this."

"I never doubted it for a moment," she said.

A few days later, Tommie Dora and Harry were there and we were just sitting down to supper when Kathleen picked up a book off the sideboard.

"Bayliss," she said, "are you reading this?"

"Oh, that's where it is," I said, taking my seat next to Tommie Dora. "I've been looking all over for it."

Kathleen sat down, still holding the book. "*Saint Pelagia, the Beardless Monk?*" She looked at me. "I've never even heard of Saint Pelagia. Where'd you get this?"

"Sister Annunciata brought it to me. It's a very good book."

Which wasn't altogether true. In my opinion, there was too little about Pelagia's wild life as a dancer and too much about the hundred or so years she lived as a saintly hermit while pretending to be a man. I couldn't quite figure out that part.

Then Daddy said grace, but Kathleen wouldn't let the subject of the book drop. She gave me a knowing look and said, "You're in trouble again and Sister Annunciata's making you read this. But how's that possible? You haven't even been in school."

And that's when I said, "I've decided to become a nun, and Sister Annunciata's gonna help me."

Now everybody was looking at me, apparently at a loss for words. Nobody said, *How exciting, Bayliss! You'll be a wonderful nun.* Nobody even said, *Well, isn't that nice?*

Then Harry started to laugh. "You're pulling our legs, right?"

I cut my eyes at him. "Wrong."

"But where did *this* come from?" Mother looked a little confused. "You've never mentioned wanting to be a nun."

And Kathleen said, "I'd have remembered that."

"The last I heard," Mother said, "you wanted to be an explorer. What happened to flying an airplane to the North Pole?"

From the look on her face, you would have thought she had her heart set on me taking off for the Arctic the very next morning. *It would have been an amazing life*, I thought, feeling both sad and noble.

"I was just a child then," I said. "Now that I'm older, it's time to move on to other things."

"For the love of Pete, you're only twelve!" Mother was getting agitated, and she was about to say more, but Daddy cut her off.

"That's right, Helen," he said in that steady voice he used to calm patients when they were all worked up, "Bayliss *is* only twelve. She could change her mind twenty times before she gets out of school."

"I could," I said, "but I won't."

"There's no use trying to talk sense into her," Tommie Dora said as she reached for the platter of fried tomatoes. "I know that mule-faced look." Then all of a sudden her chin snapped up, and those black eyes locked with mine. "It was that picture of Edna Earl. *That's* what put this dern fool idea into your head. But I want you to ponder long and hard on what it would be like living in a convent for the rest of your life."

"And think about teaching every day," Kathleen said with a smirk. "We all know how fond you are of children."

"And I bet you couldn't have a cat," Harry said.

No cat? Now, that could be a problem. "Well," I said, thinking fast, "Rosie can live here, and I'll come see her."

"Nuns can't go larking off anytime the mood strikes," Tommie Dora said.

"But Sister Boniface visits *me*," I said. "And Sister Annunciata does, too."

Kathleen sighed and gave me a pitying look. "That's because you've been sick and their visits are acts of mercy. Surely you don't think they come to see you 'cause they *want* to."

15. HOLDING ON

"Good Lord, Bayliss! What in tarnation are you doing?"

Kathleen was standing in the doorway to the kitchen, hands on her hips, looking at the table and counters where I'd laid out most everything that used to be in the pantry.

"Rearranging," I said. "It was a mess."

"Well, it's a worse mess now," she grumbled. "I swear, if you get any more helpful, I'm gonna lose my mind. I have a pot of beans to put on and a pie crust to make, and there's not one inch of space to work. You get this cleaned up right now."

I have to say, that part about losing her mind hurt my feelings. Kathleen always managed to get the wash done and put supper on the table, but she never seemed to get around to things like cleaning out the pantry or scrubbing the stove. I'd taken care of the stove right after breakfast, and it looked good, even if I did say so myself. And since I'd been doing the dishes and sweeping—and dusting, because Kathleen just gave it a lick and a promise and didn't even bother with the tops of picture frames—she'd had a lot more time to listen to her programs.

"Bayliss, did you hear me? Put all this stuff away."

So I did, one item at a time, because I still couldn't lift anything heavier than a jar of pickled beets. But then Kathleen started muttering about it taking me so long. And when I offered to mix the dough for her pie crust, she said, "No, Daddy likes the way I make it," as if stirring up flour and shortening took some kind of special talent.

She'd always griped to Mother that I didn't do my share around the house, but now that I was trying to make myself useful, did she appreciate it? I was starting to think she liked it better when she could fuss over how lazy I was and take all the glory for herself. But I had a lot of selfish years to make up for, so she'd just have to get used to the new Bayliss.

Kathleen was putting the pot of beans on the stove, and I moved to the other side of the room where I wouldn't get in her way. I was refolding the dish towels into neat squares when she looked up and asked, "Aren't you going to Tommie Dora's today?" Like she couldn't wait to get me out from underfoot.

"Soon as Harry's done mowing Miz Mayhew's yard. We're gonna pick all the ripe tomatoes."

"Well, don't be lugging heavy baskets," she said.

"Harry does the lifting. I fill a strawberry cup and empty it into a basket at the end of the row."

Kathleen had been wiping up syrup I'd spilled on the counter, but now she stopped and just stood there for a minute with her back to me. When she finally did turn around, her face was so sad, I knew she was about to say something that I didn't want to hear. Well, maybe part of me would want to hear it, but the rest of me was thinking, *No, don't do this, Kathleen. Just leave it be.* But the words were already tumbling out of her mouth, like she'd been storing them up for a long time and couldn't hold them in another second.

"The garden makes me think of Leo," she said. "How he'd come home from Tommie Dora's all dirty and sweaty and grinning from ear to ear. How he'd brag that this year's squash were twice as big as last year's. Do you remember that, Bayliss? How proud he'd be of every crop?"

Sure I remembered. Most days I was out there sweating right alongside him.

"One time I asked him why he put in such a big garden," Kathleen went on, "and he said, 'The bigger it is, the more time I'll get to spend in it.' He told me it was satisfying to watch things grow from seeds he'd planted himself. And he said that he loved being outdoors because the sky and the trees and the earth were always changing, depending on the season. I told him that it was hot or cold or wet or dusty, too, depending on the season, and he just laughed and said, 'See what I mean? Always changing.'"

Her face was pinched with remembering. And I felt that same pinching in my chest when I realized that I'd never asked Leo why he loved farming. Now it was too late, and there were things I'd never know about my brother.

"It's just so hard." Tears were spilling down her face, and she wiped at them with the back of her hand. "The other day Mother was looking through Leo's baby book, and she took out a lock of his hair and sat there holding it for the longest time. And Daddy . . . I don't think he ever sleeps anymore. I hear him go downstairs in the middle of the night, and the next morning I'll find him in the living room reading. And sometimes, when they think we're asleep, I hear them crying."

They cried? Of course I knew they were hurting, but I'd never seen them cry.

Kathleen reached into her pocket for a handkerchief and blew her nose. Then she said, "One night on my way to the bathroom, I heard Daddy tell Mother that he'd been so set on Leo becoming a doctor, he hadn't bothered to ask what Leo wanted. And then Mother said that you and Leo wouldn't have even been at the lake that day if she hadn't told you to go. She thinks she's to blame for you getting hurt . . . and Leo . . ."

"Well, she's *not*," I said, riled up all of a sudden and not exactly knowing why. "*I* was the one who couldn't wait to take that boat out."

But instead of snapping back at me, Kathleen said in a

quiet voice, "We all feel guilty, Bayliss," like she understood what I was feeling, even if I didn't. "I think about how I'd get aggravated with Leo and say mean things to him. But we didn't cause what happened. It was an accident. I just keep wondering why he didn't start back when he realized a storm was coming."

I'd gone over that in my mind about a million times. Was it because he hadn't expected the storm to move in so fast? Or because he thought he was strong enough to swim through it? I'd always believed Leo was perfect, that he didn't make mistakes. And the one time he did, it killed him.

Kathleen had gone back to wiping the counter, and I thought she'd finally run out of words. But then she said softly, "I've kept one of his shirts. Trying to hold on to him, I guess. I know—that's dumb."

"It's not dumb," I said, thinking, *No dumber than lying in bed at night saying his name and still half expecting him to answer.*

"It helps to talk about him." Kathleen had turned to look at me again. "Maybe, if we *keep* talking, it won't hurt so much after a while. Maybe we'll even be able to laugh when we remember all the funny things he did."

At that moment, I couldn't imagine a time when I'd laugh again, not the way Leo had made me laugh. But Kathleen seemed to be waiting for me to say something, like it mattered to her, so I nodded and said, "Maybe you're right."

Then she got busy with the pie crust, and I went outside to wait for Harry. But that afternoon, while we picked tomatoes, I thought about how upset I'd been in the hospital, and when I first came home, because Mother and Daddy wouldn't even mention Leo's name. It had felt wrong, like we were turning our backs on him, trying to forget him because it hurt too much. And it did hurt, remembering. Even the smallest things, the way one side of his mouth would go up a little higher than the other side when he grinned, or how he loved to eat green apples even though he knew they'd give him a bellyache. And it hurt Kathleen, too, but that didn't stop her from talking about him.

After we'd finished picking the tomatoes—which were surely the biggest and reddest Leo had ever planted—Harry carried a basketful up to the porch. And while I waited for him to come back for the second basket, it crossed my mind that even though Kathleen and I had lived in the same house for twelve years, I'd never given her much thought. The truth was, I'd decided a long time ago that we didn't have a thing in common, except for a last name, and she'd always been more of an aggravation to me than anything else. But now I found myself thinking that there might be more to my sister than I'd ever given her credit for, because today I'd seen something different in Kathleen. I'd seen that she could be brave.

*　　*　　*

116

The next day, I started down Gilly Road in the direction of Tommie Dora's. But I passed her house and kept on walking till I came to the road that led to Sweet Springs Lake. A few minutes later, I was standing on the front stoop of George Davies's cabin. Out of the corner of my eye, I could see the boat tied up at the dock, but I turned away without looking at it and knocked.

The door opened and Mr. Davies was standing there. His face showed surprise, then pleasure.

"Why, if it isn't Miss Mary Bayliss Pettigrew," he said.

My heart was beating fast. I was feeling nervous, and even a little shy with this man who'd saved my life.

"Hey, Mr. Davies. I just wanted to thank you. And your sons, too."

"Well, bless your heart." Then he opened the door wider and said, "I made a jug of sun tea. Come in and have a glass and tell me what you think."

We sat at the table in his little kitchen to drink our tea, and Mr. Davies told me about that afternoon at the lake. How Harry had come for them in a panic and how they'd followed him back to the cliffs, barely able to see where they were going because it was raining so hard and the wind was blowing in fierce, wet gusts, slapping them in the face. He told me how he'd worked to get me breathing again, while Harry and Albert had taken the boat out to look for Leo and James had gone for Daddy.

"The rain had nearly stopped by the time I saw your daddy come running down the beach toward us," Mr. Davies said, "and I'll never forget his expression. It was desperate with hope and on the brink of despair at the same time. And when I told him you had a heartbeat—and I saw that flash of pure relief and gratitude on his face—well, Mary Bayliss, it just made me want to break down and cry."

"And Leo?" I said softly.

"Albert and the Burdeshaw boy had gotten him back to shore, and your daddy tried every way in the world to revive him." Mr. Davies sniffed and then cleared his throat. "He must have kept that up for an hour or more, till it started getting dark, all the while saying, 'Breathe, Son, breathe.' The rest of us knew it wasn't any use, but nobody had the heart to tell your daddy."

Later that afternoon, I walked the four blocks to Annie Schumann's house. I was feeling anxious about seeing her, too, but this time, it was guilt that was making my palms sweat. I hadn't been kind to Annie, and I needed to set things straight between us. Right away. Because she'd be leaving any day to spend the month of August with her grandma in Mississippi.

Annie must have seen me out the window because the front door swung open and she came running out to the porch before I'd even started up the walk.

"Hey!" she called to me.

"Hey, yourself!" I called back, and I knew everything was going to be all right.

That night, my back was hurting and I couldn't get comfortable. Finally, I got out of bed and paced around the room, hoping the ache would ease up.

A crescent moon was resting on top of the trees. The sky was so clear, it looked like the stars were burning holes through the darkness. But I turned away from the window before I could start looking for the lions.

I switched on the lamp and got back into bed to finish the book on Saint Francis of Assisi, my favorite saint so far because he preached to the birds and made a peace treaty with a wolf. Then Rosie jumped up on the bed and crawled into my lap. I was stroking her when I noticed some white hairs had sprung up in the black fur on her face. That's when it hit me that she was getting old, and my heart seemed to stop for a second. Because someday, maybe soon, I'd lose her, too, and I didn't think I could bear it. What sense did it make to love a cat—or a person—when God could just snatch them away from you at any moment?

Blinking back tears, I pulled Rosie closer and kissed the orange spot on top of her head. But she didn't know anything about dying. She was just happy to have me loving her and started to purr.

16. SAINT MARY BAYLISS

The next day, I learned an important lesson the hard way, which was this: don't ever think you can predict how somebody's going to act from one minute to the next. Especially when that somebody is your sister. Or your mother.

I should have known better, but after Kathleen had talked about Leo and been so nice to me, I was willing to give her the benefit of the doubt. So I woke up that morning with the idea that I'd go out of my way to be kind to her. First, because she was my sister and it was the right thing to do. Second, because I thought maybe I'd misjudged her. And third, because nuns are supposed to be nice to everybody, whether they feel like it or not, and I figured that was something I'd better start working on right away.

I had it all planned out, how I was going to try extra hard to make life easier and more enjoyable for Kathleen, and for Mother and Daddy, too. But the fact is, you just can't please some people, as I discovered when I walked into the kitchen that morning.

Kathleen was making coffee, and Mother was mixing the dough for biscuits.

Mother looked at me and said, "You're up early."

"I thought I'd fix the oatmeal," I said. "And I'll finish those biscuits so you can get off your feet."

It seemed to me that Mother's voice was a tad on the chilly side when she said, "I believe I can manage to stay on my feet a little while longer."

"Then I'll start on the oatmeal," I said, and opened the cabinet door to get a pot.

"I appreciate you pitching in," Mother said, her fingers working that dough like she meant to strangle it, "truly, I do. It's just—"

"Bayliss," Kathleen cut in, "what Mother's trying to say is, you've been acting peculiar, not like yourself one bit, wanting to help out all the time. It's like you've turned into Saint Mary Bayliss or something, and it's giving us the willies."

"Kathleen, don't put words in my mouth." Mother frowned at her and then turned that frown on me. "But since your sister brought it up, Bayliss, I might as well tell you, if this sudden interest in cooking and cleaning has anything to do with that nun business, then I wish you wouldn't bother. If you were older . . . if I thought for a minute that you had a true vocation— Oh, what's the use? You never have listened to me, and the whole thing's giving me a sick headache. I don't want to hear another word about it."

Then Mother dropped her eyes to the ball of dough and started pounding it. "But all that aside," she said, "you still need to take it easy."

"Daddy says I'm just about healed," I told her. "Except for heavy lifting, he says I can do anything I want."

"Does he really." Mother said, and *now* it looked like she was mad at Daddy.

After all this, anybody with an ounce of sense would have thrown in the towel. But I was hell-bent on spreading joy and giving aid wherever I could, whether Mother and Kathleen appreciated it or not. So I made the oatmeal— and scorched it a little, but only Kathleen thought to mention that—and set the table. Then I twisted the napkins into bunny faces like I'd seen in the Easter issue of Miz Burdeshaw's *Ladies' Home Journal*, but for some reason, all the bunnies ended up with just one ear, a real long one. Still, I thought they turned out pretty good for my first try.

Then Daddy sat down and reached for his napkin. He gave it an odd look and said, "Helen, why is this napkin tied up in knots?"

"Heaven only knows," Mother said, pinning me down with her eyes. "I guess it's just one of life's great mysteries."

It was discouraging, especially when Kathleen plopped down in her chair and muttered, "I just ironed those napkins." And she didn't say two words to me while we ate, except to complain about the oatmeal being burned, but Daddy was quick to tell me that he *liked* his oatmeal well done.

After breakfast, while Kathleen and I did the dishes, I tried to start a pleasant conversation. But Kathleen said, "Bayliss, more work and less talk. I've got to mop the kitchen and get the wash on the line and I don't know what all."

Well, it was obvious to me that Kathleen was just as ornery as she'd ever been. But I was still trying to be nice, so when she handed me a pot to dry that had crusty stuff in the bottom, I said as politely as I could, "Kathleen, you need to wash this again."

But the words were hardly out of my mouth when she yanked that pot out of my hand and glared at it. "That's your *well-done* oatmeal," she said, which I thought was uncalled for. "It's gonna take forever to get this clean."

At that point, I was just about as fed up with her as she was with me. So I said, "Give it to me! *I'll* get it clean." And I reached for the pot.

But she jerked it away and said, "Don't bother! It's easier to do it myself." Then she gave me the meanest look and said, "Bayliss, I've had enough. You want to be a nun? Then go help *them*! March yourself on over to the convent right now and volunteer your services."

So that's what I did.

It took about two minutes to change out of my overalls into a dress. Then I marched out of the house without saying a word to Kathleen and marched down Markham Street in the direction of the convent. But all that marching made my back start to twinge, so when I turned onto Main, I slowed down some and stepped lightly the rest of the way.

The convent was next door to the church and the cemetery, set back on a wooded lot and hidden from the street by a high wall. There was a wooden gate in the wall, which I half expected to find locked. But when I lifted the handle, the gate swung open.

I'd never been inside the convent walls, but other folks went in all the time. Deliverymen and plumbers and anybody else who had official business to conduct with the nuns. Well, today *I* was here on official business, but that thought didn't do a thing for my nerves once I'd gone in and closed the gate behind me.

There was a gravel path leading into the trees, and way back, through the leaves, I could see the stone walls of the convent. I made myself start down that path, even though I was thinking, *What am I doing, listening to Kathleen? This is a bad idea.* But helping the nuns seemed like a *good* idea, even though Kathleen hadn't suggested it with the purest of intentions, so I just kept walking till I reached the front entrance. And before I could change my mind, I lifted the heavy door knocker and let it fall back against an iron plate on the doorframe.

The sound it made was so loud, it must have carried to

every corner of the convent. I could just see the sisters being jolted out of their prayers—and whatever else it was that nuns did all day—and figured they'd be hopping mad and want to know what in Sam Hill I was doing here. And since I was asking myself that same question *again*, I probably would have taken off if the door hadn't opened before I could get my feet turned back toward the street. And there was tiny Sister Agnes looking out at me, sweet and smiling as always, and she said, "Morning, Mary Bayliss. What can I do for you?"

"Morning, Sister," I said, feeling weak with relief that it was her and not one of the grouchier nuns at the door. "I need to talk to Sister Annunciata—that is, if she's not busy praying or something."

Still smiling, Sister Agnes said, "No, dear, Sister Annunciata isn't praying. She's over at the school getting things ready for classes to start. We only have four weeks, you know."

"Yes, Sister. Then I'll just go on over to the school," I said, already backing away. "Thank you, Sister."

I was probably the only student in Sacred Heart's history to have actually been on convent grounds, and that would be something to brag about later, but right now I couldn't wait to get out of there. The school, on the other hand, was familiar territory. Walking through those double doors seemed like the most natural thing in the world to do, because I belonged there. And right away I could see that nothing had changed since March. Or the March before that. The hall was still dark and dusty, and the gray tile floor was covered with skid marks and beginning to crack in spots. And there was that same stain on the ceiling from somebody forgetting to turn off the water in a clogged sink on the second floor. Even though I'd had more than my share of run-ins with some of the teachers, it felt like I was coming home.

I found Sister Annunciata in her office, surrounded by piles of textbooks. She was counting the second-grade readers, but when she saw me standing in the doorway, she waved me in and then made a mark on her clipboard. She didn't look the least bit surprised to see me, but then, I'd never known anything to surprise Sister Annunciata. Leo used to say that after teaching kids for a hundred years, she was unflappable.

When I told her why I was there, I could see that she'd forgotten all about coming up with charity work for me. But then it seemed to dawn on her what I was talking about, and the first thing she asked was, "Has your back healed?" And once I'd assured her that I was fine and raring to go, she walked around the room for a couple of minutes, pausing now and then to straighten a stack of books before it toppled, and then she turned back to me and said, "I know just the thing. The weary travelers."

This didn't ring any bells for me. So she went on to say that Sister Boniface and some of the other nuns served meals to folks every day, and I realized she meant the hoboes, only Sister Annunciata said the sisters called them weary travelers.

Then she asked me if I'd like to help serve food, and what could I say but yes? I mean, how would it have looked, me coming here telling her I wanted to help people and then turning up my nose at a chance to do good deeds? But in all honesty, I had my doubts about this.

First off, I wasn't sure about working side by side with the nuns. I'd thought maybe they'd send me to visit shut-ins, like me when I was home in bed. And I had already been imagining how I'd arrive with a book to read to some poor old soul, and maybe bring a few flowers from the yard, and brighten up her dreary days. But if I was working right there with them, the nuns would be watching every move I made. What if I didn't do things right and they sent me home? And I wasn't exactly thrilled about being face to face with the hoboes—the *weary travelers*—either, since the only time I'd been around them, I'd felt uneasy, even with Leo there. And that was the third problem. I'd heard that Eugenie Watts had left town, but seeing the hoboes would just remind me of her.

But Sister Annunciata was waiting for an answer, so I said, "That sounds fine, Sister."

"Good. I'll tell Sister Boniface to expect you tomorrow afternoon at four o'clock. Go to the side door of the convent. And don't be late."

Then she went back to counting her books, and I left. But I didn't feel like going home and spending the rest of the morning with Kathleen, so I dawdled. And when I got to the gate of the cemetery, I stopped and looked through the iron bars at the headstones and the carved angels that watched over some of the graves. I'd always liked going to that cemetery, admiring the statues and reading the inscriptions on the stones, but it didn't seem like the same friendly place anymore. Not when I thought about the families who'd brought somebody they loved through these gates and then had to say goodbye forever.

I stood there awhile, with my fingers wrapped around the rusty bars, before pushing the gate open and going inside. Then I started down the brick path that led between rows of headstones—some of them so old, they were leaning and beginning to crumble—and followed it to the back of the church and then up the hill to the spot where Mother's parents were buried.

I stopped at their graves and read the names on the granite stone. *Carl Ernst Reinhart. Kathleen Ballard Reinhart.* My grandparents. Only I'd never known them because they'd died before I was born. Somebody, probably my mother, had set jars of black-eyed Susans on the graves.

On up the hill was the Pettigrew plot. There were the graves of my great-grandparents and two stone crosses where the babies were buried, the sons Tommie Dora and Grandpa Halsey had lost before having Daddy. And there was Grandpa Halsey's headstone, with Tommie Dora's name next to his.

Then my eyes moved across the grass, past a tangle of red roses Tommie Dora had planted after she'd laid her husband to rest, to a stone carved from white marble. My first sight of Leo's grave.

I should have been prepared to find him here. *Leo Halsey Pettigrew, Born December 4, 1915, Died March 21, 1932. Beloved Son.* But seeing the words *Leo* and *Died* together, and knowing once and for all that he was really there under that mound of red clay where grass was just beginning to grow back, caught me off guard. There were more black-eyed Susans on his grave, which meant Mother came here, too. I hadn't known that, but of course she and Daddy would. Only why hadn't they mentioned it? Why hadn't they asked if *I* wanted to visit Leo?

Now that I was here, I didn't know what to do. Should I talk to him? But what would I say? And could he even hear me?

I'd been breathing too fast and was beginning to feel light-headed, so I sat down in the grass and rested my forehead against the cool stone. Closing my eyes, I listened to bees buzzing around the roses and smelled the blooms' sweet scent mixed with the dust that coated everything this time of year. But even after the swirling in my head had stopped, I couldn't think of anything to say to Leo. So, finally, I stood up and brushed the dry grass off my skirt and headed for home.

17. THE WEARY TRAVELERS

It was easier going to the convent the second time, because if anybody asked what I was doing there, I could just say, *Sister Annunciata told me to come.* And nobody messed with Sister Annunciata.

So this time, I opened the gate and walked right in. But I still had some worries about the hoboes, and I'd admitted as much to Tommie Dora when she'd come over for supper the night before.

"Oh, you'll be all right, with the sisters there," she said. And then she asked, "What did your mother have to say about you doing this?"

"Plenty," I said. "She's not fond of *anything* to do with nuns right now, but Daddy told her to leave me be."

Him saying that had surprised me, since Daddy had his own bone to pick with the church these days. But he'd told Mother that this was something I had to decide for myself. I thought maybe the reason he was letting me make up my own mind about it was because he felt like he'd failed Leo by not paying attention to what he wanted.

This time, instead of going up to the front door, I followed the path around to the side of the building, where a covered porch was crowded with a bunch of tables and mismatched chairs. Near a door that I figured went into the kitchen, the sisters had set up a soup pot, platters of bread, and a basket of apples on a long serving table. Sister Boniface was bringing out a tray of dishes, and Sister Josephine was right behind her, pushing a cart that held the biggest coffeepot I'd ever seen. And standing there doing nothing was Sister Mary Vincent.

My first thought was, *Oh no, not her!* Because Sister Mary Vincent was the only teacher I'd ever had who gave me nightmares—all through third grade and even after I'd moved on to fourth and sweet Sister Agnes. Sister Mary Vincent used to keep me after school at least once a week, just so she could reel off a list of my faults. According to her, I was stubborn, disrespectful, careless, huffish (though just what *huffish* meant I never found out, because when I asked, she accused me of being *brash*). And then she'd shake her head and say, "I know your parents are terribly disappointed, Mary Bayliss. You must be breaking their hearts." So I'd go home and study my mother and daddy and see no sign whatsoever that their hearts were breaking. But try telling that to Sister Mary Vincent.

I'd come to a full stop and was just staring at her when Sister Boniface noticed me and said, "Welcome, Mary Bayliss. We're so glad you're here to help us."

The apron Sister Josephine gave me was big enough to fit Tommie Dora, and I had to wrap it around myself twice. And I hadn't even gotten it tied when Sister Mary Vincent started spitting out orders.

"Mary Bayliss, hurry up and get that apron fixed. We haven't got all day. Then slice and butter the bread—*thin* slices, mind, and go easy on the butter. When it's gone, it's gone."

The bread turned out a little squashed and ragged, but I figured it was a miracle I hadn't chopped off a finger, what with Sister Mary Vincent breathing down my neck the whole time and muttering, "*Thin* slices. Too much butter. What did I tell you?"

Sister Boniface said, "Good job, Mary Bayliss," but then Sister Mary Vincent started in again.

"Mary Bayliss, you go stand at the far end of the serving line and put an apple on each plate. Just one, now, even if they ask for more. We're running low."

Meanwhile, Sister Josephine had opened the gate in the back wall, and people were surging past her, heading like a mob for the serving table. I just hoped I was ready for this.

But I wasn't. There were so many of them, mostly men, but a few women, too. And one woman had two little boys with her who probably weren't even school-age yet. Everybody coming through that gate looked half starved and about as worn down as they could be and still keep moving.

I was pretty sure I'd made a mistake. I had no idea what

to say to these people and was wondering if it was too late to take off my apron and light out for home. But I'd *asked* for this, and if I quit, Sister Annunciata might never give me another chance. Besides, the first weary travelers were already at the table. Sister Boniface was smiling and talking to them while she ladled soup into bowls and placed the bowls on plates, and some of the men were smiling back at her.

Now the line was moving along to Sister Mary Vincent, who was putting a slice of bread on each plate. Sister Mary Vincent spoke to the weary travelers, but she didn't smile and neither did they.

Sister Josephine was standing next to me, and I heard her say, "It's good to see you. How are you today?" to the first man as she handed him a mug of hot coffee. And now it was definitely too late to turn tail and run because that same man was stopping in front of me.

He was close enough for me to see the wrinkles at the corners of his eyes, the stubble on his chin, the black under his fingernails. Close enough for me to catch a strong whiff of body odor.

"Hey," I said to the man. "Would you like an apple? They look real good."

"Thank you, little lady," he said softly. "I will take one."

Then he left to go sit down, but in the few seconds he'd been there, I'd felt something shift inside me. A faceless hobo had turned into a man with warm brown eyes and a kind voice that sounded a lot like my daddy's friends when they spoke to me.

After the last person had eaten and left, I wiped off the tables and swept the porch while the nuns went back and forth to the kitchen carrying pots and platters and dirty dishes. They weren't letting me lift anything heavier than a dishrag, which was just as well because my back was starting to ache from being on my feet so long.

Sister Boniface came over as I was finishing up. "So how was it?" she asked me. "You think you might want to come back tomorrow?"

"Yes, Sister, I do." As it turned out, helping people in need wasn't so hard after all. And besides, there was something about being here that I liked.

"I'm glad to hear it," Sister Boniface said. "You know, Sister Josephine has been singing your praises. She said you knew exactly what to say to make everybody feel at ease. That's a gift, Mary Bayliss."

I was just turning in to our driveway when the Packard pulled up across the street. Harry was behind the wheel, and Jack was sitting on the passenger side with his big head stuck out the window.

As Harry and the dog were getting out of the car, I yelled, "You been running bootleg liquor again?"

"Why do you ask?" Harry yelled back, grinning. "You looking to buy a jug?"

I went over to join them, and Jack collapsed in the grass, resting his chin on my foot.

"So what *were* you doing?" I asked.

"Just driving around. Cars need to be run regular or they won't start. Where've *you* been?"

I stooped down to scratch under Jack's chin. The dog groaned and rolled over so I could reach his belly. "Serving meals to the weary travelers," I said.

"That's right, I forgot. You think you'll go back?"

"I reckon so."

"Then I guess Kathleen was wrong."

I stood up and looked at him. "Wrong about what?"

"She said you'd give up on the idea of being a nun after one day with those hoboes."

"Kathleen's been right about twice in her life," I muttered. "And, Harry, we *call* 'em weary travelers."

18. MORE
WEARY TRAVELERS

Most of the weary travelers moved on after a day or two, but there were some who'd made the camp by the railroad tracks their home. And after serving meals for a while, I got to know the ones who stayed.

The man with the warm brown eyes was named Pete. He had a wife and four children back in Oklahoma, but he hadn't seen them in more than a year. He'd left to find work and got a job at a sawmill in Arkansas. Then he'd busted his leg and was laid off.

Pete was still limping, but every day he'd say, "It's about mended now. Won't be long till I can work again."

He wouldn't go home still broke and without a job.

Then there was an old man who never said a word and wouldn't look anybody in the eye. The bones in his face stuck out like they were about to poke through the skin, and sometimes his hands shook. One day, I noticed him shaking so bad he was about to drop his plate and bowl of soup. So I took the dishes from him and carried them to the table where he always ate alone.

The old man followed me and sat down, and then an unexpected thing happened. He looked up at me and said in a scratchy voice that sounded like it hadn't been used in a while, "Could you sit with me a spell?"

Most of the weary travelers had already come through the line, and I figured Sister Josephine could manage to hand out a few apples on her own, so I pulled up a chair. And the man who never said a word to anybody commenced to talking my ear off for the next half hour.

His name was Homer Reid, and he said he'd seen most all of the forty-eight states through the side door of a boxcar. He told me some things that made my heart ache, like how his wife had been sick with cancer and how the illness had eaten up their savings, and how he'd lost his Frances and their home within a month of one another. But then he took me back to his boyhood, when mischief was his middle name, and he had me laughing till I hollered. And he laughed, too, but softly, because Homer Reid was a gentleman.

Sister Boniface said it was fine for me to sit with him, so every day I'd watch for him to come through the gate, and then Sister Josephine would say, "You go on, Mary Bayliss, and take him this mug of coffee." But one day, I watched and watched and he didn't come. I asked around, and one of the other weary travelers said he thought Homer Reid had hopped a freight and gone back home—to live with his sister, maybe, or was it a niece? He couldn't remember.

I worried some about Homer Reid, but mostly I just missed him.

Annie came home at the end of August and called me before she'd even unpacked. "It's so good to be back," she said. "Grandma had me *canning beans*, and it hot enough in that kitchen to make a glass of water boil. So what have *you* been doing?"

There hadn't been time before she left to tell Annie about my decision to become a nun, so I told her now. And how I was helping serve meals to the weary travelers and reading about the saints. "I guess that's about it," I said.

All I heard was silence. A long enough silence for me to figure we'd been cut off.

But then Annie yelled into the telephone, "You're gonna be a *nun?* Bayliss, what's *happened* while I was gone? Are you *really* working at the convent? With *Sister Mary Vincent?* Is this a joke?"

It's probably a good thing that Annie couldn't see my face just then, because I'm pretty sure it had a scowl on it. Not one single soul was taking my vocation seriously.

"Annie," I said quietly, wanting to shame her, "I had hoped you'd be happy for me. It's a wonderful thing to be called to serve, don't you think?"

Annie said bluntly, "What I *think* is, you've lost your mind. You're the last person on earth I can picture becoming a nun. No, wait . . . I expect Lila Grace Gilchrist is the *last* person."

We snickered about that some, which helped clear the air, and then both of us were ready to change the subject.

"School starts next week," she said. "Are you nervous about going back?"

"A little."

"You think kids are gonna gawk and ask dumb questions?"

"They're bound to," I said.

"They better not, 'cause Sister Annunciata's laid down the law. Mama told me she came by the house last week. She's visiting all of us at home and talking to our parents."

Bewildered, I asked, "What about?"

"About what happened to you out at the lake. She told everybody the facts—so kids wouldn't be making up stories—and said we're to welcome you back and ask how you're doing, but we're not to pry. And she said she'd better not hear of anybody making you feel bad."

"She said all that?"

"Every word. You reckon we've been wrong about her all these years?"

"I wouldn't go that far," I said.

A few nights later, we were having supper, and Daddy said, "I went by the children's home today. At the last board meeting, Vesta Eubanks reported that they're running out of space, so I thought I'd go see."

"That's a big building," Mother said. "I thought there was plenty of room."

"Two years ago they only had fifty-odd children. Now there's more than eighty." Daddy picked up his coffee cup and took a sip. "Most of the new ones aren't orphans, though. Their families just can't afford to keep them."

I could tell that upset Mother. She put her fork down like she'd finished eating, but she'd barely touched her food.

"Twice in the last month," Daddy said, "Vesta's come downstairs in the morning and found children sitting on the front steps, dropped off in the middle of the night. And a few weeks ago, a baby was left in a box on the porch."

"Oh, Walter," Mother said, "who could do something like that?"

"Somebody who's desperate. Anyway, I took a tour, and Vesta wasn't exaggerating. The dormitories have more beds than they were ever meant to hold, and she's had to start making up pallets in the hall. So I've promised to help find temporary homes. The problem is, folks around here can barely keep their own children fed and clothed."

I'd been listening and had an idea.

"The Gilchrists," I said. "They have that big house, and they're rich. They could take ten children—*twenty*, even.

And it might do Lila Grace good to learn how to share a little."

"Bayliss," Mother said, *"really."*

I thought she was about to laugh, but then she covered her mouth with a napkin and coughed instead.

"We've already found homes for five of the children," Daddy said. "Reverend Scarborough's taking two of the boys, and Vesta's sister and her husband are taking a little girl." He looked down at his plate as he scooped up some butter beans. "And I told them we'd take two girls."

Daddy said that last part casually, like he was trying to slip it in without anybody noticing, but it didn't work. The table went silent except for the clinking of Daddy's fork against his plate. And we all just sat there staring at him, too shocked to say a word.

Mother was the first to recover. "Walter," she said in a quiet voice, "you agreed to take two children without talking to me first?"

"I know," he said, like he'd been expecting her to be aggravated and was ready to face up to it. "I should have discussed it with you, but when I saw how those children are living, I felt I had to do something. And these little girls . . . Their father left them at the home about a month ago, and they looked so lost, Helen. If you'd been there . . ."

"If I'd been there . . . ," she repeated, frowning. Then

she sighed. "If I'd been there, I suppose I would have told Vesta that we'd take them."

Daddy was smiling now and looking at Mother like she was about the finest woman to ever walk on this earth, and wasn't he lucky to have found her before somebody else did.

"It won't be for long," he said. "We're looking for more permanent homes, even if it means going outside the county."

"Well, we have the extra bedroom," Mother said. "I guess it would be selfish not to help."

"Poor little things," Kathleen murmured.

But I didn't say anything because "the extra bedroom" was Leo's. How could my mother even think of letting strangers use his room? And kids! They'd probably be filthy like the Clark boys and tear everything up. I knew I should be feeling sorry for them, but I didn't even *like* kids! And the idea of living in the same house with them, putting up with all their screaming and banging around, made me feel sick. But most of all, I didn't want them in Leo's room.

"How old are they?" Mother asked just as Kathleen said, "What are their names?"

Daddy reached into his shirt pocket for a slip of paper. "Gwen and Isabel Truett. They're eight and five." He looked up at Mother. "Gwen, the older girl, told Vesta that their mother died when Isabel was a baby, so they don't remember her. Their father lost his job mining coal in Walker

County last year and started riding the rails looking for work."

"And took the girls with him?" Mother asked.

Daddy nodded. "Vesta said Gwen knew for sure that they'd been to Mississippi, Louisiana, and Texas, and maybe some other states. But he couldn't find a job, so he left the girls here and took off for Florida to see if there was any work down there picking crops."

"No telling what they've been through," Mother said.

"Their father told Vesta he'd come back for them if he could, but Gwen doesn't expect to ever see him again. She says he drinks."

Mother cut her eyes my way and frowned, but Daddy said, "Bayliss is growing up, and she's going to hear things like this. If not from us, then somebody else."

"That's right," I said, feeling cranky and more than willing to take it out on my mother. "I know about people getting drunk. Why, folks in this very town run down to Thetis Fowler's for a jug all the time."

Mother just rolled her eyes.

"Vesta says the girls are well behaved," Daddy said. "And Gwen reads well. I think we should enroll her at Sacred Heart and see if they'll take Isabel, too. She's nearly school-age."

Mother nodded. "Then they could walk home with Bayliss."

144

My head snapped up, and I said, "But I'll be working at the convent after school. Kathleen can bring 'em home."

"No, I can't," Kathleen said. "I've arranged to have study hall last period so I can leave early to start supper. And with everything else that has to be done around here, I won't have time to watch 'em."

Before I could protest anymore, Mother said, "Bayliss, I'm sure the sisters can get along without you for a little while. This won't be forever."

It wasn't fair! I didn't even want these kids here, and now I was the one stuck with them. And I *loved* helping the nuns. I didn't *want* them to get along without me.

I hadn't realized I'd sighed *that* loud till Mother said, "Don't sulk, Bayliss. I know the weary travelers are important to you, but we have our own weary travelers to take care of now."

I was desperate for a way out of this and pounced on the only thing I could think of that might get them to change their minds. "What about the tuition? We aren't made of money, you know."

"Tuition's low at Sacred Heart," Mother said. Then she asked Daddy, "When are they coming?"

"I told Vesta I'd pick them up on my way home tomorrow night," he said. "But if that doesn't give you enough time, we can wait a day or two."

Mother shook her head. "No, they need to get settled

145

before school starts. Kathleen, while I do the dishes, you can put clean sheets on the girls' bed. And, Bayliss, go up to the attic and find that pretty tulip quilt your great-aunt Maudie Bruce made. Oh, and look through Kathleen's and your old toys for things little girls might like."

I was making fork prints in my potato cake and refused to look at her. "I want to keep my toys nice," I said.

"For what?" Kathleen asked. "If you're a nun, you won't have any children of your own to give 'em to."

"Bayliss, I'm sure you can bear to part with one or two toys," Mother said. "These children have lost both their parents and their home, and we don't even know what else."

She was trying to make me feel ashamed. And maybe it worked, a little. But I wasn't about to let *her* know that. "May I be excused?" I asked stiffly.

"You may," Mother said.

Trudging up the stairs to the attic, I was mumbling to myself, "They aren't even here yet, and they're already getting me in trouble. Well, I don't care *what* she says, I'm not giving 'em my farm set. Or my bunny. Let 'em mess up Kathleen's stuff."

19. SLIPPING AWAY

I'd always loved the attic. When I was little, I'd carry my stuffed animals up there and tuck them into the crib that Leo, Kathleen, and I had all used as babies. Then I'd read to them from a fairy-tale book. And when I'd get tired of reading, I'd rummage through the trunks and boxes, never knowing what I might find. Little handmade baby dresses with smocking on the front, old letters and postcards, Christmas ornaments that had been brought all the way from Germany and wrapped carefully in tissue paper. And one time, I found an accordion that Mother said had belonged to her daddy. It was like a treasure hunt.

I hadn't been in the attic for a long time, so when I switched on the light, I just stood there a few minutes looking around. My stuffed animals were in the crib, with a blanket pulled up to their chins. The rest of the toys were on shelves against the wall. Leo's bow and the two arrows that hadn't been lost. His catcher's mitt. A jar filled with marbles. Another jar with real Indian arrowheads that we'd found over the years in Tommie Dora's fields. Kathleen's many baby dolls, and the only one I ever remembered getting, which still looked brand-new because I'd never cared much for dolls. And there was my farm set!

I went over and peered inside the barn, where the little wooden people and animals were stored. Leo and I used to play farm on my bedroom floor, setting up the fences for pastures and a pigsty, and making wrinkle hills in the rug for the cows and horses to graze on. Leo had mostly pretended to plow and plant crops, while I made the horses gallop and the cat rub against the ankles of the farmer's wife. And when I got bored, I'd yell, "Tornado!" and jerk the rug so everything would go flying.

I finally tore myself away from the farm set and found the quilt Mother wanted in the cedar chest. The white background had yellowed some, but the appliquéd tulips were still deep pink, their stems and leaves the color of new grass, the butterflies as bright as daffodils. I picked up the quilt and headed downstairs.

Kathleen was coming out of Leo's room carrying his quilt and a box filled with ship models. Leo had spent a lot of time building those ships from kits. They were the only things of his that he wouldn't let me touch—because they were so delicate, he said—and it grieved me to see them dumped in a box and tossed every which way.

Kathleen had already changed the sheets, so I dropped

the tulip quilt on the bed. I noticed the wooden lamp Leo had made in eighth grade, with the shade that had never hung quite straight, and snatched it up. I didn't want those kids wrecking it.

Back in the attic, I put Leo's lamp in a safe place. Then I had to go through a lot of boxes before I found Kathleen's lady lamp. It looked like a doll—a grown-up lady doll with a hoop skirt and a pink ruffled parasol for the shade. I couldn't stand the thing myself, but Kathleen had just loved that lamp till she was twelve or thirteen and decided she was getting too old for it.

I grabbed a pillowcase out of the cedar chest and tucked two of the baby dolls into it. Then I got Kathleen's bunny off the shelf. It was gray and fluffy, and the ribbon around its neck was still tied in a perfect bow. It didn't look like Kathleen had ever played with it.

The only other stuffed animals were those in the crib, the ones I'd slept with and read to and dearly loved. There was Cocoa the bear, Tootsie the dog, Gus the monkey, and Biscuit. When he was new, Biscuit had looked just like Kathleen's bunny, only his fur was light brown. Now he had bald spots, his ribbon was missing, the stitching on his nose had come loose, and one of his ears was bent so it looked like it needed a splint. But the others were in even worse shape. I looked tenderly at my four old friends, debating with myself. The *right* thing to do would be to give them

Biscuit. But those kids wouldn't take care of him, and it would break my heart to see them pick him up with their sticky hands and tug on him till his legs fell off. No, I couldn't give up Biscuit.

By the time I got back downstairs, Kathleen had the tulip quilt on the bed and was cleaning out the desk. I put the lamp on the bedside table and plugged it in.

"My lady lamp!" Kathleen's face lit up. "It's perfect in here. Those little girls are just gonna love their room."

You mean Leo's room, I thought, and started arranging the dolls and the rabbit on the bed.

We were about finished when I noticed Mother standing in the doorway, her hand on the doorframe and one foot inside, like she'd meant to come in but then something had stopped her in her tracks. Her eyes moved from the bed to the lamp and then settled on me.

"What a good job you two have done," she said.

Kathleen surveyed the room and nodded. "It does look nice."

I didn't say anything. It wasn't like I *approved* of all this. I was just doing what I'd been told to do.

"Bayliss, those baby dolls were a good choice," Mother said. "But you only brought one stuffed animal. Run up to the attic and get another one."

"There aren't any more," I said, smoothing a wrinkle in the quilt so I wouldn't have to look at her. "Just some old ragged ones."

"Well, pick out the one that looks best," Mother said.

I pretended to smooth another wrinkle that wasn't there, stalling for time. I didn't want to say straight out that I wasn't giving up any of my animals. But I didn't have to, because Kathleen said it for me.

"She doesn't want to share her toys," Kathleen said. "All these were mine."

"That's not true," I said. "The doll with the bottle was mine."

"But you didn't want it," Kathleen said, "so I took it."

Now I was starting to get irritated. "Just because you *took* it doesn't mean it was yours. It was *my* Christmas present."

"It doesn't matter *whose* doll it was," Mother interrupted, beginning to lose patience with us. "It's Gwen and Isabel's now. And we need two stuffed animals for them."

This was so unfair. Kathleen didn't have to give up a single thing she cared about. Even that stupid lady lamp didn't mean anything to her now. So I tried pleading. "Mother, you know how much I've always loved Biscuit and Cocoa and the others. I couldn't stand to see any of 'em mistreated."

But that didn't soften Mother up a bit. "Bayliss, we're talking about two little girls. They aren't going to mistreat your animals." She sounded even more impatient.

"And besides," Kathleen said, "nuns have to make sacrifices all the time and do it with a joyful heart. If you want to be a nun, Bayliss, you can't be so selfish."

I was selfish? Kathleen was the one who had to have her own way all the time. And I didn't see *her* going over to the convent every day to help people. I would have told her that, too, but Mother cut me off.

"Not another word," she said, "from either of you. Bayliss, do what I said right now. And when you come back downstairs, I don't want to see any sulking."

I stomped out of the room, thinking, *Well, maybe I won't come back downstairs. Maybe I'll spend the whole night in the attic and sulk as much as I want.*

But the attic was hot, and I was too big to sleep in a crib. So after a while, I did come downstairs, bringing Biscuit with me. I loved Biscuit best of all, but I figured he was the toughest and had the best chance of surviving whatever those kids would do to him. And I'd brought the fairy-tale book, too, just so he'd have something familiar.

Mother was gone when I went into Leo's room, but Kathleen was still there, filling a box with stuff from the desk. I walked past her without a word and placed Biscuit on the bed next to the other rabbit.

I was bending Biscuit's good ear so it would look more like the injured one when Kathleen said, "Let's try to get along, Bayliss. We upset Mother, and she needed us tonight, with Daddy catching her off guard like that. He's such a good person, sometimes he can be thoughtless."

I'd made up my mind not to speak to Kathleen, but I

couldn't help saying, "That doesn't make a bit of sense," hoping she'd pick up on the sneer in my voice. "How can he be good and thoughtless at the same time?"

"Daddy didn't stop to think how bringing children into the house and letting 'em use Leo's room would hurt Mother. He just knew helping the girls was the right thing to do. It never entered his mind that the rest of us might not be as good as he is." Kathleen sighed. "But maybe it's for the best."

"*I* don't think so."

"Honestly, Bayliss, can't you just try? For Mother's sake? Can't you see how hard this is for her?"

I almost said, *Well, it's hard for me, too!* But I didn't want to talk about that with Kathleen. The thing was, I hadn't felt Leo's presence in the house for a long time. And now we'd taken all his stuff away. When I looked at the new quilt and the lady lamp, I had a crazy feeling—like maybe this had never been Leo's room at all.

He was slipping away from me, a little more every day. And there was nothing I could do to stop it.

20. GWEN AND ISABEL

I was in the dining room setting the table when I heard the back door open and then my daddy's voice in the kitchen. I listened for little-girl voices, but all I could make out was my mother sounding way too cheerful, so I knew the girls were here even if they weren't saying anything.

Cracking the door just a hair, I could see Daddy leaning against the counter and Kathleen next to him at the stove. Mother was filling a pot with water but peering over her shoulder, smiling.

". . . won't be long," she was saying. "Can you wait half an hour, or do you need a little something to tide you over?"

My eyes shifted to the two girls standing just inside the back door. It was them Mother was talking to, but neither one answered.

"Maybe you'd like to wash up," Mother said.

They weren't exactly what I'd expected. For one thing, they looked clean. For another, they weren't making a sound.

The older girl was tall and skinny, with a million freckles and frizzy red hair that could use some brushing. This one—Gwen, it must be—looked furious, like she was letting everybody know right up front that she might have to be here, but she didn't have to like it.

The other one, Isabel, was tiny even for a five-year-old, and I don't reckon I've ever seen a prettier child. Her hair was reddish blond and silky, her skin so fair it should have been freckled but wasn't. She had her chin tucked into her chest, and she was giving my mother and sister shy looks through her lashes. But even with her head down, I could see that her eyes were very nearly Pettigrew blue.

Then Mother caught sight of me spying through the crack in the door and said, "Bayliss, come meet Gwen and Isabel."

I slunk into the kitchen, and Gwen turned eyes in my direction that were as yellow as a cat's. Or maybe they were green. But they definitely weren't friendly.

"This is Kathleen's sister, Bayliss," Mother told the girls.

Since I'd been brought up to be polite, and Mother would have something to say about it later if I wasn't, I said, "Hey." But I wasn't about to be a hypocrite and act like I was thrilled they were here.

The girls didn't open their mouths, and I was wondering if maybe they *couldn't* speak. But Gwen had told Miz Eubanks about their family, so I figured it must be that she just didn't want to talk to *us*.

While Kathleen was telling them what we were having

155

for supper, I studied them from top to bottom. Their dresses were faded and worn thin, and one look at their feet and I could tell their shoes were too small. Gwen's even had the toes cut out to give her more room. And they were clutching rolled-up paper sacks that must have held everything they owned.

"Kathleen," Mother said, "why don't you and Bayliss take Gwen and Isabel up to their room? And show them where the bathroom is."

Kathleen smiled at the girls and said, "Come on. We'll unpack your things."

Isabel edged closer to her sister, and Gwen reached for Isabel's hand as they followed Kathleen into the hall. I sighed and fell into step behind them.

Gwen was taking it all in. That red head was twisting from right to left so she could peer into every room we passed. But when we started up the stairs, I noticed that her back was as stiff as a soldier's. You would have thought she was being marched off to a firing squad.

Kathleen led the way down the upstairs hall, pointed out the bathroom, and turned in to Leo's doorway. I heard a gasp as I walked into the room and saw Isabel's hands fly up to her face.

"Ooooh," she said softly, "it's so *pretty*."

"This is your room," Kathleen said. "Yours and your sister's."

I glanced at Gwen and saw that she looked madder than ever. What was wrong with this girl anyhow? Would she rather be back at the home sleeping on the floor?

Isabel put her paper sack on the desk and walked over to the bed. She touched the quilt timidly, then ran her finger along a line of stitching. I watched as her eyes skipped from the dolls to the bunnies and then to the lady lamp.

Kathleen took Gwen's sack from her and picked up Isabel's, but there was precious little to unpack. She pulled out some dingy ankle socks and underwear with the elastic all stretched out, then hung up two worn-out sweaters and two dresses that were in worse shape than the ones the girls were wearing. At the bottom of one sack were brand-new toothbrushes that Miz Eubanks must have given them and a comb like the ones sold at Gilchrist Mercantile for ten cents. And that was it. No coats, no toys, no treasures.

Kathleen was telling them how it was good they'd come before school started, and that they'd be going to Sacred Heart with us, while I just stood there not knowing what to say and feeling foolish. And Gwen never took those peculiar yellow eyes off me.

"I have to help Mother with supper," Kathleen said. "Y'all make yourselves at home, and Bayliss'll keep you company."

I wanted to say, *Now wait one cotton-pickin' minute*, but she was already out the door and gone. So there we were,

157

just the three of us. Gwen was still staring at me, and Isabel had turned *her* eyes my way, and I was wondering, *What do they expect me to do, entertain them?* So I looked around, feeling a little panicky, and saw the fairy-tale book.

I grabbed for it and asked, "Do y'all like stories?"

Speaking her first words in my presence, Gwen said, "Isabel can't read."

It came out sharp—downright rude, I thought—but I was doing my best to be civil, so I said, "Then I'll read to both of you."

Gwen narrowed those eyes at me and said, "I don't need anybody reading to me. I could do it myself if I wanted to, which I don't. Fairy tales are stupid."

But Isabel tugged on her sister's arm and said, "Please, Gwen? I wanna hear the story."

Gwen was between a rock and a hard place. I could see it in her face. She'd probably just as soon swallow broken glass as pick up that book and read from it—much less let me do it—but Isabel's feelings mattered to her.

Well, that wasn't my problem. And I was fixing to put the book down, say, *Suit yourself,* and leave. Because I didn't care for her company any more than she cared for mine.

But then Gwen folded her arms across her chest and glared at me. "So go ahead and read," she said. "What are you waiting for?"

Isabel seemed happy as she scrambled onto the bed.

"Don't mess up that cover," Gwen said.

Isabel froze, looking stricken.

"It's all right, Isabel." I cut my eyes at Gwen. "It's *your* bed. Jump on it if you want to."

That was all Isabel needed to hear. She scooted up to the pillows and looked with interest at the baby dolls and rabbits. Then she reached over Kathleen's bunny for Biscuit and settled back to listen. I sat down next to her and opened the book.

"Gwen, come over here with us," Isabel said. "There's plenty of room."

Gwen didn't move till I looked up. Then she made a point of sitting down at the desk.

" 'The Real Princess,' " I read, and glanced at Isabel, who was holding Biscuit against her chest and stroking his fur with her thumb. "You've got good taste in rabbits," I said.

Isabel's eyes jerked up to my face, and she looked startled.

"Well, are you gonna read it or not?" Gwen demanded.

I didn't answer. I was too busy wondering what the penance would be for whacking somebody over the head with a book.

Gwen barely touched her supper, taking little nibbles but mostly watching all of us out of the corner of her eye, while Isabel couldn't shovel it in fast enough. Rosie was in her usual spot at my feet. I was fishing out bits of pork Kathleen had used to flavor the beans and dropping them to the floor when Isabel finally noticed. She lifted the tablecloth and cried out, "It's a kitty! Did y'all know you have a cat under here?"

"Bayliss, put the cat out," Kathleen said. "We can't ever sit down to a meal without her begging."

I was all set to argue, but then Mother, her eyes on Isabel's disappointed face, said, "It's all right, Bayliss. She can stay in this one time."

Isabel beamed. "What's her name?" she asked me, which opened up the first real conversation since we'd sat down, and it centered around Rosie.

Everybody joined in, even Daddy. He told the story of how, when I was about three, my grandmother had brought a full-grown Rosie to us, saying we children needed a cat and she had some to spare. As soon as she put Rosie down, the cat made her way upstairs to my room and climbed into the crib with me. A little later, when Daddy came up to check on us, he found me lying there with my eyes open wide, staring at this good-sized lump under the blanket and at the one black paw sticking out. He said I turned my head to look at him and whispered, "Daddy, there's a wild animal in my bed. I don't want you to hurt it, but could you please get it out of here?"

Isabel started giggling, then laughing out loud, and so

did everybody else. Everybody but Gwen, who lowered her head over her plate and seemed to get real interested in her food all of a sudden.

I'd been keeping an eye on Gwen, wondering if she'd been this cantankerous at the home or if it was just being *here* she hated. I figured it had to have been awful riding in noisy boxcars day after day and ending up in one strange place after another, and then having their daddy run out on them. So maybe Gwen had a right to be mad. But didn't she realize she was better off here than being dragged all over the country?

Then I looked at Isabel, who was sneaking Rosie bites of everything from squash to corn bread, and not fooling anybody, and thought how she wasn't the least bit sullen. But then, she'd always had a big sister around to take care of her.

After supper, Kathleen and I started clearing the table. Mother told Gwen and Isabel they could go listen to the radio with Daddy, but Gwen was already reaching for her and Isabel's plates.

"You don't have to do that," Mother said, "not on your first night."

Gwen just ignored her and took off for the kitchen with the dishes. And I thought, *Well, at least she's not expecting to be waited on.*

Mother and I carried the bowls of food to the kitchen,

with Isabel trailing after us. Kathleen was running water in the sink.

"What do you dry with?" Gwen asked Kathleen. "Isabel and me can pull our own weight."

Kathleen gave her a dish towel, and Mother started putting food away in the icebox. I reached for the broom and noticed Isabel watching me.

"You want to help?" I asked her.

She nodded, so I got the dustpan and handed it to her. "Just hold it steady while I sweep the crumbs into it."

Isabel squatted down and held on tight to the dustpan, frowning as she tried to do it just right.

21. FROM A TO IZZARD

When I walked into the kitchen the next morning, Mother had the ironing board up and Kathleen was on her way out the back door with a basket of wet wash.

Looking up from her ironing, Mother said, "I wanted to get the laundry on the line before we start cleaning, so you'll have to make your own breakfast. And when Gwen and Isabel come down, can you fix them some eggs? There's oatmeal and a pan of biscuits on the stove."

I got myself two biscuits and a glass of milk and sat down. "I thought Kathleen just did the wash the other day," I said, spreading strawberry jam on a biscuit.

"Gwen and Isabel need clean clothes."

"They don't hardly have anything."

"I know," Mother said. "When Kathleen told me what they'd brought, I went up to the attic and found some things of yours that should fit them. And don't tell me," she hurried on before I could open my mouth, "that you want to save the dresses you wore in third grade."

"I don't care what you do with that stuff," I said, and bit into my biscuit.

"Good. Because I think we have everything they'll need. I even found some shoes they can try on."

When the girls came downstairs, I was just finishing my breakfast. Gwen still had that fierce look about her, like she'd just as soon spit in your face as speak to you, and that rusty hair was wilder than ever. There was a big knotty tangle in the back that I figured was beyond brushing. Somebody was going to have to cut it out. Isabel's hair wasn't combed either, but everything about Isabel was soft and sweet, even her tangled curls.

"Morning, girls," Mother said. "Bayliss is fixing your breakfast. Sit down and she'll bring you some milk."

Isabel crawled up into a chair, looking bright-eyed and eager. Gwen plopped down beside her and stared out the window. When I set the glasses of milk in front of them, Gwen studied hers like she was wondering if I'd slipped in some rat poison.

"I'm ironing something for you to wear today," Mother told them. "Y'all can help Bayliss dust, and then she'll take you out to play. You don't want to bother with dresses on a Saturday."

While I digested the news that I was going to be babysitting these kids all day, I noticed that Isabel was thrilled with the idea of new clothes, and that Gwen wasn't. But then, I could have predicted that.

Mother held up overalls and a shirt I'd worn when I was three or four and said, "Why don't you try these on, Isabel, and see if they fit?"

Beaming like it was Christmas morning, Isabel was out of that chair and jerking her dress over her head before Gwen had time to get on her high horse about it. I brought the pot of oatmeal to the table, but Isabel was dancing around the room exclaiming over the deep pockets in her overalls and couldn't have cared less about breakfast. Gwen was slumped in her chair with her bottom lip poked out about as far as it would go, making it plain how she felt about taking charity from strangers. But I reckon she didn't have the heart to ruin it for her sister.

"And, Gwen, these are yours," Mother said.

Gwen took the clothes without a word and left the room. She was back in a few minutes, still sullen, but wearing the overalls.

Isabel folded her hands under her chin like she was praying and said, "Oh, Gwennie, you look *bee-yoo-tuh-ful*."

After that, it wasn't much of a struggle to get them into my old socks and shoes. But as we were leaving to go dust the dining room, I heard Gwen say to Mother, "We'll wear these things while we're here, but we're not taking 'em with us."

It turned out that Gwen and Isabel knew how to work and were quicker than I was. But Isabel had to stop every now and then to admire her new shoes or to say in a worried voice, "I just hope and pray I don't mess up this pretty outfit."

When we moved on to the living room, Gwen noticed Mother's needlepoint first thing and picked up the half-finished canvas to look at it. Mother was making new seat covers for the dining room chairs, and she'd come up with that pansy design herself. Isabel and I started dusting, but Gwen was still examining the canvas when Mother came in with the carpet sweeper.

"Do you like needlepoint?" Mother asked her.

Gwen shrugged. "I was just counting the colors. Six different purples, four yellows, and five greens."

Mother looked surprised. Then she smiled at Gwen as if the girl had just said the most brilliant thing she'd ever heard. "Would you like to learn how to do it? I could teach you."

For the first time since I'd met Gwen, she wasn't looking hateful. She actually seemed to be giving Mother's offer serious consideration. But then she caught herself and slapped that scowl back on.

"I tried to get Kathleen and Bayliss interested in needlepoint," Mother said, "but that was a lost cause. I tell you what, Gwen, after supper I'll show you some stitches and give you a piece of canvas to practice on."

Gwen shrugged again, as if she didn't care one way or the other, and put the canvas back where she'd found it.

Next we headed upstairs to Leo's room. I was dragging my feet because I didn't like going in there with the tulip quilt and the lady lamp and nothing of Leo's left.

Gwen and Isabel got right to work, but I stood looking at that silly lamp. It didn't belong here, any more than these kids did. Gwen didn't even *want* to be here and didn't appreciate a single thing we were doing for her.

Then Isabel looked up at me and said, "Your mama's nice, Bayliss, and so's your daddy. Does he ever yell at you?"

"Daddy's not much for yelling," I said, and started dusting the desk so we could finish up and get out of there.

"Does he ever take a strap to you?"

"Isabel." There was a warning in Gwen's voice.

"What's wrong with that?" Isabel asked. "I was just wondering."

"It's none of your business," Gwen said.

Lord love a duck, I thought, *she's about as bossy as Kathleen!* And that made me feel a little sorry for Isabel. I knew what she had to put up with.

So I said to Gwen, "She can ask anything she wants." Then I turned to Isabel and said, "Daddy whipped me a couple of times when I was little, but it was just a swat with his hand."

"You must've been a very good girl," Isabel said solemnly. "*Our* daddy got the strap out lots of times. When he was drinking, he could be *real* mean."

"Isabel," Gwen said sharply, "hush up."

Tears sprang to Isabel's eyes, and Gwen said hastily, "Now don't go to blubbering. I didn't mean to hurt your feelings."

Isabel sniffed and rubbed her eyes. I moved away and started dusting the bedside table, feeling like I shouldn't be hearing all this and thinking that Isabel was awfully little for somebody to take a strap to her.

"Come on, Isabel," Gwen said. "Why don't you fix the rabbits the way you want 'em?"

Isabel jumped up on the bed and turned the bunnies to face each other, placing their paws together like they were holding hands.

Gwen was watching her sister. Standing this close, I could see that her eyes weren't yellow; they were pale green with little specks of gold in them. She turned those eyes on me now.

"Daddy didn't start drinking till after our mama died." She lifted her chin and gave me a hard look, as if daring me to contradict her. "Our grandma said when Mama was alive, he was sober as a Baptist preacher."

Then Gwen whipped around to start dusting the dresser, and all I could see was her back. Isabel didn't say anything, and neither did I. Gwen had made it clear that this conversation was over.

I wasn't sure what I was feeling right then, because it was all mixed up. From what Isabel had said about their daddy, it seemed to me they were better off without him. But I still didn't want them living *here*.

And then I thought of something Gwen had said, about them having a grandmother. But I needed to find out where she lived. I couldn't ask Gwen, so I'd have to come up with a way to get Isabel off by herself. And right now seemed like the perfect time. Gwen had just started dusting the carved front of the dresser, and it was going to take her a while to get into all those little crevices.

"Isabel," I said, "let's move on to Kathleen's room. Gwen can join us when she's done here."

That was fine with Isabel, so we left Gwen and went down the hall. Once we'd started working in Kathleen's room, I said, "Gwen mentioned that you have a grandmother."

"Grandma Truett," Isabel said. "Daddy's her son, but she gave up on him. She told him the devil's just waiting inside that whiskey bottle, and that's why he turns mean as a snake when he drinks. And she said she didn't want to lay eyes on him again, not as long as there was a drop of liquor on his breath."

"Where does your grandma live?"

"Morrisville."

I'd been to Morrisville once when Daddy drove Mavis Quick up there to visit her sister. I figured it must be about fifty miles from here.

"After Daddy got laid off from the mine," Isabel said, "we moved in with Grandma and our brother for a while."

I turned around to look at her. She was dusting Kathleen's dressing table and being careful not to knock anything over. "You have a brother?" I asked her.

"Uh-huh, Frank. He's our half brother, really, 'cause he had a different mother from Gwen and me. But he loves us like a *whole* brother."

Now I was getting excited. "How old is Frank?"

Isabel stopped dusting to consider this. "Ummm . . . He's pretty old. Nineteen, I think."

This was more than I'd hoped for. Gwen and Isabel had a grandmother and, even better, a brother. A grown-up brother who loved them and could take care of them. I was sure Daddy didn't know this or he would have already taken the girls to Morrisville. And I couldn't wait to tell him.

I was thinking how surprised he'd be, when Isabel sighed, and then she said in a little voice, "Frank wanted to keep us, but he was out of work, too, and our grandma said he didn't have a say. Not till he could help put food on the table."

After dinner, Daddy had to go back to the office, so I walked with him to the car shed.

"I've just found out that Gwen and Isabel have a brother," I told him. "He lives in Morrisville, and he's at least nineteen. I'll bet he doesn't even know where they are. Isabel says he loves them, so he'll want 'em to come live with him. I know he will."

I had decided not to mention the part about their brother being out of work, figuring that he'd probably found a job by now. And I was expecting Daddy to smile real big and congratulate me on solving a problem that had been weighing on his mind. But he didn't smile.

"Mrs. Eubanks checked to see if there was family willing to take the girls," he said, "and there wasn't."

"But, Daddy—"

"Bayliss, I'm running late." He opened the car door and tossed his medical bag into the passenger seat. "I'm doing everything I can to find a permanent home for them. You'll just have to trust me, all right?"

Sometimes even the best parents can disappoint you. I was feeling really let down when I went back inside. And Mother didn't help matters when she said, "Kathleen and I can clean up. Bayliss, why don't you take the girls out to play?"

She said it like she was asking, but I knew I didn't have a choice. I'd been wanting to start a book on Saint Afra, but it looked like the days of me having a minute to myself were long gone. Kathleen could say all she wanted about nuns having to make sacrifices, but it seemed to me the nuns had it easy. *They* only had to put up with kids for seven hours a day. But I had to live with these two and do everything from A to *izzard* for them. This didn't seem right to me.

When we went outside, I noticed some piles of leaves

against the car shed that Leo and I had raked up last fall and never got around to burning. Daddy had taken over mowing the yard this year, but he hadn't bothered with those leaves. Maybe, like me, he didn't care if they were burned or not.

Isabel went running ahead, humming a song that didn't have much of a tune to it. Then all of a sudden she threw herself into the biggest pile of leaves and started moving her arms and legs up and down like she was making a snow angel.

"You'll get ticks," Gwen told her.

"Then you can pick 'em off," Isabel answered.

It was boring just walking around the yard, so I said, "Isabel, you want me to push you in the swing?"

"Yes!" she shouted, and leaped to her feet.

I pushed that old tire swing till my back was burning, but Isabel just kept screaming, "Higher, Bayliss! Higher!"

After a while, I saw Harry coming up the street pulling his wagon with a bushel basket in it. Jack was trotting along beside him.

"It's a dog!" Isabel shouted.

"Let's put the brakes on this thing," I said, "and you can go see him."

Harry was backing the wagon up to his porch when we crossed the street.

"Hey!" I called to him. "Little boy with the red wagon! What you got there?"

Harry looked up and smiled. "Apples," he said. "After I finished with the rolling store, Jack and me went out to Miz Tommie Dora's and picked some so she and Mavis Quick can make apple butter. She told me to bring these home to Mama."

Isabel had thrown her arms around Jack's neck. He was giving her sloppy kisses, and Isabel was having a giggling fit.

"Are there more to pick?" I asked Harry.

"Lots. I'm going back next week. Y'all wanna come?"

"Sure," I said. Then I introduced Harry to Gwen and Isabel. "And that pony you're hanging on to, Isabel, is named Jack."

"Bayliss, this isn't a pony," Isabel said kindly. "He's just a real big dog."

Harry had lifted the basket of apples to the porch. "How'd you like me to pull you down the street?" he asked Isabel.

"Can Jack ride, too?" she asked, already scrambling into the wagon.

"He wouldn't like it, but he'll run with us. Hold on to the sides so you don't fall out." Then he said to Gwen, "Hop in."

Gwen shook her head and stood there watching as Harry pulled Isabel out to the street and took off running, the wagon rattling behind him. Isabel was screaming in delight, and Jack was giving sharp, happy barks as he chased after them.

Meanwhile, I'd noticed Gwen peering up at an old crab apple tree in Harry's front yard. The limbs started close to the ground and spread out like sturdy arms, a great tree for climbing. Gwen must have had the same thought, because the next thing I knew, she was reaching for one of the limbs. And the way she flew up that tree, you would have thought she had wings instead of arms like ordinary people.

I hadn't climbed a tree since the accident, and wasn't even sure I could do it anymore, but I figured I might as well find out. So I grabbed hold of a low branch and pulled myself up. I felt stiff and awkward compared to Gwen, who had already climbed as high as she could go and was sitting on a limb that grew out over the street. That irked me some, because I used to be as fast as she was.

When I finally did reach the last of the weight-bearing limbs, I found one of my own a good distance away from Gwen's, so we wouldn't have to make conversation. My back was aching, but I felt pretty proud of myself. And the view from up there was something. I could see the court-house roof and the twin spires of Sacred Heart Church—and there was Harry. He'd gone to the end of the block and was turning the wagon around. Isabel was shouting out orders, and Jack was still barking.

I glanced over at Gwen, but she was too busy watching Harry pull her sister back up the street to pay me any mind. At least she hadn't said anything about how long it took me to climb the tree, but I was embarrassed all the same. I wanted to tell her that I hadn't always been that slow, that I'd hurt my back but it was nearly healed now. Only then she'd get the idea that I *cared* what she thought, and I sure as heck didn't. Gwen Truett was nothing to me, and besides, I had to believe that she wouldn't be here long enough for it to matter.

22. THE DADBLAMEDEST THING

"Perfect," Kathleen said. "Both of you look just perfect."

It was the first day of school. Mother was doing the breakfast dishes, and I was sitting at the table reading my book on Saint Afra—and wondering what a brothel was—while Kathleen fussed over Gwen and Isabel in their school dresses. Kathleen had washed and trimmed the girls' hair the night before and had spent the better part of the evening teasing that giant rat's nest out of Gwen's, with Gwen jerking and wiggling and shooting her dirty looks. Then Kathleen had put Gwen's hair up on rollers, thinking she could tame it some. But that mess of frizz had a mind all its own, so Kathleen had settled for pinning it down as best she could with two barrettes.

"You did tell Sister Annunciata that you won't be helping serve meals today?" Mother said to me.

"Not yet." I should have said something on Friday, but I'd still been hoping that Mother would come home early and let me off the hook.

"Well, see that you do," Mother said, "right after you take the girls to their classrooms and introduce them to their teachers."

I'd known I had to walk them home, but nobody had mentioned mornings. Couldn't Kathleen do even that much?

"Bayliss?" Mother's voice was edgy.

"Yes, ma'am," I muttered, and propped my book in front of my face so I could fume in private.

Mother made us leave early so that Gwen and Isabel could get settled in before all the other kids got there. As we walked down Main Street toward Sacred Heart, Isabel said, "Gwennie, don't we all look nice in our new dresses?"

Gwen just scowled, and Isabel said, "Well, I think we look nice."

And I reckon we did, although none of the dresses were new. Gwen and Isabel were wearing old ones of mine, and Mother had taken up a dress of Kathleen's for me. It was a pretty red plaid that I'd always admired. And I had new shoes because the old ones had been pinching my toes as far back as last winter. When Mother had pointed out the brown oxfords in the Montgomery Ward catalog, Kathleen had turned up her nose and said she'd just as soon go barefoot as wear those tacky things. "Fine, then," Mother had said, "but there's nothing at all wrong with these shoes. They'll last forever." And Kathleen had grumbled, "That's what I'm afraid of." So I was the only one to get new shoes and was right pleased with them, even if they were the ugliest things I'd ever laid eyes on.

We got to school so early, the first-grade classroom was still locked, so we went to Gwen's room. There was no sign of Sister Mary Vincent, but the door was standing open and the lights were on.

"Come on," I said. "We'll wait."

We went inside and took seats up front. Gwen sat staring at a world map that covered most of one wall, while Isabel's eyes flitted from the map to the blackboard to the crucifix behind Sister Mary Vincent's desk. Then she twisted around to watch the door.

Sister Josephine passed by, and Isabel said, "All these ladies are wearing the same black dress."

"They're Catholic nuns," I said, "and that black dress is called a habit."

"We're not Catholic," Isabel said.

"I know. That's why you and Gwen went to the Baptist church yesterday with Miz Burdeshaw and Harry."

Isabel nodded, but she was starting to look worried.

I could remember being a little bit scared my first day at Sacred Heart, even though I'd been around nuns all my life. And it was Leo, as always, who'd made me feel better. He'd walked me to school that morning, holding my hand, and he'd said, "You're gonna like it, little britches. Wait till you see how much fun we'll have playing tricks on the nuns." And he'd been right, we did have fun. Of course, before the week was out, I was cooling my heels in Sister Annunciata's office, and she was telling Mother that she'd never had a first grader cause so much trouble—not even Leo. And that night, after Daddy had sent me to bed without any supper, Leo had sneaked into my room and said, "Didn't I tell you school was fun?"

I was smiling, thinking back on that. Then my eyes fell on Isabel's worried face again, and I said to her, "You don't have to be Catholic to go here. Just remember, you call the nuns Sister. You say, *Yes, Sister* and *No, Sister* and *Thank you, Sister.* And your teacher, Sister Gertrude, is old and real sweet. She reads stories and lets you draw and color, and if you fall down on the playground, she'll take you in her lap and call you her little lamb."

Isabel gave a deep sigh, and then she said, "I just hope and pray I don't do everything wrong."

Gwen's eyes left the map and settled on me. "What about my teacher?"

"Well . . ." I straightened Isabel's collar, stalling for time. "Your teacher is Sister Mary Vincent."

Then I was stuck. What could I tell her that was true but wouldn't make her think I was trying to scare the living daylights out of her? That Sister Mary Vincent was a trial and a torment and maybe just a little bit crazy? Leo

179

used to call her Sister Polly Pious behind her back, because one look at her face and you knew that being a nun was grim and serious business. She'd rattle on and on about how blessed we were to have the Holy Mother and the rosary, and to know better than to eat meat on Fridays—unlike the poor heathen children, who were ignorant and doomed to eternal damnation. Hearing this from Sister Mary Vincent when I was in third grade, I'd asked her, "Where do the poor heathen children live, Sister?" And Sister Mary Vincent had waved her hand vaguely and said, "Oh, across the water." So, for the longest time, I'd imagined them camped out on the other side of Sweet Springs Lake.

"Well," Gwen said, "are you gonna tell me about her or not?"

"Uh . . . You learn a lot from her. I had trouble with the multiplication tables, and she wouldn't let me quit till I'd memorized 'em." *Till she'd pounded them into my head like she was hammering railroad spikes*, I added to myself. "And when you turn in a perfect paper or do a good job reciting in class, she puts a gold star by your name on the wall." I recalled that there had been precious few stars beside *my* name. "Oh, and she has spelling bees. Sister Mary Vincent loves spelling."

Gwen just stared at me, as if she suspected I was holding out on her.

180

Meanwhile, Isabel had gotten up and walked over to the teacher's desk. "What's that?" she asked.

"What?"

She pointed to a big goldfish bowl that was nearly hidden by stacks of books. "That," she said.

I went up to the desk and looked inside the bowl. It had about two inches of sand in the bottom where Sister Mary Vincent had arranged little chalk figures: four men in robes, a camel, and a palm tree.

"This is Sister Mary Vincent's diorama," I said.

"Her *what*?"

"It's just a scene she sets up from the Bible. In December, you can count on her having Mary, Joseph, and the baby Jesus in the stable. And one time she did the Garden of Eden, with a black shoelace for the serpent, but she hid Adam and Eve behind some rocks so we couldn't tell if they were naked or not."

Gwen had come over and was studying the goldfish bowl.

"So what's this one about?" Isabel asked.

"I reckon it's Jesus healing the sick," I said. "See how three of the men are sprawled out in the sand? They must be the cripples."

Gwen shook her head. "Jesus in a fishbowl," she muttered. "If that's not the dadblamedest thing I ever saw!"

I almost cracked a smile. But being back at school just

reminded me that I *should* have been going to the convent that afternoon, and now I couldn't. And I was discovering that I wasn't above holding a grudge.

By the time Gwen and Isabel were finally settled, the bell was about to ring, so I took off to find Sister Annunciata. She listened while I explained that two girls from the children's home were staying with us and that I had to look after them till Mother got home and wouldn't be able to serve meals to the weary travelers.

"It's just for a little while," I said, expecting her to be put out with me. "I'll be back to help the sisters before long."

But all Sister Annunciata said was, "There are different ways of helping, Mary Bayliss."

23. ACTS OF CHARITY

As the morning passed, I realized that Sister Annunciata must have put the fear of God into the other kids. Because they were friendly, and welcomed me back, but nobody asked any nosy questions. And Sister Louise was nice to me in class, but not *too* nice. Nobody even mentioned Leo, which was the only thing that felt wrong.

I'd promised myself to buckle down this year. No passing notes or pulling pranks, and I meant to study hard for all my tests because the convent wouldn't want a dummy. Plus, I'd vowed to be kind to everybody—even Lila Grace Gilchrist.

When the noon bell rang, kids didn't waste any time taking off for home or going out to the playground to eat. Annie and I headed for our usual spot under a sugarberry tree and unwrapped our sandwiches.

"Egg salad," I said.

"Bologna. You want to trade half?"

After I'd taken a big bite of bologna and cheese, I

looked around the playground and spotted Isabel sitting with some other little girls. I didn't see Gwen, but I figured even Mother couldn't expect me to hold her hand all day at school.

I was enjoying that bologna—which we never had at home because it cost too much—and was about to pop the last bite into my mouth when who should come sashaying over but Lila Grace Gilchrist, followed by her shadow, Jane Tillett. And as usual, they had smiles on their faces that had nothing at all to do with good humor and everything to do with being hateful.

As much as I despised Lila Grace, I couldn't deny that she had pretty hair, which was even blonder than Annie's and fell in perfect waves to her shoulders. And her clothes were nice, too. Today she was wearing a blue dress with pearl buttons—new, of course, and definitely not ordered from Montgomery Ward. Lila Grace was always bragging how her mother took her to Birmingham to shop. But all the fancy dresses in the world couldn't hide the fact that she had squinty little eyes and a face as round and flat as a cast-iron skillet. Even so, the way she flounced around, you could tell she thought the sun rose every morning just to hear her crow.

"Hey, Mary Bayliss," Lila Grace said in that high-pitched voice that would start a coon dog howling. "What you been doing all summer?"

Annie shot Lila Grace a look like she was warning her, but I just said, "Nothing much. That's a pretty dress, Lila Grace. You get that in Birmingham?"

Lila Grace smoothed her skirt and said, "Mama and I went to Atlanta last week to shop. You can't hardly find anything worth buying in Birmingham these days. This Depression's just awful."

Jane Tillett, who was dressed better than most but not so fine as Lila Grace, nodded. "Just awful," she echoed.

Now Lila Grace's sharp little eyes were fixed on me again. "Haven't I seen that dress before? Oh, I remember; it's one of Kathleen's old ones. You know, Mary Bayliss, red's not your color. You should see if Kathleen has anything blue you can wear."

My insides were starting to churn, but I caught myself before I gave Lila Grace the satisfaction of making me lose my temper. Besides, I was going to be kind—to *everybody*.

But since that was easier said than done where Lila Grace was concerned, I thought I'd best cut this conversation short. So I stood up and fixed my mouth into what I hoped would pass for a smile. "I reckon clothes aren't that important," I said. "Not with folks all over the country losing their homes and going hungry."

Annie had scrambled to her feet, too, probably expecting the shouting to commence at any moment and clearly puzzled that it hadn't.

"It's not *my* fault they're hungry," Lila Grace burst out, her face turning pink. "My daddy says most of 'em are just lazy. They could find work if they wanted to. My daddy says they're just looking for a handout."

"Then your daddy," I said quietly, "doesn't know what he's talking about."

Lila Grace looked mad enough to spit nickels, and I could tell she was about to let loose with every insult that was rattling around in that empty skull of hers. But then Jane Tillett nudged her and whispered something, and the two of them snickered.

They were being awfully rude, but that wasn't what bothered me. It was how Lila Grace was smirking when she turned to look at me again. I had the uneasy feeling that she knew something I didn't and was fixing to use it against me.

"I reckon you understand all about folks looking for a handout," she said. "We heard how your daddy brought home those two orphans."

"Miz Eubanks told my mother that your daddy's right taken with 'em," Jane said.

And looking smug, Lila Grace added, "She figures he'll adopt 'em."

Lila Grace had always been able to get to me, as far back as first grade. And even though I was sure Daddy wasn't planning on adopting Gwen and Isabel, Lila Grace had touched a nerve all the same. Because I'd already been stewing over what we'd do if we couldn't find somebody else to take them. And I knew Daddy wouldn't kick two little girls out on the street to fend for themselves, even if that meant keeping them for months. Or *years*!

But I couldn't let Lila Grace think she'd upset me, so I shrugged like it didn't matter to me one way or the other. "They aren't even orphans," I said. "They have a daddy."

"I heard he didn't want 'em," Lila Grace shot back, "and that's why he left 'em at the home. That's the same as being orphans."

"My mother says your daddy's just the kind to take 'em in," Jane said. "She says he's too soft, letting folks get by without paying their bills, and that he always was one to take Christian charity a step too far."

They could say anything they wanted about me, but *nobody* bad-mouthed my daddy and got away with it. My whole body had tensed up, and I could feel the heat rising in my face. But then Annie put her hand on my arm and squeezed till it hurt.

"Most of us don't take it far enough," Annie said, "and I, for one, admire Bayliss's daddy for helping those little girls."

Jane started to say something, but Lila Grace cut her off. I was taken aback when she said, "Annie's right, Jane. What Mary Bayliss and her family's doing for those orphans

187

in their time of need is a true act of charity, and it's to be commended." But I knew she wouldn't stop there, and a second later, she added, "Now, I'm not sure *I'd* want to take strangers into my home, not knowing anything about 'em. I just hope they don't *steal* from you, Mary Bayliss."

Annie still had her hand on my arm, but she didn't need to worry. I was fed up with listening to Lila Grace run her mouth. So I said to Annie, "Come on, let's find a spot where we can eat in peace," and walked away.

I had never, *ever* turned my back on a fight with Lila Grace Gilchrist, but that day I did. And I reckon there was nothing I could have said or done that would have riled her more.

We still had fifteen minutes left before the bell rang, but I'd lost my appetite. So after we'd moved to the other side of the playground, I gave the rest of my egg salad sandwich to Annie.

"Those two get worse every year," she grumbled. "Somebody ought to tell Sister Annunciata what they just said to you. I'd like to see how high and mighty they'd be when *she* got through with 'em."

It was an old daydream of mine—Sister Annunciata lighting into Lila Grace and making her beg for mercy— but I wasn't going to be the one to tattle on her. I might be stubborn and disrespectful, like Sister Mary Vincent said, and I might even be *incorrigible*, to use another one of her favorite words for me. But I was no stool pigeon.

Annie bit into my sandwich, chewed awhile, and swallowed. Then she said, "You don't reckon your daddy does mean to adopt Gwen and Isabel."

"No!"

"Well, you don't have to bite my head off."

"I didn't mean to," I said. "It's just that I didn't want 'em staying with us in the first place, and I sure don't want Daddy adopting 'em. Did I tell you they've taken Leo's room?"

And once I got started, it all came pouring out, the many grievances I'd been holding in because Mother and Daddy and Kathleen didn't want to hear them. But Annie listened to every word, and when I was through talking, she said, "I think I understand how you feel, Bayliss."

"It's selfish," I said, hoping that she'd tell me it wasn't.

But Annie was one of the most honest people I'd ever known, right up there with Tommie Dora, only more delicate about it. "I guess it is a *little* selfish," she said. "But in your place, I'd probably feel the same way."

She finished the last of my sandwich, and while she was brushing crumbs off her skirt, she said, "You know, Lila Grace was right about one thing. No, wait—hear me out. When she said that taking Gwen and Isabel in was an act of charity, she didn't really mean it, but it's true."

"What if it is?" I was in no mood to admit that Lila Grace had been right about anything.

"I was just thinking that maybe you should be looking

189

at this a different way," Annie said. "You wanted to do something good, so you helped the nuns with the weary travelers, only you can't do that with Gwen and Isabel here. But you can still do good by taking care of *them*. Don't you see, Bayliss? It's the same thing."

"No," I said, "it's *not* the same."

"Why not?"

"Because the weary travelers didn't move into Leo's room," I said. "And besides, helping with *them* was easy. I'd hand out apples for an hour, feel good about it, and then go home and forget it till the next day. But I *can't* forget Gwen and Isabel, not when they're living with us. I have to take care of 'em *all the time*. And it's a burden, Annie. It's just too hard having 'em here."

"I think helping the nuns sounds hard," Annie said. "Seeing all those people every day, with no homes and no hope. And weren't you scared?"

"I was at first," I said, "but the weary travelers weren't what I'd expected. I got to know 'em, and *like* 'em."

"Maybe you'll get to know Gwen and Isabel and like them, too," Annie said. "Or maybe it doesn't matter if you like 'em or not."

"What?"

"You know, like Father Mueller's always saying. It's easy to do the right thing when it makes you feel good. But when it doesn't, and you do it anyway, just 'cause you know it's right—that's when it really counts."

This wasn't what I'd wanted to hear. I had thought, being my friend, she'd take my side and give me a little sympathy. Instead, she was preaching a sermon. And the worst part was, I knew she was right.

"If it was just Isabel," I said, "maybe I wouldn't mind as much. But Gwen's so contrary, *nobody* could warm up to her. And, anyhow, she won't *let* folks help her."

"You could just try being nice to 'em," Annie said, "and see what happens."

Isabel came out of her classroom chattering away with another little girl. But when she saw me, she said a hasty goodbye to her new friend and made a beeline for me.

"How was your first day?" I asked, but I could already see the answer in her grinning face.

"I had a *very* good time," she said. "You were right, Bayliss, Sister Gertrude's the sweetest old lady. She let us sing and draw pictures. And a girl named Ruby ate bugs at recess and threw up in the cloakroom, and another girl told me my dress was pretty."

"That sounds real exciting," I said. Then I reached for her hand, something that didn't come naturally to me. But Isabel's fingers curled around mine as if she'd been waiting for me to do just that.

"Well, come on, Miss Hope and Pray," I said, "let's go get your sister."

Gwen was waiting for us outside her classroom. She didn't

look exactly happy, but then, she didn't look unhappy either. With the words *be nice* running through my head, I asked her, "Did you have a good day?"

"It was all right," she said as we started down the hall.

"What do you think of Sister Mary Vincent?"

"She's all right."

Gwen's face was still a blank, but I saw something—a brightness in her eyes—that I knew hadn't been there before. *Keep trying*, Annie would have said.

"You think the work's gonna be hard?" I asked her.

"I don't reckon."

I thought she was going to leave it at that, but then she glanced up at me, and I swear, if she didn't look a little bit excited. Then she dropped her eyes and said, "Sister Mary Vincent put me in the first reading group. That's the best. And she gave us some words to spell, and I was the only one to raise my hand on the word *onion*."

"Did you get it right?"

Gwen nodded. She was trying to act like it didn't matter, but I could tell she was proud of herself.

"What did Sister Mary Vincent say?"

"She said, 'Very good, Gwendolyn.'"

Isabel's head snapped up. She looked shocked. "You let her call you Gwendolyn? But you hate that name. You throw a fit when I call you that."

Gwen shrugged. "You can't very well throw a fit with a

teacher. And besides, she said she likes Gwendolyn, 'cause she has a sister by that name. A real sister, not a nun."

All I could think was, this didn't sound *anything* like the Sister Mary Vincent I knew. "Did she get aggravated with anybody?" I asked. "Because sometimes she does."

"All day long," Gwen said, "but not with me. She gave me a gold star."

"You got a star? On your very first day?" I was flabbergasted, since I hadn't gotten more than two gold stars from Sister Mary Vincent the whole year!

The apple trees were in a field behind Tommie Dora's house. Each of us had a sack with a shoulder strap, leaving our hands free for climbing and picking. Gwen was a natural. She scurried over those branches like she'd been born in a tree. Isabel was too little to move fast, but she was a hard worker. Before long, we had two bushel baskets filled.

All the while, I couldn't help thinking about how I used to help Leo pick Tommie Dora's apples, and how quick he was, but careful, too, so he wouldn't bruise the fruit. And how he'd keep me in stitches with some tall tale or other so it never seemed like work.

Just about every day I'd find a new reason to miss Leo, something else we should be doing together and couldn't. And it didn't feel right having Gwen and Isabel climb our trees—Leo's and mine—and pick our apples.

Harry loaded the baskets into his wagon, and we took them to the kitchen.

"Y'all go around to the front porch," Tommie Dora said from the door, "and I'll bring you something to drink."

My back was aching, and it felt good to sit down in one of the rockers. Harry took the chair next to mine, Gwen sat in the swing, and Isabel squatted on the steps to pet a gray tabby who'd been dozing in the sun.

Tommie Dora brought out a pitcher of lemonade, and while she poured it for us, I said, "Tommie Dora, this is Gwen. And the cat girl down there is Isabel."

Isabel grinned up at us, then picked up the cat and started rocking it like it was a baby.

Tommie Dora sat down and proceeded to study Isabel for a minute, then Gwen for another minute. Finally, she said, "I'm much obliged to you girls for picking my apples. I'll have Mavis Quick make you a pie. So, Gwen, where are you from?"

Staring at the porch floor, Gwen said, "Walker County."

"You have people in these parts?"

"No, ma'am."

"So your daddy's gone looking for work?"

"Yes, ma'am."

"Have you heard anything from him?"

"No, ma'am."

Well, I could see where this was going. Tommie Dora

would just keep pestering Gwen with questions till she'd satisfied her curiosity. And we could be here till dark.

This seemed like a good time to show Gwen just how nice I could be. So I jumped in while my grandmother was pausing for breath.

"School started today," I said in a bright, chirpy voice that didn't sound a bit like me. "And, Tommie Dora, you'll be glad to know that Isabel is already in the first grade, even though she's only five. And Gwen is the best reader in third grade, and Sister Mary Vincent gave her a gold star."

Tommie Dora looked at me and raised an eyebrow. "You don't say."

Then I let my eyes slide over to Gwen's face. Instead of seeming grateful, she was staring hard at me, like she was trying to figure out just what kind of funny business I was pulling.

"Miz Tommie Dora, this is good lemonade," Harry said.

"This is *real* good lemonade," Isabel said.

About that time, a big orange tom rubbed against Tommie Dora's legs and then jumped into her lap.

"Oh, I *like* that cat," Isabel said. "What's its name, Miz Tommie Dora?"

"This is Jim Dandy," Tommie Dora answered. "Come on up here and the two of you can get acquainted."

24. MICE IN THE ATTIC

I tried. All *week* I tried, and Gwen wouldn't give an inch. After that first day at school, when she'd been excited about her gold star and whatnot, she'd clammed up again, and I couldn't get two words out of her. And by Saturday, I was sick and tired of being nice, not to mention desperate for some time to myself.

So when Harry came over at noon to eat with us and remarked that Jack was in need of a bath—due to a bad habit of cozying up to skunks—I said, "He's so big, I reckon you'll need some help," knowing that Isabel would jump at the chance to offer her services. Which she did. And then she said, "And Gwen'll help, too."

It was an answer to my prayers.

As soon as Kathleen and I finished the dishes, I went upstairs and stretched out on the bed to read my book on Saint Afra. But it couldn't have been more than ten minutes later when Mother stuck her head in and said, "I need you to run down to Gilchrist's and get me a spool of white thread."

"Soon as I finish this chapter," I said.

"The mending's supposed to wait till you're ready? I don't think so, Bayliss."

So what could I do but close my book and trot down to Gilchrist's for her?

When I got back, I found Mother at her sewing machine in the living room, waiting for me. She'd taken the collar off one of Daddy's white shirts and turned it over so the worn part wouldn't show.

"Here's the thread," I said, and started to leave. But her voice stopped me at the door.

"Before you take off," she said, "go over to Harry's and get Gwen and Isabel. Saturday's the only day Mrs. Burdeshaw has to do her housework, and she doesn't need them underfoot all afternoon."

Well, neither did I! It never seemed to enter Mother's mind that Gwen and Isabel got in *my* way all the time, and I just had to live with it. But then she looked up from threading the bobbin as if to say, *Are you still here?* So I got the message and left.

Harry was sitting on the front steps drying Jack with an old towel. The smell of skunk made my eyes water.

"He still stinks."

"But not as much," Harry said.

Poor old Jack was hanging his head like he knew how bad he stunk and was feeling mighty low about it. I scratched him behind the ears, hoping to cheer him up some, but he just looked at me with those big, mournful eyes and sighed.

"I came to get Gwen and Isabel," I said to Harry. "Are they with your mother?"

He shook his head and reached for another towel. "They went back to your house a while ago. And don't be surprised if they stink, too."

"Just what I wanted to hear," I said. "Now I'll be expected to give *them* a bath."

When I got home and didn't find Gwen and Isabel in the kitchen, I went looking for them, figuring Mother would have a conniption if I told her that I didn't exactly know where they were at the moment. I searched the whole downstairs, then went upstairs to look. But they weren't in Leo's room. Or mine. Or Kathleen's. And they weren't in the bathroom either. I was on my way to check Mother and Daddy's room when I heard some thumps and thuds overhead.

The first thing I thought of was the time we'd had bats nesting in the attic, which had inspired Leo to tell me a story about bats turning into vampires. That one had made me wake up screaming for a week. Only the sounds I was hearing now were more like things being dropped and slid around, and it seemed likely that I'd found Gwen and Isabel. But before I went up there, I ran back to my room.

Since there wasn't a baseball bat handy, I grabbed the big atlas, which weighed a ton, off my desk and took that with me. Just in case.

The door to the attic was open and the light was on, which pretty much convinced me that I didn't need to worry about bats. And when I was halfway up the stairs, I could hear voices, then Isabel giggling. So I wasn't surprised to walk in and see Gwen and Isabel sitting in the middle of the floor, but I was plenty surprised to find Kathleen there with them. And I couldn't believe my eyes when I saw that Kathleen was helping them set up my farm.

"The horses shouldn't be fenced in," Isabel was saying. "They like to run free."

Kathleen lifted two horses out of the pen. "All right, then why don't I put them over here?"

"That's good," Isabel said. "And the cows need to be near the barn, so we can get to 'em easy to milk 'em."

About that time, Kathleen looked up. She was smiling, but when she saw me, the smile froze and then slid right off her face.

"Bayliss," she said, her expression putting me in mind of a little kid who'd been caught snitching candy. "I heard a noise up here and guess what I found."

"Us!" Isabel exclaimed. "I saw your farm set on the shelf, Bayliss, and Kathleen said we could play with it if we were careful. I just love this farm," she added blissfully. Then she held out her hand to show me the cat and two kittens she was holding. "These are my favorites. I've named the mama cat Cotton, 'cause she's white, and the little ones Bayliss and Kathleen."

"Isn't that sweet," Kathleen said, "her naming the babies after us?"

She was trying to soften me up, but it wasn't going to work. Kathleen *knew* how much I treasured that farm set. What had she been thinking, letting them strew it all over the attic? I couldn't tear my eyes away from Gwen, who was lining up the piglets at their mother's belly, and Isabel, who was trying to balance the mama cat on top of the barn.

"Did Mother send you up here to get me?" Kathleen asked.

"No," I said, glaring at her. "I heard something. I thought it might be—" I couldn't very well say *bats* without sounding like a fool, so I said, "I thought it might be mice."

Kathleen's eyes shifted to the atlas in my hands. "And what did you mean to do with *that*? Give 'em a geography lesson?"

Isabel giggled like this was the funniest thing she'd ever heard, and even Gwen made a little snuffling sound that might have been a laugh.

"Bayliss, you want to play with us?" Isabel asked.

But I was already heading for the door. I didn't slam it, and I didn't stomp down the stairs, because I wasn't so much mad as I was hurt. It was bad enough seeing them mess with my farm set—and Kathleen letting them. But then she'd made that joke to embarrass me, which just proved how little my feelings mattered to Kathleen.

I kept going till I reached the downstairs hall—creeping past the living room in case Mother had thought up more running for me to do—and slipped out to the back porch. Rosie was asleep on the top step, so I sat down next to her and stroked her head. She didn't open her eyes, but I could feel her starting to purr.

"They were having fun," I said. "Kathleen hasn't spent five minutes with 'em since school started, but they'd rather be with her. And I've tried to be nice, Rosie, but Gwen still hates me. So this proves that Annie was wrong. You *can't* help somebody when you don't like each other, especially somebody as smart as Gwen. But what do I care? If they'd rather be with Kathleen, that's fine with me. Maybe they'll stay out of *my* hair now."

But I couldn't shake my hurt feelings. And then it hit me that I was jealous. I might not like Gwen, but I didn't want *her* liking Kathleen more than me. And when I'd found them all in the attic having a good time together, I'd felt left out. This was a new experience for me. When Leo was here, I'd *never* felt like an outsider, because we were a team, six of one and half a dozen of the other.

Then I found myself wondering if Kathleen had ever

been jealous of Leo and me. When we were up to our shenanigans and not thinking about anybody else, had *she* felt left out? She must have. Not too often, maybe, because lots of stuff we did seemed childish to her. But I was willing to bet that there had been times when she'd seen us taking off together and wished that she'd had somebody like Leo.

Then I remembered the look of pure joy on Isabel's face when she'd said, "I just love this farm," and all of a sudden I wasn't quite sure why I'd made such a fuss over them having my toys. It wasn't like *I* was ever going to play with that farm set again. And I'd been wrong about them wrecking everything. Isabel was taking good care of Biscuit.

It didn't make any sense. I'd been so sure of how I felt, and now I couldn't figure out why I'd felt that way. The farm set wasn't doing anybody any good up in the attic, and since Isabel loved it, she should have it. I kept seeing that look on her face, and thinking how she loved the animals as much as I used to, and how the cats had been my favorites, too. I sat there stewing about it for a long time and finally decided that somebody ought to be playing with that farm again, enjoying it as much as Leo and I had. But I still got this sinking feeling when I pictured myself handing it over to Isabel and it not being mine anymore.

That evening, while Kathleen was washing Gwen's and Isabel's hair for church, I went up to the attic and brought down the farm set. I placed the barn on top of their book-case and put the fence around it. Then I got busy arranging the animals. I'd expected to have it all done and be gone before they came back, but I was still debating where to put the chickens when Gwen walked in with a towel wrapped around her head.

She looked surprised to see me, and then she narrowed her eyes. But they popped wide open when she saw what I was doing.

"This is for you and Isabel," I said, and left.

I was getting my pajamas, figuring I'd stake a claim on the bathroom before Kathleen took it over for her usual hour, when Isabel came running into my room. She threw her arms around my waist and then looked up at me and said, "Oh, Bayliss, thank you. I *love* that farm, and I'll take real good care of it."

That's when I noticed Gwen standing in the doorway. She had those cat's eyes fixed on me, but she didn't seem fierce or sullen. It was more like she'd just stumbled across some peculiar-looking animal—the likes of which she'd never seen before—and didn't quite know what to make of it.

25. THE SMART ONE
AND
THE PRETTY ONE

Gwen and Isabel were at the kitchen table cutting out paper dolls from an old Sears, Roebuck catalog Mother had given them while Kathleen dried the dishes from dinner and I mopped, as best I could, around them. I was just about done when the back door flew open and Tommie Dora came lumbering in, tracking dirt all over the part I'd just cleaned.

"*Whoa!*" I said, scowling at the muddy size 12 footprints on the linoleum. "Didn't you notice the floor was wet?"

"I must've overlooked it," she said, and then tromped across another clean part to set her sewing bag down on the counter. "I'm here for your mother's knitting party."

Gwen and Isabel had looked up from their cutting. "There's gonna be a party?" Isabel asked eagerly.

"Not the kind where you eat cake and play games," Kathleen said. "It's just some ladies from the church getting together to knit things for the weary travelers."

Of course, Isabel's next question was, "What's a weary traveler?"

"A hobo," Gwen said.

I looked at her, surprised. "How'd you know that?"

Gwen shrugged, "Sister Mary Vincent talks about 'em all the time," she said, and went back to cutting.

"Every year the sisters give the weary travelers a special Christmas dinner," Kathleen explained to Isabel. "The whole town pitches in. Merchants donate canned goods, and some of the men go hunting and bring back turkeys. And the ladies knit socks and gloves so the weary travelers can have a Christmas present."

I stopped mopping to stare at her. "How come *I* never heard anything about this?"

"Beats me," Kathleen said.

"Didn't you ever wonder who your mother was knitting all those gloves for year after year?" Tommie Dora asked. "And last Christmas, your sister got involved. Didn't you finish three pairs of socks, Kathleen?"

"Four," Kathleen said. Then she looked at me again. "Don't you remember the nuns asking us to bring in food?"

Sure I remembered. And I'd known that food was for the poor; I'd just never realized it was going to the weary travelers. But that was before they'd become *my* weary travelers, so I probably hadn't been paying much attention.

"Mary Bayliss, you might want to join us this afternoon," Tommie Dora said. "We do most of the work at home, but it's nice to get together at the beginning so everybody can say whether they'll be doing socks or gloves, and how many. The sisters told us they'll be needing sixty presents this year, so we could use the help."

"Except Bayliss doesn't know how to knit," Kathleen said.

Tommie Dora's eyebrows shot up. "You never learned to knit?" And the way she said it, you would have thought I'd committed a *crime*. "Well, it's time we fixed that."

I could see I was about to get roped into spending the whole afternoon with a bunch of gossiping ladies, and every last one of them shaking her head because I couldn't knit and determined to remedy the situation. I'd tried to learn back when Mother had taught Kathleen, but I'd found out quick enough that I didn't have the knack for it. And besides that, it was boring.

So I said, "I'd love to join y'all, Tommie Dora, but Daddy wants me to straighten up the car shed. And it has to be today, 'cause it's such a mess, there's barely room to get the car in there."

"Daddy's been saying that for two years," Kathleen said. "I'm sure he wouldn't mind you waiting till next Saturday."

But then Tommie Dora, bless her, said, "It's up to you, Mary Bayliss. Kathleen, are the other ladies here yet?"

"They're not coming till one-thirty. I was just fixing to make the tea, and Mother's moving the chairs around in the living room so we can talk while we knit."

"Then I'll go see if I can help," Tommie Dora said.

After she was gone, Isabel looked up at me and said, "I'd rather help you with the car shed, Bayliss."

Gwen didn't open her mouth, but I hadn't expected her to. She still didn't really speak to me unless I spoke first, and I'd just about quit speaking first because I didn't see the point anymore. She seemed to have settled in all right, but, with Gwen, you never knew. It wasn't like she'd say straight out what was going on inside her head.

"All right," I said to Isabel. "Let me go over this floor again, and then we'll get started."

The sun was bright, but I could feel a nip in the air when we stepped outside. And the big maples out front were turning red and yellow, a sure sign that fall wasn't far off. But I was thinking beyond that, to Christmas, when the nuns would be fixing their special dinner for the weary travelers.

I could see it in my mind, all of them gathered on the porch enjoying turkey and mashed potatoes smothered in gravy, and maybe slices of pecan pie. And when the travelers couldn't eat another bite, the nuns would start handing out presents, and I could imagine all the surprised faces when they unwrapped a new pair of socks or gloves. It wouldn't seem like much to some folks, but having warm toes and fingers would mean a lot to the weary travelers.

Then, I figured, everybody would sing carols, and it

would be just wonderful. But since I wasn't helping serve meals anymore, I wouldn't be there to share it with them. And I wanted to, more than anything.

"So what do we do first?" Isabel asked, bringing me back to the here and now.

With Daddy's car gone, you could see what a mess that car shed was in. There were stacks of old newspapers everywhere, and untidy piles of kindling and sticks that Leo had used to stake tomato plants. There were hoes and rakes and shovels leaning against the walls, towers of bushel baskets that looked ready to topple over, and all sorts of junk heaped up on the shelves. I hadn't realized this was going to be such a big job.

"I reckon we'll have to clear out some of this stuff before we start organizing," I said. "Isabel, you can carry those baskets out to the yard while Gwen and I unload the shelves."

We worked all afternoon, taking most everything out of the car shed, going over all the shelves with an old broom to get the worst of the dust and cobwebs, and then bringing everything back in and storing it neatly. There were hooks on one of the walls for tools, only Leo and I hadn't bothered to use them. And there were crates to hold the kindling and stakes. We stacked baskets in a back corner and put odds and ends on the shelves.

Finally, wiping my filthy hands on the sides of my overalls, I looked around. "Well, it's better than it was," I said. "We still have to find places for the newspapers and flowerpots,

208

but I could use a break. Come on, let's go get something to drink."

From the kitchen, I could hear the ladies jabbering as they prepared to leave. And that got me to thinking all over again about the Christmas dinner and how much I wanted to be there. Daddy just *had* to find Gwen and Isabel another home by then, so I could be.

We took our glasses outside and sat in the grass, watching the ladies get in their cars or take off on foot down the street while we sipped our tea. Only Isabel lost interest in that real fast and ran over to the swing.

"There's Miss Ida Henderson," I said, "and Miz Eubanks." I didn't much care who'd come to the knitting party, but I'd gotten used to Isabel's chatter filling the silences between Gwen and me, and now it seemed like I had to say *something*.

"But I forgot," I said, glancing at Gwen, "you know Miz Eubanks."

Gwen didn't bother to answer.

So I turned my head to look at Isabel, who had draped herself belly down through the tire and was pushing off from the ground with her feet to get the swing going. She was belting out a song that sounded like she might be making it up as she went along.

"Isabel always has a good time," I said, "no matter what she's doing."

I didn't expect Gwen to comment on that either, but then

she said, "Miz Eubanks says it's good that Isabel's so fun-loving. She says folks like a happy child, and somebody might adopt her if our daddy can be found to let 'em." She was pulling at blades of grass and didn't look up.

"And adopt you, too," I said.

Gwen's eyebrows came together in a frown. "Isabel's little, and pretty. That'll make her easier to place. Miz Eubanks says Isabel's the pretty one, and I'm the smart one."

Not that I especially cared *what* Miz Eubanks thought, but her saying that got my dander up. Like being smart was second-best. So I said, "I'll bet lots of people would want to adopt you."

"Miz Eubanks says I shouldn't get my hopes up."

"*Dadburn it!* What's *wrong* with that woman?"

Gwen's head snapped up, and she looked startled.

"Being smart's a dang sight better than just being pretty," I said. "Look at Kathleen, how pretty *she* is, but ask her the last time she read a book—for fun, I mean. Ask her how long it took Amelia Earhart to fly solo across the Atlantic. Thirteen hours and thirty minutes! See, I know that. Because I read. Because I'm the smart one in this family. And that suits me just fine."

Gwen was studying my face like she thought she might be living with a crazy person. Then she dropped her head and went back to pulling up grass.

26. WILD AND WOOLLY

Nights had been chilly for a while, but one Sunday in October, I woke up to—*cold!* I pulled my bare foot back under the covers and lay there shivering. When Isabel wandered in a few minutes later, she was wearing a flannel shirt over her pajamas.

"Bayliss," she said in a pleading voice, "aren't you ever gonna get up? I don't have anybody to talk to."

"Where's Gwen?"

Isabel made a face. "Sewing. That's all she ever does. And when I say something to her, she just says, 'Huh?' like she's not even listening."

Sewing was Isabel's word for needlepoint. And she was right, Gwen didn't seem to know anybody else was around when she was working on the canvas Mother had given her.

"Well, she won't be sewing for long," I said, jumping out of bed and jerking open a dresser drawer in search of something warm. I grabbed an old sweater and pulled it over my head. "She'll have to get ready for church. Have you two eaten?"

"Yes. Uh-oh, that's what I was supposed to tell you. Your mama says if you're not downstairs in two minutes, you won't get any breakfast 'cause she's got to clean up."

"What's the rush? We've got time."

"Uh-*uh*," Isabel said. "Some lady's had a baby, and your mama and Kathleen have to go sit with her."

We went downstairs, and I saw Gwen in the living room bent over her needlepoint. Kathleen was coming down the hall carrying Gwen's and Isabel's Sunday shoes.

"All polished," she said, and handed the shoes to Isabel.

"Who had a baby?" I asked Kathleen.

"Jewel Clark. A little boy."

I rolled my eyes. Another Clark boy!

"She had a hard time," Kathleen said. "Daddy's gone back to check on her. He says she'll need somebody with her for a few days."

"What about her husband?"

Kathleen had started up the stairs, but now she looked back and said, "Flat-out useless. Can't fix a meal, and I don't think he's ever changed a diaper. Mother and I have to relieve Miz Scarborough in a little bit, so hurry up and eat."

There was a plate of food waiting for me on the stove. Mother was washing dishes. I carried my plate to the table and, after pushing the fried potatoes aside, took a bite of egg. Isabel crawled up into the chair across from me.

Mother looked over her shoulder and said, "Bayliss, did Isabel tell you about Jewel Clark's baby? You'll have to help the girls get ready for church while I change and do something with this hair. You can go to Mass by yourself, can't you? I *know* I can trust you to behave yourself, and, anyway, your grandmother'll be there. Isabel, you want another biscuit?"

"Yes, ma'am," Isabel said. "Can I have boysenberry jam on it?"

Mother dried her hands and said, "Of course you can, sweetheart."

I watched Mother spread jam on a biscuit and thought, *She never talks to me like that. It's always, Hurry up, Bayliss. If you're not at the table in two minutes, you'll just have to starve, Bayliss.* Then I noticed the circles under her eyes. She'd probably been up all night waiting for Daddy to get back from the Clarks'.

"I can finish the dishes and clean up," I said. "Why don't you go get ready?"

"I think I will," Mother said as she brought Isabel her biscuit. "Thank you, sugar."

Isabel was sitting on my bed, already dressed for church and watching me circle the room in my slip trying to find my Sunday shoes.

Mother stuck her head in to let me know she and Kathleen were leaving. "There's a pot of stew for dinner,"

213

she said. "Daddy should be here when you get home, and y'all can heat it up."

After she left, I looked in the closet again, but my shoes seemed to have walked off by themselves. I was giving some thought to wearing my brown oxfords—since Kathleen wouldn't be there to tell me how hideous they looked— when Gwen appeared in the doorway.

"Isabel, you forgot these," she said, holding out a pair of white gloves. "And I've got your nickel for the collection plate."

"Well, bring 'em on over here," Isabel said.

Meanwhile, I'd flopped on my belly to look under the bed for my shoes. About the time I spotted them, I felt the mattress sink down under Gwen's weight. And then I heard Isabel ask, "Bayliss, is this you?"

I dragged the shoes out and got up. Isabel had crawled the length of the bed to the bookcase and was holding the photograph from my birthday.

"Yep, that's me in the middle."

"And there's Kathleen," Isabel said, "and your mama and daddy. But who's the boy?"

I sat down next to Gwen and started putting on my shoes. Isabel was looking at me, waiting, but all of a sudden my stomach didn't feel quite right.

"Bayliss?" Isabel bounced across the bed toward me.

This was the first time I'd been asked about Leo, because

everybody in town had known him. So I'd never said the words before—*I had a brother who died*—and I didn't know if I could say them now.

Rubbing at a scuff mark on the toe of my shoe, I said, "That's Leo, my brother." When I raised my eyes, they fell on Gwen, and I saw her surprise. "He died last spring."

Gwen's face seemed to freeze. But Isabel's was open and tender when she crawled over to me. "Oh, Bayliss," she whispered.

And all of a sudden I wanted to tell them—to tell *somebody*—about Leo.

"It was right after my birthday," I said. "Leo had given me a rowboat, so we'd gone to the lake to try it out. But a storm came, a bad one, and he drowned."

I took the picture from Isabel, and she inched closer to look at it with me. "Leo was nice to give you a boat," she said.

I nodded, studying his grinning face. "He *was* nice, and fun, too. He always had the best ideas. Brilliant notions, he called 'em. This one time he made stilts for us out of lumber left over from building the back porch, and we walked all over town on those things—till Leo fell off and broke his collarbone."

Now Gwen had leaned over to look at the picture.

"And another time," I said, smiling as I remembered, "Leo and I took candles from Tommie Dora's kitchen and went out to the woods and lit 'em, pretending to be altar boys. But I dropped mine and caught some brush on fire, and it spread so fast our grandpa had a dickens of a time putting it out. He was so mad at us."

Isabel sighed and said in a dreamy voice, "We have a brother who's fun like Leo."

"Half brother," Gwen corrected her.

"His hair's even redder than Gwennie's," Isabel said, "and he's very handsome. I bet he misses us."

"He'll come get us once he's on his feet," Gwen said quietly.

"Remember that time when he made us kites?" Isabel asked her sister.

Gwen drew her knees up and rested her chin on them. "I remember," she said.

Harry stopped by for Gwen and Isabel, and I was about ready to leave for Mass when Daddy came home looking plumb tuckered out. I figured he'd sleep till we got back, but then he said, "I think I'll go with you, Bayliss," like it was a sudden decision. "Just give me a minute to put on a clean shirt."

I must have looked surprised because he smiled a little and said, "I reckon that'll make Father Mueller's day—the prodigal son returns."

This sounded awfully close to blasphemy to me—leastways, that's how Sister Mary Vincent would have seen it—and coming from *Daddy*, of all people. I couldn't help grinning at him.

After he'd washed up, we set off down Markham Street side by side, and I liked the feel of it. Daddy was hardly ever home during waking hours anymore, and I couldn't remember the last time we'd done something together, just the two of us. So I figured I'd use this walk to church to get to the bottom of something I'd been mulling over.

"Daddy," I said, "I've been wondering why you haven't been going to Mass with us."

He glanced down at me, then looked away. It was a few seconds before he said, "Because I'm not sure the church has anything to offer me. I'm not proud of feeling that way, and I don't want to set up doubts in *your* mind, but that's the reason."

I'd been hoping he would bring up Leo, maybe say right out that he was mad at God for letting Leo die. And then I could have told him that I wasn't too happy with God myself, and it might have been a comfort, us knowing that we both felt the same way. But his mind seemed to have drifted off someplace else, and he didn't say any more.

"I can understand you feeling like that," I said, trying to keep the conversation going. "There's been plenty of times when *I've* wanted to stay home from Mass."

He looked at me again, and that little smile came back.

"I never would have guessed it," he said. "Not from somebody who's planning on becoming a nun."

For a minute, I didn't see his point. Then I realized that he was thinking about nuns going to Mass and praying all the time, being a lot holier—and quieter—than regular folks. But for me, being a nun was all about doing good deeds. Like giving food to the weary travelers. And comforting the sick—lepers maybe, who'd be especially grateful to me since nobody else much wanted them around. And with lepers, I'd have to go to some far-off place, maybe the jungles of Africa, and I might even run into some crocodiles and headhunters. I'd imagined myself doing any number of things as a nun, but the truth was, praying all day had never been part of the picture.

Only that seemed like a lot to explain, so I just said, "Well, I'm working on it."

And he said, "Well, so am I."

We were nearly to Sacred Heart, and I could see Tommie Dora standing on the front steps watching for me, when Daddy remarked, "Gwen and Isabel seem like nice girls. How are you getting along with them?"

"All right," I said.

"You've been a big help. Mother and Kathleen and I don't have a lot of time to spend with them, and I appreciate you taking on the responsibility."

"But you said it was just for a while," I reminded him.

"Then I can go back to helping the sisters. I'd *like* to help 'em with the Christmas dinner," I added, sneaking a look at him.

But it seemed like his mind had wandered off again, so I didn't push it.

After we'd eaten, Gwen, Isabel, and I cleaned up while Daddy read the paper. Then I told the girls to get their jackets, because I had an idea.

When we stepped out on the back porch, a gust of wind swooped down, grabbing at our hair and sending leaves skittering across the yard. *Perfect,* I thought, and headed for the car shed.

While I picked through sticks in the kindling box, I said, "Isabel, can you get a newspaper off that stack? And, Gwen, there's a ball of string on the shelf behind you. Bring that and a couple of those rags, too."

"I know what we're doing," Isabel said as we carried everything back to the kitchen. "We're making a kite."

"Yes, ma'am," I said, "that's exactly what we're doing."

Gwen and Isabel tore the rags into strips while I cut sticks and tied them together in the shape of a cross. Then I marked and cut the newspaper, and Gwen and Isabel did the pasting and knotted the rags for a tail.

When it was finished, Isabel said softly, "Oh, Bayliss, it's *bee-yoo-tuh-ful.*"

Gwen carried the kite out to the street, with Isabel

trailing behind and twirling its tail like she was turning a jump rope. Harry and Jack saw us from their yard and walked over to join us, and then Daddy came out and said, "That's a mighty fine kite. But you can't fly it here. Too many trees."

So we all headed for the hill behind the courthouse. And with Daddy, Harry, Isabel, and me calling out advice, Gwen took off running with the kite. When she let it go, the kite soared and we all cheered. Then it went into a sharp dive, and everybody groaned. But Gwen kept running, and the kite started rising again. It went up and up and up, with us screaming and hollering, and after a while, Gwen was able to just stand there, letting out more string as the kite kept climbing.

"I wanna fly it," Isabel said.

Gwen handed her the ball of string. Isabel looked scared—and thrilled—as she clutched the string and watched the kite float across the sky. Then it started drifting toward the ground.

"Oh no, it's falling!" Isabel cried out. "What do I do?"

"The wind's dying down," Daddy said. "Start rolling the string around the ball. Slowly . . . That's it. Just keep rolling."

When the kite had made a smooth landing, Harry said, "There's still a little breeze. Gwen, try running with it again."

"Can I do it?" Isabel asked.

"You don't run fast enough," Gwen said.

"Why don't we do it together, Isabel?" Daddy hoisted her to his shoulders and said, "Gwen, can you hand her the kite? All right, Isabel, don't let go till Bayliss tells you to."

He started to run, holding on tight to Isabel's legs, but she still managed to bounce up and down on his shoulders, screaming, "Look at her go! Faster, Doc, faster!"

Jack raced after them, barking, and the rest of us stretched out in the grass and shouted encouragement. Daddy kept running back and forth till he was out of breath and had to slow down.

"Hey, Isabel," Harry called to her, "let me be your horse for a while!"

Isabel shook her head. "I want Doc! Run, horsey, run! *Good* horse!"

When the wind stopped blowing altogether, we headed for home. Daddy was limping, and everybody was covered with burrs and beggar's-lice.

"Maybe we'll have time to clean up before your mother sees us," Daddy said, and smiled at me.

Gwen was carrying the kite, which had a little tear in it, but Daddy had assured her it could be mended. Isabel held up the tail for a while so it wouldn't drag on the ground, but then she dropped it and ran to catch up with me.

"Do I look happy?" she asked. "'Cause I *feel* happy."

I peered down at her red face and tangled hair and said,

"You *look* wild." Then I turned around to Gwen. "And *you* look woolly."

Isabel started to giggle. "That's our new names, Gwennie! Wild and Woolly!"

Gwen gave her a look as if to say that she didn't want any part of such foolishness, but Isabel and I kept making up names for the two of them all the way home.

"Fuzzy and Wuzzy!" I called out.

And Isabel came back with, "Cheese and Crackers!"

"Topsy and Turvy!"

"Biscuits and Gravy!" Isabel screamed.

That's when Harry put an arm around her shoulders and said, "Isabel, I reckon you haven't quite got the hang of this naming thing yet."

"Food," Gwen said. "That's all she ever thinks about."

27. DRIVING
THE ANGELS CRAZY

Annie and I were sitting under the sugarberry tree eating our sandwiches when all of a sudden she muttered, "Aw, heck, she's coming over here."

I looked up to see Lila Grace Gilchrist barreling toward us.

"Just ignore her," Annie whispered, knowing full well that Lila Grace wasn't somebody you could ignore.

And when her shadow fell over us and she screeched out, "Hey there," I had to at least pretend to be polite.

"Hey, Lila Grace," I said.

Annie just grunted, but Lila Grace didn't seem to notice. Her color was high and her little pig eyes were as wide open as they'd go, and I could tell she was chomping at the bit to tell me something.

"Mary Bayliss," she said, "I wanted you to be the first to hear. Sister Mary Vincent stopped me in the hall this morning and asked me to help serve meals to the unfortunates after school." She paused to let this news sink in, and then

223

she said, "I knew you'd be interested, since *you* were helping with that. Before you quit."

"She didn't *quit*," Annie said, but Lila Grace kept right on talking.

"Sister Mary Vincent said there's so many coming to the convent looking for a handout these days, and Sister Josephine's down with her rheumatism, so they need somebody to step in, somebody *reliable*. And I said I'd be happy to do whatever I can."

She was looking down at me like she was the Queen of Sheba and I was no better than beggar-trash, and I just wanted to haul off and smack her. Except I was starting to have this sick feeling in my stomach, and it occurred to me that I might be fixing to throw up all over Lila Grace's shiny new shoes. But then something worse happened. My eyes welled up, and I realized that I was this close to crying. In front of my worst enemy in the whole world!

I acted like I'd finished eating and got busy gathering up things so I wouldn't have to look at her, all the while fighting back tears and trying as hard as I could not to mind that Lila Grace Gilchrist had taken my job—a job I *loved*!—and that even when Gwen and Isabel went someplace else, the nuns wouldn't need me anymore because they'd have Lila Grace. And she'd be helping with the Christmas dinner, too!

Luckily, Annie gave me time to collect myself. She told

Lila Grace that folks weren't looking for a *handout* when they came to the convent, and if she felt that way about it, she wasn't the right person to be serving them. And then Lila Grace got riled and commenced to telling Annie that both of us had always been ugly to her because we were jealous, and that she reckoned Sister Mary Vincent knew best about who should be helping—and who could be counted on to stick with it and not just up and quit at the drop of a hat. But about that time, we all caught sight of Sister Annunciata on the back steps, eyeing us like a hawk about to swoop down and grab a mouse for its supper, and Lila Grace had the good sense to take off before we all got Bible verses to copy.

After she was gone, Annie tried every way she knew to make me feel better, but it was no use. Lila Grace had won again. But if I thought I was feeling so bad that it couldn't get worse, I was wrong.

That afternoon, Gwen and Isabel and I were walking home, and Isabel's mouth was running a mile a minute. Which was fine with me because talking was the last thing I felt like doing. She was telling us how everybody in the first grade was going to have a part in the Christmas pageant, and how Sister Gertrude had told them they'd have to stay after school some to practice, when Gwen said, "I might have to stay late, too. Sister Mary Vincent wants somebody to help out at the convent."

And right then and there, I felt my stomach knot up again, because I knew what she was talking about. Even before Isabel asked, "Help with what?" and Gwen answered, "The nuns fix supper for the hoboes, and they need somebody to clean the tables and wash dishes. Sister Mary Vincent says we're never too young to start practicing charity, and she'd like somebody from her class to set the example."

"So you're gonna be the example?" Isabel asked.

"Maybe," Gwen said. "I have to think on it."

It wasn't Gwen's fault. This was all Sister Mary Vincent's doing. I knew that. But how fair was it that Mother had made me quit because of Gwen and now *she* was going to get to help with *my* weary travelers? Her and Lila Grace both!

But this time, I wasn't even close to bawling. I was too furious to cry. So when Isabel asked me if Gwen could work at the convent even though she wasn't Catholic, I said, "If there's a rule against that, I reckon they'll overlook it. For *Gwen*."

Gwen cut her eyes at me, and Isabel said, "Bayliss, you sound so mean. Are you mad?"

"No."

"You *look* mad."

"Well, I'm *not*."

Nobody said another word the rest of the way home, and then I went to my room and shut the door. I should have been feeling bad for taking things out on Gwen and Isabel when they weren't to blame, but I was thinking more about myself just then. After all, *I* was the one who wanted to be a nun. I just couldn't see Lila Grace trading in her fancy dresses for that ugly black habit. And as Isabel had pointed out, Gwen wasn't even Catholic. *I* should be the one working at the convent. So why couldn't God see His way clear to help me out a little? Unless He was trying to tell me something. Could it be that God didn't *want* me to be a nun?

When we sat down to supper, I was still stewing over Gwen and Lila Grace edging me out of where I most wanted to be, but my temper had cooled down some. And now my conscience had started poking at me, and it wouldn't quit, not till it left me feeling pretty bad about how I'd treated Gwen and Isabel. So I made an effort to talk to them while we ate and went out of my way to be nice. And that did the trick with Isabel. She was all smiles and forgiveness. But Gwen kept her eyes on her plate and wouldn't look at me. I'd hurt her feelings, and she was letting me know that she wasn't about to let bygones be bygones that easy.

After I'd helped Kathleen with the dishes, I said I had homework and went upstairs. I was supposed to be doing a report on General Sherman's march through the South, but after writing four sentences, I was stuck. Sister Louise had made it sound exciting. She'd called the Yankee general a no-account scoundrel, which had caught my attention because it wasn't like Sister Louise to be so hard on folks. But after I read about the march in a book from the library, it seemed to me the Yankee soldiers just did the same goldurn thing in every town they came to. And after I'd written that they'd burned everything to a crisp and made off with all the horses and bacon, what more was there to say?

A breeze from the window was blowing my papers, and I got up to shut it. I stood there a minute, looking out at the darkness, and my eyes lifted on their own to the sky. But I knew I was safe. It was too late in the year for the lions to be there.

I went back to my desk and sat down, wondering how in tarnation I'd ever get five pages written by Friday, when I heard Isabel yelling for me up the stairs. Grateful for any excuse to leave the Yankees be, I went down to see what she wanted.

They were all in the kitchen roasting peanuts. A patient had given Daddy a croker sack full, and everybody was sitting around the table waiting for them to get done. Mother was patching a pair of my overalls, and Gwen was working on her needlepoint, which by this time was kind of limp and covered with smudgy fingerprints.

"Sit here, Bayliss." Isabel patted the chair next to her.

Gwen straightened up, bleary-eyed, and seemed surprised to find me across the table from her.

"You've almost got it finished," I said.

"She's a wonder," Mother declared. "I've never seen anybody catch on so fast."

Gwen gave Mother a shy look, then dropped her head to study the blue forget-me-nots that were taking shape on the canvas.

"They're ready," Kathleen said, and took the pan of peanuts out of the oven.

"Isabel, I'll get some for you and Gwen," Daddy said. "Be careful now, they're hot."

The only sounds in the kitchen after that were the cracking of shells and crunching as we chewed. Then Isabel sighed and said, "I could eat forty-eleven dozen of these."

"There's no such number," Gwen informed her.

"Then I could eat the whole panful!"

"If you eat many more," Gwen said, "you're gonna turn into a monkey."

"A monkey with a bellyache," Mother said. "Y'all finish what you've got, and we'll save the rest for another night."

I was looking around the table at everybody, and a fanciful notion suddenly popped into my head. I was thinking if somebody who didn't know us peered in through the window right now, they'd figure we were a real family. Because that's how we'd look to them, the six of us sitting at the table together. And for about a second, it almost seemed like that to me, too. Till I remembered Leo.

Isabel was sneaking peanuts from Daddy's pile, and he was pretending not to notice, when the telephone rang three times, our signal on the party line. Kathleen got up and went out to the hall to answer it. Most calls were for Daddy, but right away I could tell this one was for Kathleen. Her voice got high and kind of breathless, like she was nervous and tickled to death at the same time.

She came back and sat down, trying to act natural, but anybody could see she was in a dither.

"Who was it?" Mother asked, and Kathleen got busy brushing up peanut shells.

"Ray Vanzandt," she said. "His mother's having a birthday supper for him next Saturday night, and he asked me to come."

Mother just nodded, as if boys called Kathleen every day of the week. "You should wear your green dress," she said. "And you can borrow Grandma Reinhart's pearls."

Kathleen looked thrilled. "Really, Mother? I'll be careful with 'em."

"Is that boy your sweetheart?" Isabel asked. "Are you gonna marry him?"

Kathleen's face turned pink, but it was Daddy who said, "Kathleen's too young to be thinking about marriage."

He sounded so gruff, I thought he might be mad at Kathleen—or at Ray for calling. But then I saw that he was looking more down in the mouth than angry, and I figured he was thinking the same thing I was, that he wasn't ready for any more changes.

Gwen and Isabel were tucked in, and I was sitting on the side of the bed with Rosie in my lap. Gwen was no longer making a point of not looking at me, and I was trying to forget about her and Lila Grace helping the nuns. I reckon you could say we'd called a truce, but it was a shaky one.

"You'll like this," I said, holding up a book so they could see the picture on the front. "It's called *Heidi*."

Gwen frowned. "Those are goats. You're gonna read us a story about *goats?*"

"It's *about* a girl named Heidi," I said. "See the girl? And that's her grandpa behind her. Those are *his* goats."

"I like goats," Isabel said.

She was holding Biscuit, with her chin resting on his head. And I noticed that she had a fistful of peanuts.

"How'd you get those past Mother?" I asked her. "Give 'em to me, rabbit girl. You've already brushed your teeth."

Isabel snickered and handed over the peanuts. "We can read about goats some other time," she said. "Tell us a story, Bayliss. One about you and Leo."

"Well . . ." What should I tell them? About all the tricks we'd played on folks? I'd have stories for the next ten years. "All right," I said, "I've got one. I'll tell you about a prank Leo and I pulled when I was in second grade. Only it turned

231

out Sister Annunciata wasn't the least bit scared of snakes, so that part was a big disappointment."

For the next twenty minutes, I turned the adventures I'd had with my brother into bedtime stories. Isabel loved them, and even Gwen seemed to be paying attention.

Finally, I said, "That's enough for tonight. It's getting late."

Isabel snuggled down under the quilt. "You and Leo had a fine time, didn't you, Bayliss?"

I was feeling warm inside from remembering those fine times. But with all his brilliant notions fresh in my mind again, I was missing him something terrible.

"You reckon Leo's happy in heaven?" Isabel asked.

"I don't know if there *is* a heaven."

I hadn't realized I was going to say that, and it left me feeling like I couldn't catch my breath. No heaven? But that couldn't be. If there was no heaven, then Leo couldn't be there. He was just lying in a box in the ground. But now that I'd admitted to having this one doubt, a whole bunch more seemed to be elbowing their way in. All the things the nuns had taught us about God and Jesus and the saints—I'd never questioned any of it. But now I couldn't help wondering if it was true. Nobody had any proof, one way or the other, not even the nuns. They just took it on faith. And that's when it hit me that I had a problem. How could I entertain the notion of becoming a nun when I didn't even know what I believed?

"I don't think there's a heaven," Gwen was saying, "or a God either."

"And *you're* gonna be helping the nuns?" Isabel asked.

"Nah." Gwen shook her head. "I don't reckon I'm the good example Sister Mary Vincent's looking for. Besides, if I want to clean up after supper, I can do that right here."

I didn't say anything, but I was awfully glad to hear that Gwen wouldn't be working at the convent.

"So why *don't* you believe in God?" Isabel asked her sister.

"Well, if there is one," Gwen said, "then why did He let Mama die when He knew we needed her? And why didn't He make Daddy do better?"

"The nuns say we'll know the reasons for things when we get to heaven," I said. "I *hope* so. I hope there *is* a heaven, and a God. I'm just not sure."

"Was it Leo dying that made you not sure?" Gwen asked.

Since she'd go for days without even speaking to me, and had *never* asked anything personal, I figured my answer must be important to her. So I nodded and said, "I can't understand why He didn't save Leo, just like you wonder why He'd let your mother die."

"Well," Isabel said, "*I* believe in God. I see Him all the time."

Gwen was staring at her sister. "*When* do you see Him?"

"At night, after I'm in bed. He stops by to visit."

233

Gwen snorted. "You just dreamed it. God doesn't visit you."

Isabel's chin came up, and she folded her arms across her chest. "He does too—after you're asleep. And I don't blame Him for not visiting *you*, when you don't even believe in Him! And I believe in heaven, too," she went on stubbornly. "And, Bayliss, I bet heaven's a lot more fun now that Leo's there. He's probably driving the angels crazy."

28. WALKING IN KATHLEEN'S SHOES

I was stretched out in the window seat in Tommie Dora's living room watching raindrops run down the glass in squiggly streams. The book on Saint Margaret of Cortona was open in my lap, but I hadn't made much headway. It's probably sacrilegious to say, but the truth is, most saints led pretty dull lives.

"That doesn't go there."

I turned my head toward Tommie Dora's voice. She was frowning at Kathleen across the card table, a giant jigsaw puzzle between them.

"Don't you see the red on the tip of that piece?" Tommie Dora asked her. "There's no red in this part."

"But it fits," Kathleen said, frowning back.

Tommie Dora grunted. "Then leave it there. Just remember where it is when we're looking for a little bit of red."

Gwen and Isabel were on the floor going through a box of old clothes that Kathleen and I had used for dress-up when we were little. Isabel was holding a black cat in her arms, trying to get the poor thing to stay still long enough for her to tie a lace collar around its middle like a skirt. The cat had a wild and desperate look in its eyes.

It was a cold Sunday afternoon in late October, the perfect day for tea cakes and hot cocoa. Isabel finally let the cat go and took a noisy slurp from her cup. Then she bit into a tea cake.

"These are good," Isabel said. "Did you bake 'em just for us, Miz Tommie Dora?"

Tommie Dora looked up. "Mavis Quick made 'em. I don't bake."

Isabel raised her eyebrows. "I thought *all* ladies baked."

"Not this lady," Tommie Dora said, and went back to her puzzle.

Gwen pulled a white hat with a big silk rose on it from the box and squashed it down on her head. She went to a wall mirror to see herself.

"Hats look good on you," Kathleen said. "You have the face for 'em."

But Gwen's attention had wandered to the family photographs on the mantel, mostly pictures of men and women in stiff, old-fashioned clothes. But there was one of Tommie Dora and Grandpa Halsey standing on the front porch with Leo, Kathleen, and me. This was the one Gwen was studying.

I got up and went over to look at the picture. "I remember when this was taken," I said. "It was Leo's birthday, and Grandpa made peach ice cream. In *December*! Just 'cause Leo liked it."

"And it never got hard," Kathleen said. "He and Daddy cranked it for hours. Y'all want some more cocoa?"

Tommie Dora shook her head, but the rest of us said we did. Kathleen collected the empty cups on a tray and headed for the kitchen.

Gwen had gone back to rummaging in the clothes box with Isabel, but I was still looking at the photograph, trying to recall everything I could about that day. It was Leo's twelfth birthday. I remembered because Grandpa Halsey had given him a hunting rifle and Mother thought he was too young to have a gun. But Leo had pulled her aside and said it didn't matter, that he wasn't planning on hunting anyhow, but he didn't want to hurt Grandpa's feelings.

Tommie Dora came over and stood next to me. "He was a handsome boy," she said. "Just look at that smile."

"He'd beat Grandpa and Daddy at horseshoes and was real happy about it," I said.

"They probably let him win, it being his birthday."

"I don't know. . . . Leo was good at everything."

Tommie Dora turned her head to look at me. "You make it sound like he was perfect."

"Well, I reckon he was," I said, "or pretty near. Good at

school and sports—and any job y'all ever gave him to do. And he was good with people. Everybody loved him."

Tommie Dora nodded. "They did. And loving was something he was good at, too. But I don't want you thinking your brother didn't have any faults, because he did. No human being's perfect, Mary Bayliss."

"Maybe not," I said, beginning to get aggravated with her, "but he was so much better at everything than me, he *seemed* perfect."

"That's not true. He *wasn't* better at everything."

I made a face. "I bet you can't name one thing I was better at."

"One thing? That's easy. You were always stronger than Leo."

I shot my grandmother a look, but before I could tell her she didn't know what she was talking about, she said, "Yes, you *are* stronger. Inside, I mean. Leo was such a sweet boy, he never wanted to upset anybody or hurt their feelings. But that meant holding back how he felt and what he thought a lot of the time. We can't go around trying to please everybody, Mary Bayliss, and stay true to ourselves. You seem to have been born knowing that."

I knew she was paying me a compliment, and that I should have been basking in it, but it seemed to me that she was calling Leo weak. And I didn't like hearing that.

"You've always made up your own mind about things,"

Tommie Dora went on, "even when the whole dadgum world disagreed with you. Now, I'm not saying you couldn't be a little more obliging—that might be nice for a change—but one thing's for sure: you've got backbone. And something else, Mary Bayliss. Leo thought *you* were the one who was just about perfect."

I hadn't expected that. My breath caught in my throat, and I couldn't make a sound. Because it was such a wonderful thing for her to say, and because hearing it filled me with more joy and more sorrow than I knew what to do with.

Then I noticed how quiet the room had gotten, and I looked over at Gwen and Isabel. They were sitting perfectly still, watching us and listening.

Kathleen came back with the cocoa. She stopped in the doorway when she saw everybody frozen like statues and said, "What's going on? Did something happen?"

"Not that *I'm* aware of," Tommie Dora said, and went back to the jigsaw puzzle.

I took my cocoa to the window seat. Isabel came, too, and sat down next to me.

"Bayliss, I've been thinking," she said. "We should take a ride in your boat."

Everybody's eyes were suddenly directed at me, and Gwen burst out, "Isabel, don't you ever know when to keep your mouth shut?"

Isabel dropped her head. "What did I say wrong?" she mumbled.

"Nothing," I said. "And I reckon you're right. We *should* take the boat out sometime, maybe have a picnic at the lake."

Tommie Dora was still looking at me from across the room. "I just might go with you," she said, "one day, when the weather's nice."

"Then I reckon I will, too," Kathleen said, but she seemed uncertain. "Tommie Dora, do you think Mother and Daddy would go with us?"

Tommie Dora pursed her lips, studying on it, and then she said, "They might need a little time to get used to the idea."

That evening, we were all in the living room listening to the radio, but I was fidgety and couldn't keep my mind on the program. I was thinking about the boat and whether it was really a good idea to take it out. Part of me never wanted to lay eyes on it again, but another part kept thinking how proud Leo had been the day he'd shown it to me, and how that was the last present he'd ever give me.

Everybody was howling over Jack Benny playing the violin when Isabel tugged on my sleeve and said, "You're not even laughing, Bayliss, and it's funny."

"She's probably thinking deep thoughts," Kathleen said. "I don't reckon nuns see the humor in Jack Benny."

The way she said it was kind of snotty, and it hit me the wrong way. My nerves were on edge anyhow, what with worrying about the boat and wondering how Mother and Daddy would take it if I mentioned us going out to the lake. But mostly, Kathleen just had a way about her that ruffled my feathers.

I decided to ignore her and said to Isabel, "I was thinking about the book I'm reading. I'm not even halfway through, and it's due this week. I reckon I'd better get back to it."

Then I went upstairs, but I had no intention of spending the rest of the evening with Margaret of Cortona. I'd had a bellyful of reading about saints. All they ever did was pray till they died some really horrible death—like being roasted alive or chopped to pieces—and didn't have a scrap of fun along the way. I was starting to realize how much I missed reading about aviators and explorers. Now, *their* lives were exciting!

So I went to my desk and dumped all the saints books into my schoolbag to take back the next morning. Then I found the book Daddy had given me for my birthday and spent the next hour stalking through the African jungles with Mary Kingsley and the snakes and the crocodiles.

I'd gotten to a really good part, where Mary Kingsley was captured by a tribe of cannibals who were butt-naked except for some red paint and a few leopard tails, when

241

Mother came in to say good night. Kathleen was walking down the hall and stopped at my door, too. I'd nearly forgotten about being put out with her.

Mother said, "Daddy's driving over to Winston County tomorrow to see some patients who can't make it into the office, and he wants me to go with him."

I was anxious to get back to Mary Kingsley and the cannibals, so I just nodded and said, "All right."

"We'll probably be late, but you and Kathleen can fix supper and help the girls with their homework."

That's when Kathleen came flying into the room and said, "But I have choir practice tomorrow. Remember, Mother? I told you last week. Sister Winifred said I should try out, and I did, and they gave me a solo. And after practice, I said I'd stay and help Ginny Cunningham with her part. But Bayliss can see about the girls and get their supper."

I just wanted to get back to my book, so I was ready to agree with whatever Kathleen said, only Mother was shaking her head and saying, "I'm sure it won't matter if you miss one practice, Kathleen. You know how that old stove acts up. I don't want Bayliss lighting it with nobody else here."

But Kathleen wasn't giving in that easy. "Why do you have to go with Daddy anyhow?" she wanted to know. "He's always making house calls by himself."

"He has two widow ladies to see," Mother said, "and he thought they'd feel more comfortable with me there." She looked steadily at Kathleen and added, "He needs me with him, so that's that."

Then there was dead silence. I could see Kathleen's face working, the disappointment she was feeling and the unfairness of it fighting to get out while she struggled to hold them in. And I have to say, at that moment, I felt sorry for her. For the first time in my life, I could see just a little bit of what it was like to walk in Kathleen's shoes, and that it wasn't as easy as I'd thought. And it *was* unfair to make her miss choir practice. I might have told Mother that, too, except she said good night and was out the door before I could decide whether to put my two cents in or not.

Kathleen just stood there, staring past me, with neither one of us saying a thing. Then I heard Mother and Daddy's door click shut, and I said, "Go on to your practice, Kathleen. They'll never know. I'll tell Gwen and Isabel not to say anything, and we can eat cold corn bread or something."

But instead of being grateful, she looked like she was fixing to explode. And then she did.

"I just get so *sick* of it!" She was keeping her voice down, but I could hear it shaking. "All I do is *work*! If I'm not in school, then I'm scrubbing or cooking or washing or ironing—I don't ever get ten minutes for myself. I don't even have time for friends! And being in the choir may not seem like much to you—or to Mother—but it's important to me. Sister Winifred says I have a good voice. Do you know, that's the first time anybody's ever said I was good at something?"

"That's not true," I said. "Mother and Daddy are always telling you—"

"Oh, sure! That I make good corn bread and put just enough starch in Daddy's shirts." Tears sprang to her eyes, and she made a swipe at them. "I'm a *great* maid."

I'd never seen Kathleen this worked up before, but I couldn't help remembering all the times I'd tried to help her out, and she hadn't appreciated it one bit. And besides, I'd always thought she *liked* Mother and Daddy relying on her. Lord knows, she strutted around like a peahen when they bragged on her cooking.

So I was still working on what to say to her when all of a sudden Kathleen said, "I just wonder when it's going to be *my* turn to be the special one in this family, 'cause I never have been. It was always Leo, how sweet and dear and funny Leo was. And this last year, it's been all about you, Bayliss."

Her saying that was so unexpected, you could have knocked me over with a feather. And Kathleen must have seen it in my face because she said real quick, "That came out wrong. You were hurt, and I just wanted you to get better—all of us did. But then you did get better, and we were still walking on eggshells, with Mother and Daddy telling me not to mention Leo or anything else that might upset you." Her eyes filled with tears again, and this time she didn't bother to wipe them away. "All anybody seemed to think about was sparing your feelings, like you were the only one who'd lost him."

I slammed down my book and jumped up off the bed. "Well, I didn't *ask* y'all to spare my feelings. And another thing—I *tried* to take some of the load off you and Mother, but you wouldn't *let* me!"

"Because you weren't helping," Kathleen shot back. "Did you ever think to ask what needed to be done? No! You just jumped in with both feet and did whatever you felt like doing—and made *more* work for us. After you cleaned the pantry, I couldn't find a blessed thing. It took me all afternoon to straighten it out!"

Kathleen was glaring at me, and I was glaring at her, and I think it's safe to say that she didn't like me at that moment any more than I liked her. But I couldn't really argue with what she'd said, because I *hadn't* asked what needed to be done, and I *had* jumped in with both feet.

"At least I was *trying* to help," I muttered.

"Maybe so," Kathleen said. Then she sighed and flopped down in the chair at my desk, looking like all this carrying on had worn her out.

"Bayliss," she said in a tired voice, "I didn't mean to make you feel bad. I was just upset, all right? I get tired of having so many responsibilities, but you've had 'em, too. I know you didn't want Gwen and Isabel coming here, and them taking Leo's room was hard on you. But you've done a good job. You've made 'em feel welcome and not let on."

Then she stopped, and her eyes darted to the door. I looked, too, and saw a flash of bright red hair and two bare feet sticking out from under one of my old flannel nightgowns just before those feet took off running down the hall.

29. MULE FACE

Kathleen made a sound like a dog groaning in its sleep. The look on her face told me she felt awful, and so did I.

I started for the door, and she said, "I'll go with you. I'll explain."

"Explain what? Everything you said was true."

She was trailing me down the hall. "Bayliss, I'm sorry. I didn't know Gwen was standing there. Oh, me and my big mouth."

That just about summed it up, but all I said was, "Hush. Mother and Daddy'll hear us." And when we reached her room, I whispered, "Just go to bed. I'll talk to her."

The door to Leo's room was closed. I was about to knock, but then I realized that I didn't have any idea what I was going to say. Everything Gwen had heard about me not wanting them here *was* true. Only Kathleen had been wrong about one thing: I *hadn't* made them feel welcome, at least not Gwen. And now all I could think about was how ugly I'd been to her. Even when I was trying to be nice,

I'd still had those ugly feelings inside. And Gwen had known that.

There didn't seem to be any way to fix this, and I was tempted to go back to my room and not even try. I didn't want to face her. I didn't want to see the fury in her eyes and know that I deserved every hateful thing she was thinking about me. But then it dawned on me that, for all her fierceness, Gwen was just a little kid, and she was hurting. Because of me.

I still didn't want to knock on that door, but I made myself. And when nobody answered, I opened it and went in.

The lamp was off, but light from the hall fell in a wide streak across the bed. Isabel was asleep, curled up in a ball under the covers with her arms wrapped around Biscuit. Gwen was lying beside her, eyes wide open.

I walked to the bed and sat down near Gwen's feet. She rolled over and turned her face to the wall.

Since I hadn't rehearsed what to say, I just let the words come out any way they wanted. "I know you heard Kathleen," I said, keeping my voice low so as not to wake Isabel. "It's true, I didn't want y'all using Leo's room. I didn't want to pack up his ship models or even get rid of his quilt. Because they were *his*, all I had left of him."

Gwen didn't move a muscle.

"I haven't been very nice," I went on, "but that had nothing to do with you and Isabel. I'd have felt the same way about *anybody* using Leo's room. And I'd started help-ing the nuns in the afternoons, and Mother said I couldn't do that when we found out y'all were coming, so I was dis-appointed. No, I was *mad*. But it was wrong to take it out on you. None of this is your fault, and I should've seen that. I'm sorry."

At this point, I reckon I would have been relieved if Gwen had reared up out of that bed and given me a piece of her mind. Because I was running out of things to say, and it was hard not knowing what was going through her head. But it seemed like she'd decided to let me stew awhile—either that, or she'd washed her hands of me once and for all—and she still wouldn't look at me.

"The thing is, you and Isabel aren't what I expected," I said. "I didn't know you'd be smart. Or funny. Like what you said about Sister Mary Vincent's diorama—*Jesus in a fishbowl*. I had to work at not laughing at that. Because I'd already made up my mind not to like you. But sometimes I'd forget—when we were flying the kite, and when I was telling you stories about the pranks Leo and I used to play on folks—and I'd find myself having fun. With Leo gone, I thought I'd never have fun again. But I did, Gwen—because of you and Isabel."

There was movement under the covers, and then Gwen flopped over and raised herself up on her elbows. Her eyes were narrowed to slits and her mouth was set in a thin line, and I knew she hadn't forgiven me and didn't intend to.

"We were your *job*." She spit out the words like they had a bitter taste. "Kathleen said so. You *had* to tell us stories and fly that kite. Your mother *made* you."

"No, I had to walk you to and from school," I said, "but I told y'all stories and built the kite because I wanted to. That's what I meant—when I stopped sulking and just let things happen, I ended up having a good time."

Gwen lay back down and scowled at the ceiling. "I *thought* maybe you were starting to like us, especially Isabel—and me, too, a little. But then tonight I came to tell you something and heard what Kathleen said—and I knew you'd just been putting on an act."

"No," I said. "It wasn't always easy for me to be nice, but the times you thought I was starting to like you? I was. I've never been good at pretending."

She just kept staring at the ceiling.

"You said you came to tell me something. What was it?"

"Doesn't matter," she muttered.

"Please, I want to know. What were you going to say?"

She was still scowling, still refusing to look at me, so I figured I'd never get an answer. But then she said grudgingly, "It was about the boat. I didn't want you feeling like you had to take it out just 'cause Isabel wanted to. She's too little to understand." Her eyes darted to me and then away.

"But I should've known you wouldn't do it just for her. I was being stupid."

"It wasn't stupid," I whispered, staggered by what she'd just said. I hadn't bargained for this, Gwen thinking about *my* feelings, and how hard it would be the first time I stepped into that boat. Only eight years old, and she was way ahead of me when it came to understanding what was in people's hearts.

"You were being thoughtful," I said, "and I haven't done anything to deserve it. But if you'll give me another chance, I'll try to change that. It took me too long to realize it, but I do care about you and Isabel."

Gwen just lay there a minute. Then she turned her head to look at me. "I don't believe you," she said.

On the surface, nothing changed. I still walked Gwen and Isabel to school and spent the better part of my waking hours with them when we were home. Gwen would answer when I asked her a question, and the rest of the time she'd ignore me. Isabel was the same as always, so I knew Gwen hadn't told her about overhearing Kathleen. Now, if somebody had hurt *my* feelings like that, I would have wanted to talk about it, needing the comfort, but Gwen hadn't said a word. Because she was thinking of her sister instead of herself.

Every time I looked at Gwen, I'd remember the mean

things I'd said or done or thought, and I couldn't stand how that made me feel. So I'd rack my brain for a way to make it up to her. I considered everything from gathering up every single toy in the attic and bringing them down to Leo's room—which was how I still thought of it—to begging Gwen for her forgiveness. But I knew that a bunch of old toys wouldn't change how she felt, and that she wasn't going to forgive me just because I wanted her to. It didn't work that way.

There was only one thing I could have said to her that might have made a difference. Telling Gwen that I cared about her and Isabel wasn't enough. She needed me to say, *I want you and Isabel here with us. This is where you belong.* If I could have said that, and meant it, I was pretty sure she would've come to believe it eventually.

But as much as I wanted her to feel better—and me to feel better, too—I couldn't say it. Because I *wouldn't* have meant it. My feelings for them had changed, but I was still hoping Daddy would find them a home someplace else.

So I was right back where I'd started, looking for a way to ease Gwen's hurt without lying to her. And one night, as I was drifting off to sleep, it came to me. The boat. We *would* take it out, and I'd tell Gwen and Isabel how important it was to me for them to be there. I didn't think Gwen would refuse and disappoint Isabel, and maybe she'd realize that I wouldn't be sharing Leo's gift with them if I didn't really care.

But since I wasn't sure what Mother and Daddy would think of the idea, I figured I'd wait to bring it up till the girls weren't around. And the perfect time seemed to present itself a few days later.

Mother had come home early, and she and Kathleen and I were fixing supper when Daddy got there. Gwen and Isabel were over at the Burdeshaws', helping Harry clean the inside of his daddy's car.

I was mulling over how best to bring up the subject of the boat when Daddy said, "I have something to tell y'all."

He sounded so serious, Mother, Kathleen, and I all turned to look at him. He was staring down at the linoleum, frowning, and when I saw that, my heart started thumping. Whatever he was about to say wasn't good. I could feel it.

"You all know," he said, "that we only planned to keep Gwen and Isabel till we found something more permanent, and Vesta Eubanks has two families who'll take them."

I'd been waiting all this time for Daddy to tell us that Gwen and Isabel were leaving. But now that he'd finally said it, I was stunned. And I could see that Mother and Kathleen were, too.

Mother managed to say, "*Two* families?"

"Nobody can take both girls," Daddy said, "but they'll only be living a few miles apart. They can see each other all the time."

"No, that's not right." Mother was shaking her head. "They're sisters, Walter. They need to be together."

253

"Isabel would be lost without Gwen," Kathleen said. "Daddy, isn't there some other way?"

"I wish they could stay together, too," he said, "but I've talked to just about everybody in the county. We're lucky to have found families willing to take *one* child."

My head felt like a tornado was spinning around inside it. This was what I'd been wanting, for Gwen and Isabel to go someplace else, and I hadn't much cared where. But it made me sick to my stomach to think of them not being together. It would be *terrible* for Isabel, but even worse for Gwen. What would she do without her little sister?

And the next thing I knew, I was blurting out, "Well, if that's the best you can come up with, they'll just have to stay here."

They all turned to look at me, obviously surprised by what I'd said, but no more than I was.

Then Mother said, "Bayliss, I thought you couldn't wait for them to leave."

"Not if they're going to be separated."

"It's already been decided," Daddy said. "They can't stay here."

"But why? *Why* can't they stay?"

Before he could answer, Mother asked, "Who's taking them?" And Daddy seemed relieved to have a reason to turn away from me.

"Aubrey and Clarice Dunn offered to take Isabel, and Gwen's going to the Neismiths out near Four Corners."

"But the Dunns are seventy if they're a day," Mother said, "and Floyd Neismith works his own children so hard, the older girls couldn't wait to get away from home."

Daddy was rubbing his neck. He looked tired. "Aubrey's only sixty-two," he said. "And as for the Neismiths, they're country folk, Helen. They need everybody to pitch in to keep the farm going. But they're decent people. They'll do right by Gwen."

They won't have to, I thought. There was another way, and I had to tell them even if Daddy did hit the roof.

"I told you about their brother," I said. "Remember? They can go live with him."

Daddy didn't even look at me when he said, "And I've told *you,* Bayliss, Mrs. Eubanks has already checked with everybody in the family. Nobody's willing to take them."

"She must not have talked to their brother. *He'd* take 'em. I know he would."

"She *has,* Bayliss," Daddy said. "There's nothing more we can do."

And all of a sudden I didn't care if he got mad at me or not. I was mad enough for the both of us. So mad I couldn't see straight!

I must have *looked* mad, too, because he said, "Not another word. Go to your room. Now."

His voice was iced over, and I couldn't see anything kind or loving in his face. And that just about killed me.

"Kathleen, you go, too," Mother said quietly. "I want to talk to your daddy."

So Kathleen headed for the hall, and I followed her. But once I was through the swinging door, I stopped and eased it open just enough so I could listen.

"Come on," Kathleen whispered. "You'll get in trouble."

I waved my hand for her to go away, and she did, leaving me to eavesdrop on my own.

Mother was saying, ". . . doesn't cost that much, Walter."

And he said, "You know we're barely getting by. Is it fair to make our own children do without, more than they already are?"

There was a silence, and then Mother said, "I suppose not."

I didn't wait to hear any more. I hurried down the hall to the front door and ran outside. It was getting dark, but the Burdeshaws' porch light was on, and I could see Gwen and Isabel leaving Harry's yard. I ducked back inside and waited till they'd gone around the house to the kitchen. Then I headed across the street.

Harry was still outside, picking up rags they'd used on the car. He could tell something was wrong the minute he saw me. "What is it?" he asked.

"Gwen and Isabel are leaving," I said, "going to different families. At least, that's what my daddy thinks."

"You've got that look—what Miz Tommie Dora calls your mule face," Harry said. "I reckon there's no use trying to talk you out of whatever it is you're fixing to do. What *are* you gonna do?"

"I can't do anything on my own," I said. "That's why I need your help."

30. DESPERATE MEASURES

Mother and Daddy talked to Gwen and Isabel after supper. I stood in the hall outside the living room, listening, and heard Daddy tell them they'd be coming over to eat and seeing us all the time, but Isabel still cried. And Gwen sounded bitter when she said, "There's no use taking on so, Isabel. I told you from the first we wouldn't be staying."

After Mother and Daddy were in bed, I slipped into Leo's room. I could hear the girls whispering in the dark and switched on the lady lamp.

"Oh, Bayliss," Isabel said mournfully, "Doc says Gwen and me are leaving on Saturday. And we won't be living together."

"That's why I came to talk to you," I said, and sat down on the bed. "I have another idea."

When I told them what Harry and I planned to do, Gwen said sharply, "You're wasting your time. She won't take us."

"But you're blood kin," I said. "And even if your

grandma says no, your brother won't, not when he finds out your daddy's gone. Don't you want to live with Frank?"

Gwen hesitated, then she muttered, "I just don't want Isabel and me to be split up."

"Me neither." Isabel started to cry.

"Well, this way you won't be." I couldn't stand watching the tears roll down Isabel's face, so I got up and went over to the dresser. "I brought some sacks for your clothes."

"We're leaving the stuff your mother gave us," Gwen said.

"No," I said, "you're not."

I packed everything in the drawers and closet, except for what they'd be wearing the next day. Then I put all the little pieces of the farm set inside the barn and was placing that in a sack when Gwen said, "We don't *want* anything that belongs to you. Isabel and me can do fine on our own."

"Oh, Gwennie, don't be mean," Isabel said in a whispery voice. "It's not Bayliss's fault."

That's when my eyes met Gwen's, and I saw as clear as day that they were saying, *It is your fault. You never wanted us here, and you're glad we're going.*

I went back to my room and lay down to wait for morning. I didn't close my eyes all night. That was the only way I knew to make sure that we'd be up and gone before anybody could stop us.

Harry had thought I should try talking to Daddy again.

But Daddy would just say no, and Mother would back him up, so why bother? Finally, Harry had agreed to drive the Packard to Daddy's office and meet us there at five o'clock. There was a chance somebody might see us and start asking questions, but I figured that was safer than slamming car doors right outside the house.

At a quarter till five, I put on my jacket and went down the hall to get Gwen and Isabel. They were already dressed and sitting on the bed. I picked up Biscuit off Isabel's pillow and handed him to her.

"Thank you, Bayliss," she said softly. "I didn't know if I should take him."

"Course you should. He'd miss you something awful."

I thought about the times Leo and I had left the house through my window. But this time, sneaking out wasn't a game. I gathered up the sacks that held their things and said, "Come on. It's time to go."

We went downstairs to the kitchen. Every time a board creaked, I stopped to listen, afraid I'd hear feet hitting the floor overhead. And when the back door groaned like somebody was dying, I fully expected Daddy to come up behind me and ask what in Sam Hill we were doing. But the house was quiet when I closed the door behind us.

It wasn't till we turned off Markham onto Main that I started breathing easier. All the stores were dark, and we didn't see a soul except for a farmer passing by in a wagon loaded down with milk cans. But he didn't pay us any mind.

The Packard was parked in the alley beside Daddy's office. Harry was leaning against the door on the driver's side.

"Morning," he said, and then to me, "You sure you want to do this?"

"I'm sure," I said, and opened the back door for Gwen and Isabel.

Once we were on the road, I saw that Harry drove carefully. And slowly. I'd figured it wouldn't take more than two hours to get to Morrisville, but Harry was only doing about fifteen miles an hour, so it was going to be a long trip.

The mood inside the car was anything but cheerful. Harry was gripping the steering wheel like it might get away from him, and all his attention was on the road ahead. I looked into the backseat and saw Isabel leaning against Gwen's arm. I felt worse about Gwen than Isabel, because I knew I'd let Gwen down. And because just about anybody would warm up to Isabel's sweetness, but you had to be around Gwen awhile before you realized that she was every bit as lovable as her sister. I'd only gotten a peek at that side of her, and I worried that she might not be willing to let folks see it again.

I turned back around and watched the road, thinking how Mother and Daddy were going to be mad as heck. But I'd just have to deal with that later. Then I thought about

Sister Louise telling us how Southerners had been left penniless after the War between the States and how some had eaten dead mules and even rats to keep from starving. "Desperate situations," Sister Louise had said, "call for desperate measures." That's what I'd tell Mother and Daddy, that Gwen and Isabel's situation had been desperate, and this trip to Morrisville was the only way I knew to fix it.

It took us nearly four hours to get there. Driving through town, we passed a little grocery store with a gasoline pump out front, a diner, two churches, and a handful of neglected houses. Then we were on a country road again. There was nothing to see but plowed-up cotton fields and rows of broken cornstalks.

Harry glanced over his shoulder into the backseat. "How do I go from here?"

Gwen took her time answering, but finally she said, "There's a bridge up ahead. After you cross it, take the next left."

We went over an old wooden bridge that shimmied under the Packard's weight, then turned onto a road that was so grown up, I wasn't sure we'd make it through the tall grass and weeds.

We'd gone about a mile, with the car rocking and dropping off into deep ruts, when Isabel leaned forward and said softly, "There it is."

Up ahead was a ramshackle farmhouse, its boards buckled

and weathered gray. The house was raised up on rocks at its four corners but didn't seem to rest easy. It was leaning so far to one side, I was pretty sure a stiff wind would tip it over.

Looking at that house, I wondered for the first time if I'd made a mistake. There was nothing welcoming about it. Not one flower bed or bush that would bloom in the spring. No curtains at the windows. No sign of life anywhere except for a few skinny chickens pecking at the dirt without much spirit.

Harry pulled into the yard, and we all sat there a minute. Then I said, "Well, let's go see your grandma and brother."

I opened the door and got out. Gwen and Isabel were still in the car, not moving, so I opened the back door. Isabel looked worried. Gwen was more sullen than ever.

"Do you not want to live with Frank?" I asked them. "If you don't, just tell me and we'll turn around and go back."

I was reminded of that first night in our kitchen when Gwen and Isabel wouldn't open their mouths. But now Gwen said, "Come on, Isabel," and they scooted across the backseat to the door. Harry had come around the car and was standing there looking ill at ease, with his hands in his pockets.

We walked across the yard and climbed the rickety steps to the porch. Then Isabel came to a stop, seeming afraid to go any closer. Gwen dropped back to take her hand, and Harry took the other one, leaving me in front of the door by myself.

263

Before I could knock, the door swung open and a woman was standing there. She wasn't much taller than me, and thin as a rake handle, with gray hair pulled back into a knot and a dirty apron tied around her middle.

She shot me a hateful look and said, "Whatta you want?" Then she noticed Gwen and Isabel, and her face didn't soften a bit when she barked out, "What are y'all doing here?"

"Ma'am, my name's Bayliss Pettigrew," I said, "and I'm a friend of Gwen and Isabel's. You see, their daddy left 'em at a children's home so he could look for work, and you and their brother are the only other kin—"

"I've heard all this before," she said, waving a hand like she was swatting at flies. "A woman from the home and some preacher's already been here, and I'll tell you what I told them. I can't take care of no children. Can't feed 'em and don't have the patience."

She made a move to shut the door, but I stepped in to block the opening.

"What about their brother?" I asked quickly. "Could we talk to him?"

"Frank's been gone two months or more."

Then I heard Gwen's anxious voice behind me. "Where'd he go, Grandma?"

"How should I know? He's trying to find work, same as everybody else. Now y'all go on," she said. "And don't be bothering me again."

31. FACING FACTS

Nobody said a word as we drove away. Harry was concentrating on easing the car over the ruts and trying to make it back to the road, and I was too miserable to speak. I'd seen the girls' faces when they crawled into the backseat, and even Gwen hadn't been able to hide how crushed she was. And it was all my fault. I'd known it was risky bringing them here, but I'd been counting on their brother to love them too much to turn them away. And I'd never dreamed a grandmother would be so cruel.

I glanced at Harry, who was gripping the wheel tighter than ever as he turned carefully onto the main road. Harry was always careful. He'd tried to make me see that this was a mistake. But no! I was so all-fired sure that I knew best, I wouldn't listen, and I'd just ended up making everything worse. Now Gwen and Isabel had *proof* that nobody wanted them.

Then all of a sudden Gwen said, "Pull over. Isabel's sick."

I twisted around and saw that Isabel had her hand over her mouth and was heaving like she was about to throw up. Harry was already easing the Packard into the weeds at the side of the road. The second the car stopped, Gwen flung the door open and lifted Isabel out. Isabel took a few steps, then bent over and vomited.

I scrambled out of the car and started toward them, but Gwen's head shot up and her eyes flashed like heat lightning.

"I can take care of her," Gwen said. "Just leave us be."

And that stopped me cold. The anger in Gwen's voice cut right through me, even though I knew I deserved it. I felt helpless standing there watching as she led Isabel toward a big oak tree in the middle of the field. When they got to the tree, Isabel slumped against it and then slid down its trunk to the ground. Gwen squatted beside her and smoothed the hair back from her sister's face.

Harry had gotten out of the car and was coming toward me. I couldn't make myself look at him. I knew I'd see disappointment in his face—and maybe fury. I deserved that, too. But instead of waiting for him to tell me what a mess I'd made of everything, I took off across the field, away from the girls and away from Harry. The ground was soft and wet, sucking at my feet and probably ruining my new shoes. But I didn't stop till I came to a barbed-wire fence and couldn't go any farther.

Harry was stalking through the grass and weeds after me. His jaw was clenched, and so were his hands. He didn't look anything like the old easygoing Harry I'd always known. I figured he was fixing to blister my ears good for letting Gwen and Isabel down, and I braced myself to hear him out and take the blame. I'd earned it. But when he reached the fence, he just stood there a minute. Then he leaned against a post and squinted back at the girls huddled together under that tree.

"We never should've done this," he muttered. "Just look at 'em, Bayliss. We got their hopes up, and now . . ." His voice trailed away.

He didn't sound mad, just weighted down, the same as me.

"Listen," Harry said, "I know one of the reasons you wanted to get 'em back with their brother was because you miss Leo so bad and wish you could be with him. But, Bayliss, you gotta face facts. Gwen and Isabel don't have a family that wants 'em, and Leo's gone. And there's not a thing you can do about any of it."

I just stood there, feeling splintery inside, staring down at my muddy shoes. But finally, I looked up and said, "Don't you think I *know* Leo's gone? I wake up every morning not remembering, and then it hits me. And every morning I think, *He didn't have to die. If only we hadn't taken that boat out . . . If I hadn't gone to sleep . . .*"

"But we didn't know a storm was coming," Harry said softly, his brown eyes fixed on me. "It was a pretty day, not a cloud in the sky when we started out. Bayliss, we didn't *know*."

I let the words roll around inside my head. *We didn't know.* That was the truth, and for an instant, I felt something comforting, even hopeful, in those words. Then other truths started pushing their way in. *Leo's still gone,* I thought, *and I can't do anything to help Gwen and Isabel. So what difference does it make who's to blame?*

The silence stretched out mile after mile. For the first time in my life, I dreaded going home. Not because of the trouble I'd be in—I didn't care about that—but I figured Daddy would take Gwen and Isabel off to the Dunns and the Neismiths right away now. Before I could come up with any more bright ideas. They'd probably be gone by nightfall, and I'd have a whole new reason for needing to look away from that bedroom when I walked past it.

Harry pulled up in front of our house and cut off the engine. Before we were even out of the car, I saw people rushing down the steps. Daddy was in front, with Mother and Miz Burdeshaw behind him. Tommie Dora and Kathleen were sitting on the porch and didn't get up.

Our mothers looked worried, but it was Daddy's face, all pinched and white, that made me feel the worst. His eyes moved over me anxiously, darted to Harry and the girls, and snapped back to me. Then the burst of energy that had brought him bounding across the yard left him. His shoulders slumped and his face went still, and even the light in his blue eyes seemed to dim.

"What were you thinking," he asked quietly, "going off without telling us?"

He didn't seem angry, but Gwen must not have realized that, and words started pouring out of her mouth. "Don't blame Bayliss," she said, as scrappy and full of fight as I'd ever seen her. "It's not her fault. She just wanted Isabel and me to be together."

I couldn't believe Gwen would stand up for me, after all I'd done. And then it hit me—she *did* know I cared about her.

But Daddy didn't seem to be listening. He was still staring into my face, looking bewildered.

"We didn't have any idea where you were," he said. "Not till we found out that Harry had taken the car and we started putting two and two together. Bayliss, do you have any idea how frightened we were to get up and find you gone?"

It hadn't entered my mind that they'd be scared. But now I could see why they would be. Because something terrible can happen without any warning. It already had once this year, and losing Leo had left all of us primed for heartbreak, left us waiting for it.

Gwen moved away to where Isabel was standing with Mother, Harry, and Miz Burdeshaw. Isabel was leaning against Mother's leg, and Mother was stroking her hair. At the sight of Isabel's soft, baby-round face, I felt a rush of tenderness. Her lips were parted, on the verge of smiling, even while tears glistened on the tips of her lashes. Too much had happened since last night. She was tired and hurting and not really understanding it all, just knowing that she needed the comfort my mother could give her.

Then I looked at Gwen and thought, *I don't want them to go*, and something inside my chest cracked wide open. That's when I started crying. Quietly, so that nobody except my daddy, the only one looking at me, would have noticed. I could hold back the sounds of aching and wanting, but not the tears.

Daddy's face was a blur. I sensed him reaching out to me, and I stumbled past him, first walking, then running, for the house. I bolted up the stairs to my room and threw myself down on the bed. Everything I'd been keeping inside all these months came gushing out in a flood of tears and wails and whimpers. The tears backed up in my throat, choking me, but I couldn't make them stop coming.

A long time later, I pulled the quilt around me and lay there staring at a square of sunlight on the floor. I felt worn out and empty, but words were beginning to fill my head again. *I've messed up everything, and there's no way to make it right. When all I wanted was to get Gwen and Isabel back with Frank.*

In my mind, I could see the girls running to their brother. His face was shadowy, but I knew he was grinning at the sight of his little sisters as he squatted down to catch them in his arms. I could see the three of them holding on to one another, Frank's blond head bent toward the girls. But wait . . . Frank had *red* hair.

Then I knew who I was seeing in that perfect daydream, and it wasn't Frank Truett. It was Leo's head bent to comfort his sisters. Leo's arms holding them tight, like he meant to never let them go.

32. ON THE ROOF AGAIN

When I woke up, the room was dark, with just a wedge of light coming in from the hall. I pushed the quilt aside and got out of bed. My head was aching, and my eyes were tight and gritty. I stood there a minute trying to think what I should do next. Gwen and Isabel would already be gone, most likely, and there was nobody else I wanted to see just then, especially Mother and Daddy. I thought it was peculiar that they hadn't already been up here to bawl me out. But that was surely coming, and I'd just as soon put it off as long as I could.

Harry would have tried his best to explain why I'd taken off with the girls. It was because of Leo, he'd have told them. But that was only half right. Because Harry didn't know how much Gwen and Isabel had come to mean to me. How could he, when I was only beginning to figure that out myself? But Gwen had known. That's why she'd taken my side with Daddy and told him I'd just wanted her and Isabel to be together. And I did. But now I realized—too

272

late—that I wanted something else, too. I wanted them to stay. Even if Daddy were to find them the best home in the world someplace else, I wanted them here, with us.

I started pacing, needing to move. My room felt like a cage, too small and close all of a sudden. And then it was as if something was pulling me toward the window. And when I got there, something told me to open it. So I did and crawled outside.

It was just me this time, sitting alone on the roof in the cold, tilting my head back to look at the stars. I knew the lions wouldn't be there, but my eyes searched the sky anyhow, and I said, "Leo, I hope you can hear me, 'cause I need your help."

I sat real still, trying to feel his presence, waiting for a sign that he was out there somewhere, listening. I waited till the cold seeped into my bones, till anybody with good sense would have given up. And who knows? I might have kept waiting all night long, but then I heard the sound of floorboards creaking. Somebody was walking across my room toward the window.

"It must be freezing out there," Kathleen said.

I twisted around and saw the outline of her head and shoulders in the darkness, her elbows resting on the windowsill.

"But you and Leo used to go out there in all kinds of weather, didn't you?"

She'd known about that? I'd always thought the roof had been Leo's and my secret. "You never told on us," I said.

"Nah." She lifted her face like she was studying the sky. "Y'all were having fun. Sometimes I even wished I could join you."

"So why didn't you?"

She didn't answer me, but I already knew the reason. Because we hadn't asked her to. Because she'd known this was something Leo and I wanted to keep for ourselves.

"You can come out here now," I said. "It's not that cold."

Kathleen hesitated. Then she said, "I'd probably fall and break my neck."

But I could tell she wanted to. So I scooted over and said, "Come on, Kathleen, I could use the company."

"Well . . . ," she said. And then, "Aw, heck, why not?"

As I watched her wiggle through that little space, it occurred to me that there's an art to climbing out a window gracefully, and Kathleen hadn't mastered it yet. She landed like a sack of potatoes beside me, with her arms and legs stuck out in all directions and her skirt pulled up so high I could see her panties. And I couldn't help it; I started to giggle. Then Kathleen was giggling, too, all the while tugging at her skirt and muttering, "Don't you dare tell a soul about this. Bayliss, it's not funny." But I could just barely make out that last part because now she was laughing her head off.

It took some time, but Kathleen finally got situated and was sitting there next to me with her skirt pulled down over her knees, and both of us more or less recovered. Except I was still grinning. My ladylike sister wallowing on the roof with her drawers showing. What I wouldn't have given for a picture of that!

She tugged on her skirt one more time and then looked around. "You know, it's nice up here. I can see the lights on Main Street."

I leaned back on my elbows and peered up at the stars. "So are Gwen and Isabel already gone?" I asked, working at keeping my voice steady.

"No, they're over at Harry's having dessert. Miz Burdeshaw made an apple pie."

"What's everybody been doing?"

"Daddy was at the office all afternoon," she said. "And after supper, he and Mother shut themselves up in the kitchen, so Tommie Dora and I took the girls to the living room to listen to the radio. But when Harry came over for Gwen and Isabel, Tommie Dora couldn't stand it another second and went to check on Mother and Daddy. That was twenty minutes ago, and I haven't seen her since."

"Do you know what they're talking about?"

"I listened at the kitchen door," she admitted, "but I couldn't hear a word."

We just sat there awhile, not saying anything, and then

Kathleen looked up at the sky again. "Show me where you and Leo are," she said. "What's the name of that constellation of yours?"

"Leo Minor."

"Where do I look?"

"You can't see 'em this time of year."

She must have heard the catch in my voice because all of a sudden I felt her arm slip around my shoulders, and then she said, "It's going to be all right, Bayliss. I know it doesn't feel like it, but Mother and Daddy are trying to sort things out."

"It's probably too late for that," I said, "after all I've done."

"Oh, Bayliss, none of us have been thinking straight since Leo died. Just look at me—what a grouch I've been. I should've been more patient with you. I'm gonna try to do better from now on."

A big coppery moon was rising up over the trees, and in its glow, the stars seemed to have lost some of their brightness. Kathleen still had her arm around me, and I could feel her shivering, but she didn't make a move to go back inside and neither did I. We'd have to pretty soon, and face up to whatever was waiting for us. But not yet. I was feeling a kind of ease out there in the darkness, and I wanted to stretch out this time with my sister just a little bit longer.

I was thinking that nobody would ever look at the two

of us and say, *Six of one and half a dozen of the other*. And it also occurred to me that Kathleen *would* lose her patience with me again, just as surely as I'd find myself getting aggravated with her. Because that's how we were. Like Tommie Dora said, no human being is perfect. And sitting there next to Kathleen, the two of us huddled together against the cold, I decided I was all right with that.

"You know, I just realized something," she said, her teeth beginning to chatter. "I should've been having more fun, like you and Leo. I'm such a Goody Two-shoes."

"Not anymore," I said. "Listening at doors, crawling out on the roof at night—Kathleen, you're turning into a regular wild woman!"

"You think so?" she said, and I could hear the smile in her voice. Then she sighed. "I kind of like the sound of that, but it's not the real me. I reckon I was born to play by the rules."

"Well, that's all right, too," I said.

33. SORTING THINGS OUT

The radio was on when Kathleen and I went downstairs. *Sherlock Holmes*, one of Leo's favorite programs. But nobody was in the living room to listen to it.

Kathleen said, "They must still be talking."

I turned toward the kitchen, and she caught my arm. "Wait, we can't just barge in."

"Tommie Dora did."

"But Daddy wouldn't tell *her* to get out."

When Mother and Daddy had private talks, they'd usually go upstairs to their bedroom, and it never would have crossed my mind to interrupt them. But this was different. If they were trying to sort out what was wrong in this house, shouldn't Kathleen and I be part of it? And if they were talking about me, and about Gwen and Isabel, I figured I had a right to hear it.

"You do what you want," I said to Kathleen. "I'm going in there."

Kathleen still looked unsure, but when I opened the

door and walked into the kitchen, she was right behind me.

Mother, Daddy, and Tommie Dora were sitting at the table with coffee cups in front of them, only nobody was drinking, and they didn't seem to be talking either. Mother had been crying, I could tell that much, and Daddy looked rumpled and worried and tense. Tommie Dora was about the same as always.

Mother saw us and said, "I've kept your supper warm, Bayliss." She got up and went over to the stove.

I wasn't the least bit hungry, but eating gave me an excuse to stay, so I sat down next to Daddy. And Kathleen slid into a chair across from me.

"Well, Mary Bayliss," Tommie Dora said, "I expect you know you can't go gallivanting around in a stolen car once you take your vows. They frown on that sort of thing at the convent."

I started to tell her that the car wasn't stolen. But she would have just pointed out that Harry wasn't its rightful owner and hadn't gotten permission to drive it all the way to Morrisville, so all I said was, "Yes, ma'am."

"Helen," Tommie Dora said, "are you sure this is really Mary Bayliss and not some polite, soft-spoken child who just bears a striking resemblance to her?"

Mother managed a weak smile and set a plate of food in front of me. I picked up my fork and stabbed at some string beans, wondering why Daddy wasn't saying anything, why he didn't just go ahead and chew me out.

But it was Mother who said, "Bayliss, we understand why you took the girls to Morrisville."

"We understand," Daddy cut in, "but there's no excuse for you going off on your own that way. You should have talked to your mother and me about it."

When I heard that, I realized I was still mad at him for sending Gwen and Isabel away. I wanted to say, *I tried—and you wouldn't listen.* But what came spilling out of my mouth was a whole lot worse. "And you should've talked to me about Leo," I heard myself saying, and wished I could take it back when I saw Daddy's face crumple.

Right then, I wanted to jump up and throw my arms around his neck and tell him that I hadn't meant it, that I was sorry. I wanted to say something—*anything!*—to make it all go away. But nothing would do that. So I just kept going.

"Everything's all wrong," I said. "It has been since Leo died, and I don't know what to do about it."

He was bent over the table so I couldn't see his face, just his jaw working. Then he lifted his head to look at me, and he was blinking back tears. I hadn't meant to hurt him. Or maybe I *had* meant to. I didn't know anymore.

He was nodding his head, eyes swimming. "Everything *is* all wrong," he said. "After Leo . . . died, we should have

280

talked about what happened. I just—I couldn't bear . . ." His voice broke and he didn't go on.

I sat there feeling hopeless and horrible, wondering if anything would ever be good again, while he took out his handkerchief and blew his nose.

"We'll talk about Leo," he said, "but not now. We're all upset. It's not the right time."

"It never is."

This came from Kathleen, and we all turned to look at her.

"What did you say?" Daddy asked.

"It's *never* the right time," she said. "It's been almost eight months since Leo died, and we've hardly mentioned his name. We're all hurting, and we should be talking about it, helping each other. But we don't. We just act like it's not there. And that makes it worse. It's bad enough losing my brother, but it feels like I've lost the rest of you, too, like we aren't even a family anymore."

"Oh, Kathleen," Mother said, her eyes filling with tears, "of *course* we're a family. But we have to go on. Daddy's patients depend on him. There's a house to run and meals to fix, and school for you and Bayliss. Dwelling on what we've lost won't help."

"Neither will running away," Kathleen said. "We haven't even admitted that Leo's gone."

I had the strangest notion just then. It was like I didn't

even recognize this girl sitting across the table from me. But she was my sister all right, looking Mother and Daddy square in the face and saying exactly what was on her mind. And it occurred to me that Kathleen was a little bit like Tommie Dora, not one to shy away from something just because it was hard. Then this feeling swelled up inside me, and I realized that I was proud of Kathleen. She was a whole lot braver than I was, and even braver than Leo, because she'd say the hard truths straight out, whether we wanted to hear them or not.

Daddy was shaking his head, and then he muttered, "That's ridiculous."

"No, it isn't," I said. "Kathleen's the only one who's tried to talk about Leo, only I shut her out because it hurt too much. But she's right. If we won't even say his name, it's like we've forgotten him."

Daddy's eyes snapped to my face, and he said, "What we should be talking about is you running off with Gwen and Isabel. It was an irresponsible thing to do. You let them down, thinking more about your own needs than theirs."

Tears were pressing on my eyeballs, and my throat had closed up. I couldn't have gotten a word out if my life had depended on it. But there was nothing for me to say anyhow, because he was right.

"Now, Walter," Tommie Dora said, "I can see a positive side to her taking off with the girls. It was wrong—I reckon even Mary Bayliss knows that now—but it's brought everything out in the open and gives us a chance to do something about it. To grieve for Leo together. And maybe help those little girls, too."

"I've been *trying* to help!" Daddy threw up his hands. "That's why I brought them here in the first place."

"But now you're sending 'em away," I said, "and I don't understand why. They don't cost *that* much."

He seemed confused, like everything had gotten out of hand and he wasn't sure how it had happened. "There's something *I* don't understand," he said. "Until last night, I thought you *wanted* Gwen and Isabel to leave. So you could go back to helping at the convent."

"I don't care about that anymore," I said.

"What about becoming a nun?" Kathleen asked.

"I don't care about that either."

Mother started to say something and then stopped, looking flustered. "I was about to ask why you've changed your mind," she said. "But then I realized that I'd never asked why you wanted to be a nun in the first place. Why did you, Bayliss?"

"Because everybody kept telling me that God must've saved me for a special purpose," I said, "and I figured He wouldn't have brought me back for something piddly like traipsing through the jungles of Africa. It had to be something important, some *mission* I was supposed to dedicate my life to. And I liked the idea. It was so awful after Leo died, and I needed . . ."

"You needed something to hold on to," Tommie Dora said. "And when you saw that photograph of Edna Earl, you thought you'd found it."

"I was sure of it," I said. "So I threw myself into doing good deeds, and it made me feel better. But I got so wrapped up in it, I didn't see that I was only making *more* work for Mother and Kathleen, or that everything I was doing for the weary travelers was for me, not them. And *then* Gwen and Isabel came."

My voice was shaking a little, so I stopped to take a breath.

"What *about* Gwen and Isabel?" Mother asked.

"I couldn't stand them taking Leo's room," I said, "and I couldn't help the nuns anymore, and Gwen rubbed me the wrong way from the beginning. I just wanted 'em to go someplace else. I knew I was being selfish—Kathleen said I was, and so did Annie—but I didn't care."

"Bayliss," Kathleen said quietly, "I never should've called you selfish."

"No, you were right," I said. "I liked being charitable when it suited me, when it was easy and made me feel good. But helping Gwen and Isabel was hard, and I didn't want any part of it."

Tommie Dora was nodding. "You had to make real sacrifices when Gwen and Isabel moved in. That's hard for anybody."

"But if I'd been a truly good person," I said, "I wouldn't have minded making sacrifices."

"That's a bunch of nonsense," Tommie Dora said. "Good people struggle with doing the right thing all the time. And they fail, too. But when they keep on struggling, like you've been doing, they sometimes come to understand the true meaning of charity. That it's just plain old-fashioned generosity, putting somebody else's needs ahead of your own."

"I should've been doing that all along with Gwen and Isabel," I said, "whether I cared about 'em or not."

"But you do care now," Kathleen said.

"I didn't want to," I said. "It just happened. And then everything started looking different to me. It's Gwen and Isabel that matter, not whether I have a special purpose or not. And helping the sisters is something I might want to do later on, but it's not something I *have* to do. Just like I don't have to become a nun. I don't *need* to anymore."

After all the talking that had been going on, the room was suddenly quiet. And when I turned to look at Daddy, he was staring down at his hands, hardly seeming to breathe.

"Daddy, I've been thinking about something," I said. "When Gwen and Isabel moved in with us, I was afraid they'd take Leo's place. And I was wondering if maybe you'd been worrying about that, too. But they *couldn't* take his place. And besides, I think Leo would want 'em here with us. I think he'd love 'em, Daddy, just as much as I do."

Kathleen was crying softly, and so was my mother. Even Tommie Dora had tears in her eyes. But Daddy just sat there, and I couldn't tell what he was thinking. Then he took a deep breath and lifted his head.

I was on pins and needles, not knowing what to expect. He might break down or lose his temper, or maybe get up and leave. But what he did was reach out and touch my face, just a brush of his fingertips across my cheek before he dropped his hand.

"All I ever wanted was to take care of my patients and my family," he said, his voice low and hoarse. "To keep my children safe. That seemed easy enough in a place like Lenore. What dangers are there here? Whooping cough, the grippe—I could fight those. But what happened to you and Leo . . . How do you fight a storm nobody expected? A sixteen-year-old boy believing he's invincible? How do you lose your child and still trust yourself to protect what's left when you've already failed so badly?"

Still crying, Mother said, "Walter, you didn't fail. It was an *accident*."

"But what I'm trying to tell Bayliss," he said, seeming determined to get it all out, "is that . . . I was afraid. Of being responsible for two more children and maybe failing them, too. Of coming to love them and then having somebody show up and take them away from us. That's why I wouldn't even consider Gwen and Isabel staying here permanently, Bayliss. I thought I'd failed enough, and that we'd lost too much already."

Tommie Dora leaned across the table toward Daddy, her face softer than I'd ever seen it. "Walter," she said, "you can't live your life being afraid of what *might* happen. That's no life at all. I know how hard it is, truly I do. Every time you let somebody into your heart, you leave it open to pain, the worst kind of pain there is. But you and I both know it's worth it. And if you doubt that, Son, just ask yourself, would you give up those sixteen years with Leo? Even now, with everything you know?"

Daddy's eyes slid away from hers, and he reached for his coffee cup. He turned it round and round in his hands like he didn't know what to say, like all the feelings in that room were just about too much for him. But then he put the cup down and looked into Tommie Dora's face. His voice cracked when he said, "I *wouldn't* give up those years. Not for anything."

There was a long silence, with Daddy's words still hanging in the air around us, till Kathleen said, "So what are we going to do? About Gwen and Isabel, I mean. Couldn't they stay here a little longer, just till we find a place where they can be together?"

We all looked at Daddy, waiting, and finally he said, "Before you and Bayliss came in, Kathleen, your grandmother offered to let the girls live with her."

My heart lurched, then started to pound. I shot a look at Tommie Dora.

"Only your daddy thinks that wouldn't work out," Tommie Dora said. "He's of the opinion that I'm too old and ornery to care for children."

My hopes crashed.

"Now, Mother," Daddy said, "you know I didn't say any such thing."

Then he looked at Mother. He seemed to be asking her something. I didn't know what the question was, but she did, because she said without a moment's hesitation, "You know what *I* want, Walter."

Well, he might know, but I didn't. At least, I wasn't sure. And impatient as I was for somebody to tell me, it seemed like he kept studying her face for the longest time before finally turning back to me. And then he said, "I guess we all want the same thing, don't we? For Gwen and Isabel to stay where they are."

I reckon they all expected me to whoop and holler, and when I didn't, Tommie Dora gave me a sharp look. "Mary Bayliss? Did you hear what your daddy said?"

I'd heard; I just wasn't sure I believed it. So I said, "You mean the girls don't have to go live with the Dunns and the Neismiths? They can stay *here?*"

Daddy nodded. "Yes, Bayliss, that's what I mean."

I'd been feeling so anxious—and hopeful, and afraid of hoping—I'd grabbed the edge of the table and was holding on for dear life. Daddy reached out and covered my hands with one of his. The warm weight of it was a comfort. And then he smiled. It was almost like the old smile I remembered, the one that lit up his whole face and did your heart good just to see it, and I thought I might float up out of my chair till my head bumped against the ceiling. I was that happy.

"But we can't forget that Gwen and Isabel still have family," he said, his expression serious again. "If their father or brother ever comes for them, we'll have to let them go."

"I know," I said.

It didn't seem likely that their daddy would ever show up, but if Frank Truett got back on his feet, he might come looking for his sisters. And if he did, I'd be the first one to say they belonged with him.

Tommie Dora was eyeing me as she sipped her coffee. Then she said, "And one more thing about doing what's right, Mary Bayliss. When you put somebody else's needs ahead of your own, you just might end up getting something *you* need in return."

"Yes, ma'am," I said, grinning at her.

I could testify to the truth of Tommie Dora's words. And to another truth that had just dawned on me: that Tommie Dora Bayliss Pettigrew was the best grandmother in the county. And maybe in the whole state of Alabama.

289

We didn't sort out everything that evening, but it was a start. And we all knew that we'd have to keep talking to each other, even when it scared us, and even when we knew that some things can never be fixed.

But sitting there in the kitchen with my family that night, I wasn't thinking about being scared. I was too happy, not to mention hungry. And all of a sudden everybody else seemed to have an appetite, too, so Mother heated up what was left from supper, and we were all eating like we hadn't touched food in a week when we heard voices coming from the living room. Harry stuck his head in the kitchen, looking uncertain at first, then surprised that we were having a big meal so late.

"I brought Gwen and Isabel home," he said.

"Thank you, Harry." Mother motioned him over to the table. "Sit down and I'll fix you a plate."

Harry was never one to turn down Kathleen's sweet potato casserole, and he seemed to have picked up on the changed mood in the house, so he grinned and said, "Thank you, ma'am," and pulled out a chair.

"Harry, I'm glad you're here," Tommie Dora said as she buttered a piece of corn bread. "I want to talk to you about all those walnuts in my yard. Mavis Quick slipped on one yesterday and fell so hard I thought she'd break a hip. You've been saying for two weeks you'll pick 'em up for me."

"It's been raining most every day," he said. "How about tomorrow after school?"

Tommie Dora nodded and then looked at me. "You come, too, Mary Bayliss, and bring Gwen and Isabel. It'll keep y'all out of mischief."

"Speaking of Gwen and Isabel," Mother said, and I noticed how her face, especially her eyes, seemed to come alive, "we need to go tell them they'll be staying."

Kathleen was already out of her chair. "Well, come on then," she said.

From the hall, I could see Gwen and Isabel lying on their bellies in front of the radio, with their coloring books and Crayolas. They looked up when we trooped into the room, and I dropped to the floor between them.

"All right, Miss Wild and Miss Woolly," I said, "listen up. Doc's got something to tell you."

34. NOW

Over the winter, some good things happened. Kathleen started keeping company with Ray Vanzandt, and Daddy didn't seem to mind. Gwen got more gold stars from Sister Mary Vincent and won so many spelling bees, Mother said we had a genius on our hands. And Isabel was picked to be an angel in the Christmas pageant.

Folks are still talking about that pageant. The night of the performance, Kathleen was in the loft with the choir, Gwen was backstage waiting to come on as a shepherd, and I was sitting in the audience with Mother, Daddy, and Tommie Dora. The auditorium was pitch-black. Then all of a sudden light flooded the stage, and there was Isabel. She was perched on a stepladder behind the cardboard stable so that she seemed to be hovering over it, wearing a long white robe and angel wings. Folks commenced to oohing and aahing, and I could hear them whispering how beautiful she was and how she was perfect for the part.

Only I reckon they'd made up their minds too fast. Because about that time, the boy playing Joseph came out from behind the curtain leading a mule with Mary on its back, and right on cue, Isabel let out the loudest *"Heeeee-haw!"* you ever heard. Joseph was so startled, he came to a dead stop, and the mule, still moving, knocked him flat on his face. Then the mule jerked back, and Mary toppled to the floor, taking the stable with her.

The audience just sat there, dumbstruck, till somebody started snickering. And before you knew it, everybody was howling like it was the funniest thing they'd ever seen. Everybody but the nuns, that is.

It didn't surprise me much when some of the sisters turned around in their seats in the front row and stared straight at me. Mostly, they looked shocked, but Sister Mary Vincent's eyes were shooting off sparks, and there was no doubt in my mind that she'd dearly love to strangle me. And Sister Annunciata—well, it was kind of hard to tell, but if I hadn't known better, I might have thought she was smiling.

Not long after that, I told Sister Annunciata that I'd given up on the idea of becoming a nun.

She just nodded and said, "That's fine, Mary Bayliss."

"I've stopped looking for my special purpose," I said. "I reckon you were right. I'll just wait for it to find me."

"It will," she said. "And something tells me it's going to be a humdinger."

Then I went home and dug out my Big Chief tablet. I'd

put it away months ago, thinking I'd never need it again, but all of a sudden I couldn't wait to find new ladies to write about.

With spring just around the corner, Tommie Dora hired the Putnam brothers to plow up her garden. And Harry, Gwen, Isabel, and I will do the planting. All spring and summer long, we'll be walking up and down those rows, weeding and thinning at first, then picking ripe tomatoes and okra and beans for Tommie Dora and Mavis Quick to can.

And later on, when it's warmer, Mother says we'll go out to the lake for that picnic. Tommie Dora and Kathleen have it all arranged, down to the fried chicken and potato salad. And Miz Burdeshaw's offered to bake a pie. Harry says he'll just bring a hearty appetite.

But I could tell that Mother was still uneasy about the boat, and to tell the truth, so was I. Maybe Daddy realized that, because one Saturday afternoon about a month ago, when the sun was bright enough to remind us that spring wasn't that far off, he said, "Bayliss, I think it's time you picked up those oars again. You'll need some practice before you row all over the lake this summer." So Gwen, Isabel, Kathleen, and I piled into the Model T, and he drove us out to Sweet Springs Lake.

I wanted to go, and at the same time I didn't. But when Daddy pulled up in front of Mr. Davies's house, I decided that I mostly didn't. Because for nearly a year I'd been thinking, *That boat killed Leo.* It wasn't the boat. Only it's hard to get past feelings that have that kind of grip on you.

But then Gwen and Isabel jumped out of the car and took off for Mr. Davies's dock at a run, so what could I do but follow them? And I have to say, when I saw the *Mary Bayliss* bobbing in the water, the sight of her nearly took my breath away.

"Oh, Bayliss," Isabel said, "your boat is just *bee-yoo-tuh-ful!*"

"So what do you think?" Daddy asked me. "Are you ready to try her out?"

I hesitated for just a second, and then I said, "I'm ready."

So we've been going back to the lake every Saturday afternoon. When we first get there, we take turns riding in the boat with Daddy at the oars, and then Kathleen and Gwen and Isabel play on the beach while Daddy and I work on my rowing. It's *hard* work, too, and I've got the sore muscles and blisters to prove it. But yesterday, when I slid over the side of the *Mary Bayliss* and set foot on that island for the first time, I don't reckon I could have been any prouder if I'd just landed at the North Pole.

Daddy pulled the boat in and sat on the beach while I did some exploring on my own. After circling the island, which didn't take more than five minutes, I climbed the slope to the trees. And through the branches I saw it, the most amazing thing. Right in the center of the island was a big chunk of sandstone, a smaller version of the cliffs back onshore, rising up to the tops of the water oaks and cedars.

The sides of the stone were uneven, with little ledges and rocky points for me to grab on to. So, naturally, I had to climb it. And it wasn't long before I was standing at the top, looking out over the lake and the woods, at Daddy lifting his face to the sun and, way across the water, Gwen and Isabel burying Kathleen in the sand.

A light breeze was blowing, tickling my face. And that's when I heard him—I swear I did—whispering in my ear. I reckon I should have been surprised, but I wasn't. It just seemed like the right time and the right place for it to finally happen.

He said, *You did real good, little britches. Didn't I tell you?*

You did, I said. *I just wish you were still here to tell me things. I wish . . .*

I know. But don't think about that now. This is a day to feel happy. And remember, you can do anything you set your mind to, even when it's hard. And you can teach them, too, everything they need to know.

Gwen and Isabel, you mean.

Yep. You can teach 'em how to row and how to hit a baseball. And don't forget the constellations, he said. *You have to show 'em the lions, little bit.*

I won't forget, I told him, already picturing it in my mind. Gwen and Isabel and me climbing out through my window and lying back on the roof to look up at the star-bright sky. And me pointing out every constellation I know. Starting with the ones named for Leo and me.

ACKNOWLEDGMENTS

My deepest gratitude goes to my agent, Barbara Kouts, who has supported me through thick and thin and thinner with enthusiasm, patience, and unerring judgment. And heartfelt thanks to my editor, Michele Burke, who has the instincts and sensibilities of a very old soul. She understood better than I the story I wanted to tell and gently guided me in that direction.

I owe a special debt to the late Thelma Harding, a beloved teacher in Cullman, Alabama, who shared her memories from the Depression years and gave me the idea of writing about a Catholic family in the predominantly Protestant South.

Thanks to Max Hand and Lesia Coleman, of the Cullman County Public Library, for helping me find everything I needed to know about the real Sacred Heart, the Oddfellows' Children's Home, the acts of generosity of the Benedictine sisters during the Depression, and much more. And thanks to everyone involved in establishing the library's Special Collections, particularly the books, articles, and other documents pertaining to regional history. It's a gold mine!

And to Jeanne and R. C. Phillips: your house and its surroundings are a writer's dream, and without them this book might never have been completed. Thank you.